Trust Me

For Eve,

Trust Me

I really admire your ability to persevere with authenticity, and I'm grateful for your dedication to building healthy lives — both for yourself and for all of us in your community.

Kaija Leona

Kaija Leona

iUniverse LLC
Bloomington

TRUST ME

This is a work of fiction. All of the characters, names, incidents, organizations, and dialogue in this novel are either the products of the author's imagination or are used fictitiously.

iUniverse books may be ordered through booksellers or by contacting:

iUniverse LLC
1663 Liberty Drive
Bloomington, IN 47403
www.iuniverse.com
1-800-Authors (1-800-288-4677)

ISBN: 978-1-4917-0349-6 (sc)
ISBN: 978-1-4917-0350-2 (ebk)

Printed in the United States of America

iUniverse rev. date: 09/05/2013

ACKNOWLEDGEMENTS

Huge thanks go to Jorja Fox and the writers of CSI for Sara Sidle. Without them, this book would not exist.

I'll never stop being overwhelmed by Sir Terry Pratchett, who arranges existing words so brilliantly that each of his novels is profoundly inclusive, enlightening, entertaining, and inspirational.

I want to thank my boys, Thomas and Ben, for putting up with the crazy busyness that takes over our lives about 96% of the time, and for being amazing, fantastic, talented, compassionate, intelligent and occasionally responsible kids.

Thank you to everyone who's ever had a part in the smallest, pluckiest and most amazing middle school in the world—the past, present and future students, parents, and staff of Island Pacific School.

Somewhat awed thanks also go to Dana Railey, Maija Liinamaa, Nel Dumbrille-Meyrink, Nicole Hurtubise, and Patrick Fillion for reading early versions of the manuscript, and liking it.

This one is for my Mom, of course.

CHAPTER ONE

"Good morning, class, and welcome to Eighth Grade Advanced English," our new teacher greeted us on the first day of real classes, which didn't happen until the second week of school because we had to spend the whole first week in assemblies listening to lectures about good citizenship.

Well, that's what I did. The people who probably *should* have been listening to the lectures were making spitballs, colouring on each other in permanent marker or painting their nails with felts and highlighters.

I studied the ordinary-looking man standing comfortably at the front of the room. Well, sort of ordinary-looking, with an overall browny-greyness from his short brown hair and thick brown beard, both shot through with grey, to his grey pants and shirt. He actually wore tweed, and looked like he'd been teaching for centuries.

As he waited for everyone to settle down and give him their full attention, he took our measure as frankly as I'd taken his, his eyes passing rapidly over each student in turn.

I know what he saw when he looked at me, because I seem normal, in the right shirt and shorts and shoes. The only thing that's not totally normal is my really bright and wildly curling red hair. Well, and I'm a lot smaller than anyone else in my class, which is good for the gymnastics I used to do and the figure skating I do now, but not so handy for real life.

It was more intimidating than I thought to be the smallest person in a high school of over 4000 loud, jostling students, but I didn't look away as his eyes passed over me.

As the silence spread throughout the room, I rubbed at the skin on my nose. My last sunburn was still peeling, and a thousand freckles that would fade away during the nine or ten months of the endless rain that was on its way made me look perpetually mud-splattered.

As the teacher's inspection passed over my hair and came to settle on my face, I chewed on the inside of my cheek. His eyes were sharp, knowledgeable, and grey, although the last part might have just been the reflection from his clothing. When I looked closer, I realized they were actually a very clear, light blue.

"I'm Mr. Bowman," he said simply, and the silence was now absolute. "This year will be a little different from your other years in English. First of all, this sheet I am handing out contains the list of all the assignments that you must complete before the end of term. You may hand them in any time on or before the second to last week of classes, except for the oral report, for which I will assign you a date."

Mr. Bowman handed me six sheets and I automatically took one and passed the other five back. Teachers generally read directly to you from whatever handout they're giving you, and since I can read faster than they can talk, it saves time to ignore them. Plus, I find it really annoying to be told things I can see for myself. I'm twelve, not illiterate.

"Because this is an Advanced class, I'm going to assume that you can all read, so take a few minutes to look over the handout. I will take questions in . . ." he looked up at the wall clock and narrowed his eyes, ". . . 4 minutes."

Huh. My eyebrows raised a little in surprise and, I admit, re-evaluation as I quickly looked at the marks composition beside each item to decide how much effort I should give to each assignment. Tests and essays made up most of the final mark, with only 5% for the oral report. It figures. Teachers know that we're going to work hard for the oral anyway, since we don't want to humiliate ourselves in front of the class. Why wouldn't they make other things count more towards our grade?

Way less than four minutes later, I'd barely finished skimming through the overview when he began to call our names. A teacher who doesn't read simple material out loud and expects us to multi-task? Excellent. I'm so tired of waiting through five sets of explanations just because half the kids don't think it's worth listening unless the teacher's speaking to them individually.

My name was the first one called and Mr. Bowman didn't get it right, which was okay because nobody ever does.

"Seelee?" he called out.

"It's Kay-lee," I told him politely.

"I'm sorry," he apologized, a response that always confuses me. I don't expect anyone to pronounce it right, so why would they be sorry? My whole name is even worse. Who names their kid Caeliana Dax? *Star Trek* freaks, and not the good kind. I go by Caelie.

"It's okay," I said out loud, since he was still looking at me, and then he went on to the next name.

After the allotted four minutes, Mr. Bowman started calling on kids with their hands up, and they began asking predictable questions like what happens if you're sick and miss a test (beheading) and other lame things like that. I played around with a highlighter on my assignment sheet and stopped listening for a bit but perked up when I heard, "What about the letter writing? It tells us what's supposed to be in it, but to whom are we supposed to write? Can it be anyone?"

Trust Jeffery to artificially 'prove' his intelligence right away, but none of us reacted, partly because we'd had a break from him and his brother all summer, so our twin tolerance was higher than normal, but also because we shared the universal and fervent desire of all students everywhere to please not be assigned pen pals our own age somewhere.

"Ah," Mr. Bowman smiled. "I thought we'd get to that part. You will be writing to a celebrity of your choice. It will be your responsibility to find his or her correct mailing address and to compose an original letter that, you hope, will provoke a response. This is a personal letter, so please note that you are not required to show me the letter, just as you are not required to hand in any of the journal entries that you will be writing in class."

"So how do we get marks for it, then?"

I was wondering that, too, but I let the smartest boy in the class ask the question because somebody was bound to, and this was turning out to be a bad year for me already. Pretty much anything

I said would be ridiculed, so I was planning to keep quiet unless a teacher asked me a direct question.

"If you choose not to share what you've written, then you have to write a second letter to me including a description of your celebrity, your reasons for choosing that person, and a few other things. You can come and see me for more details if that is what you decide," he added.

He didn't expect anyone to do it, and from the reactions of most of the kids in the class, he was right. Why do twice as much work for the same mark?

You'd have to have a really good reason . . . and I did.

Less than ten minutes into my first class, I found myself abandoning my 'stay quiet and hope to become invisible' plan.

"Can you write to a character portrayed by a celebrity, or does it have to be the celebrity herself?" I asked.

"It has to be a real letter," Mr. Bowman said slowly, dashing the hopes of some of the lazier kids in the class who were already imagining hilariously superficial letters to SpongeBob, "but if your character is currently portrayed on a regular basis by one celebrity, then yes, you can write to the character, as long as you are writing to a human and not a cartoon."

Some of the kids who used to be my friends rolled their eyes at me, but I ignored them and there was silence for a few seconds before Mr. Bowman asked if there were any more questions. More silence, with a few people shaking their heads or glancing around the classroom.

"Okay, then," Mr. Bowman went on, rubbing his hands together. "The novels that we will be reading together are on your desks. When I call your name, please come up to the front and sign them out. Those of you who are waiting for your turn to come up may begin composing your letters or reading quietly. The first novel we will be tackling is *The Outsiders*. I expect there to be no talking. Caelie Aimes," he nodded briefly to me, proving he'd remembered how to pronounce my name, "you're up first."

I always am, at least since Jacob Aarons moved away to the prairies at the beginning of Grade 2.

Obediently, I grabbed the five paperbacks sitting on the corner of my desk and brought them up to the front, where he copied the numbers into his book, had me initial it, and was preparing to call the next person when I interrupted him.

"I don't want to hand in my letter," I stated lowly, getting it over with quickly. Surprise flashed through his eyes briefly and was replaced with speculation before he began flipping through his book to review my grade history.

When he got to my name, he studied the overview of all my final letter grades for every grade and subject since kindergarten. They were all A's. Wasn't that true for everyone in this program?

He glanced at me briefly and then turned to the second page, which showed the percentage I'd gotten in each course. Everything was above 96% except for Math, where I never get higher than 89%.

"Not a Math fan?"

"I don't understand Math," I replied evenly. My friends helped me with it before, but this year I'll have to start reading my textbook thoroughly or something.

Currently, my friends and I are not speaking to one another because they somehow became completely new people between the last day of summer vacation and the first day of school, and I didn't. I can't be a new Caelie who's desperately interested in boys, makeup and feckless celebrities who'll be lucky to live past their eighteenth birthday, and they don't want the old Caelie.

He looked up at me questioningly. "Do you have a character in mind?"

It was a polite question instead of a direct one, but he expected an answer I didn't want to give. I worry that if I tell anyone anything that's real about me, they'll immediately guess everything else, and I can never let that happen. Even my old friends don't know anything about me. Anything important, that is.

"You have to hand your letter in to me," Mr. Bowman reminded me, "but you can hand it in already sealed. I won't read it, but I will know where it's going."

That last part sounded like a warning, but as long as he didn't read what I wrote, would it matter? I chewed my bottom lip before answering.

"Amy Anderson," I said. "From the original *Last Line of Defense*."

There are two LLD shows on the air now, because the first one was so hugely popular, and Amy's been there since the beginning. She works in the lab to process evidence from crime scenes, but she's also the head of her unit and she tends to make people feel angry or upset a lot, even if they don't know why.

Nothing about her past has been on the show, but she's so much like me that I know anyway. You can't tell that anything's wrong from looking at her, of course; she has long, silky-smooth hair that's almost black, and the brightest, bluest eyes imaginable. She's also taller than most of the guys on the show, and she's supposed to be very athletic, but I can tell she's not. At least, her actress is definitely not.

A slight frown wrinkled Mr. Bowman's forehead as he studied me, and I hoped he wasn't going to start a new line of questioning, but he ended up just nodding to me slightly. "I'll print out the requirements for the other letter and give it to you next class."

I started to say thank you, but he was already calling out the next person's name. I walked by her on my way back to my desk, both of us looking anywhere but at each other because it was Allie, who'd been my very best friend since kindergarten. Her straight, blond hair bounced perkily at her shoulders with every step, and that was only one of the ways she'd changed.

She's had boy-short hair her entire life, but she grew it out over the summer so she'd look like everyone else. It was working. All the makeup probably helped, too.

Ignoring the stab of loneliness, I sat down, flipped open my laptop, and turned my desk so that my back was to the wall. I like to sit in the front of the class so there's never anything between me and the teacher, which also means I don't get distracted by anything other people are doing, but I didn't want anyone to see what I was writing.

Mr. Bowman looked up at the noise I made swiveling my desk around, but didn't comment. Once I was sideways to the class, my back to the wall, and everyone in my field of vision, I began to write.

Sept. 8

Dear Amy,

Hi. You don't know me at all but I watch you all the time. I've never seen anyone like me before on TV. Or in real life, either, so I hope you won't mind me writing to you because I think I might go crazy if I have to keep lying about everything all the time. I don't know what to tell you about me except that I'm a 12 year old version of you. I'm really good at school and sports, just like you, and I totally don't fit in, also just like you . . . but this is my absolute worst year ever!

My best friends hate me and I think they're stupid but now nobody ever talks to me. I'm in a really small class because I'm in a special honours program (why does anyone ever think it's good to be smart?), so all my friends and I have been together practically since kindergarten.

Sometimes a new kid comes in, but not very often. They always fit in somewhere because even though there are only 12 of us, there are the smart and athletic and popular girls, the smart and athletic and popular boys, and then everyone else. I used to be the leader of the popular girls until this year.

Last year, everything was totally normal. My friends and I organized sports at lunch in the summer and traded books in the library during the winter. We did everything together—even felt ashamed together when we made the sub run out of the class crying one day. We always get the same one and she's always pretending to be our "friend" and I think she and Professor Snape went to the same school of hairdressing but it looks a *lot* worse on her. None of us can stand her at all, but making her cry felt pretty bad.

She'd kicked me out of class for reading a book instead of working, which is what I always did with our regular teacher, and when she came out to the hall to say I could come back in, I told her I'd come back after I finished my book. I don't know for sure what the other kids did, but it wasn't long before the principal was in our room.

Anyway, the bell just rang, so I gotta go, okay? I'll write again soon.

Love, Caelie.

I saved my letter, shut my laptop, and hurriedly stuffed it into my bag. Next period was Socials and it was way at the other end of the school. I scurried through the halls trying to find the classroom, but just seemed to get more and more lost, despite the week of orientation. Sometimes, it's a tiny relief to have no friends because at least I spend less time lying, as measured in hours or days in a row, but mostly I miss them, especially at school.

Even more so while being lost alone in the hallways, I decided. Allie is a serious perfectionist who always knows everything practical and, on the off chance that she didn't have a fully functioning internal map of the school, at least we'd all be lost together. Instead, it was just me and the hundreds of Grade 12 students who never seem to have anything to do except hang out in the hallways glaring at Grade 8 students. Like it's our fault the government eliminated middle schools.

When I did find the classroom, hidden at the end of an obscure corridor, I was the last one there. I ignored the scornful looks and muffled laughter that greeted my arrival, and grabbed a desk at the front. The teacher was clearly waiting for me and had been staring warningly at the class until I got there. She began speaking as soon as I sat down.

"I am Ms. Ganett. Good morning, and welcome to Eighth Grade Advanced Socials." Yes, we know. We're geeks. Go on . . .

"Today, we're going to do a quick review of your last year's work so I have a good idea of where to start you."

She wasn't the sort of teacher you should mess with, so we sat and waited patiently as she put a sheet up on the overhead. None of us attempted to answer the first question and she sort of sighed and asked another one. Still no answer. All her questions were about someone called Louis Riel and one, or possibly more, railroads. We hadn't studied any of that at all and after three or four more questions, she demanded impatiently, "What *did* you study last year?"

There was a general mumbling and shuffling of feet before Allie put up her hand.

"We didn't really do any Socials last year," she said politely.

"Well, you must have done something," Ms. Ganett huffed.

"Callie?" she asked, consulting her seating chart.

"It's Kay-lee," I corrected her. When we met during locker assignments last week, I'd told her then, too.

"And did you do any Socials last year?" she asked, smiling in that fake-nice way teachers do when they're smugly sure of making you look stupid no matter what you say.

"I'm not sure what you mean by Socials," I told her. What specific topics we were supposed to have covered?

"And you made it into an Honours class?" she asked.

Great. One of those teachers who don't actually like kids and only want one thing from them: quiet, prompt, exact obedience. The smart thing to do would be to look down at my desk and cede the point, but I just couldn't do it. Even though I felt my cheeks turning red as everyone else laughed and whispered, I stared back at her defiantly.

"Did any of you do anything last year?" she asked the class, after smiling at me pityingly and moving to stand right in front of my desk.

I half turned in my seat and watched my classmates exchange questioning looks. Finally, Aidan put up his hand.

"We did some Math," he offered. A general nodding and murmured agreement followed this pronouncement. It was true, we had done some Math on those semi-regular occasions when our teacher bothered to assign us some pages from the textbook. When we finished, we marked each other's work.

"And Art," came another voice. I didn't remember doing any Art.

"And P.E." If being handed the key to the equipment room and being told to come back in an hour counted as P.E. instruction, then yeah, okay.

"We played Crazy Eights a lot," came a whisper from the back. A few muffled giggles followed this remark, but the teacher quelled them with a cold glance.

She looked narrowly at us for a few minutes and then theatrically rolled her eyes and dropped her head in her hands. After several aborted attempts at what we assume would have been less than complimentary comments (What was she *thin* . . . *How* could she . . . Didn't *anyone* . . . ?) about our prior teacher, she managed to get a grip on herself.

It was a good tactic, to tell us how stupid we were and then set herself up as the person who was going help us all out of that mess, but that's all it was: a tactic. None of us is stupid and she knows it.

When everyone else smiled tentatively at her, or at least gave her their full and respectful attention to avoid being the one in trouble, I began tracing designs on my desk with my fingertips.

She ignored me, except for a kind of challenging smirk. I'll lose this battle and we both knew it, but I still planned to fight it. One manipulative bully in my life is more than enough, and Ms. Ganett was a complete amateur. A petty and persistent one, probably, but still an amateur.

"We have a lot of work to catch up on," she said, walking purposefully over to her shelves where she took out a huge binder, and opened it up to the beginning. "We will spend this month catching up on the material you should have learned last year, and the next two months doing your work for this term. Because it will be very compressed, I expect that no-one will miss any classes. Or be late," she added, looking down at me. "Because Socials, Caelie, is the study of people, and if you don't know anything about people, you can't learn anything about yourself."

As I reached down for my laptop, I rolled my eyes. I know a lot more about people than she could ever imagine, and I'd still managed to set myself up as the class scapegoat, a circumstance I didn't have time to dwell on because we all opened up our computers and started taking notes as she launched into a very detailed and comprehensive summary of North America in the

19th century. I missed half of what she was saying because she was talking fast and I can't type as fast as someone speaks.

I need to learn shorthand or borrow a copy of last year's textbook, was my only recurring thought as I scrambled to get as much information down as I could. It didn't help that, under the onslaught of massive boredom tinged with panic, my mind was wandering back to Amy. It had felt so good to write to her, like I had a friend again, but even better than a real friend.

I have to lie and pretend around real people, but I'll never have to lie to her.

Normally, I like Socials, but . . . not this time. Ms. Ganett droned on through the whole hour and twenty minutes, and I managed to get through it without *too* many gaping holes in my notes. Had she really said that Russia tried to sell Alaska to Canada first, but Canada declined because all of its money was in railroads? How did Russia even have Alaska in the first place?

I was definitely in trouble, and once again, I rued losing my friends because I'd have nobody to compare notes with.

I watched Allie mouth "I'll email mine to you" to Jill and Vanessa and they nodded back, perfect ponytails bouncing in unison, that they'd send theirs to her, too. I looked away and got busy putting my stuff into my backpack.

I spent lunch in the library, reading *The Outsiders*.

The afternoon wasn't much better.

CHAPTER TWO

In fact, the next two weeks didn't get any better, and I was having a much harder time in school without anyone to share the work with, so I spent all of my extra time doing schoolwork. Especially after we got our first Socials assignment marked, and I realized I really did need last year's textbook.

It seemed like forever before Mr. Bowman gave us a free period to work on whatever we wanted, and by that time Amy was more real to me than all the people I saw every day.

Sept. 23

Dear Amy,

I got a C+ on our first Socials assignment and now I'm grounded. At least I got permission to re-do it, so it won't affect my GPA too much. I'll lose 10% for re-doing it, but if I get it done perfectly, it shouldn't bring my final mark down more than half a percent, as long as everything else I do is perfect. I'll just have to be very careful in the future. I also asked Ms. Ganett (our Socials teacher) for extra help and she gave me a bunch of alternative texts and books to read so I could understand the history better. It killed me to ask her because we hate each other, but I can't let that affect my grades.

If I don't get straight A's, I get grounded until the next report card. I used to get grounded from sports too, instead of just school, but now that I'm winning a lot of competitions, my dad doesn't want me to miss practices. Thank goodness, because the last thing I need is to spend more time in my house. Or at school. Honestly, Amy, if I'd known what Grade 8 was really going to be like, I'd have stayed in Grade 7.

Love, Caelie.

When I closed my letter file, I felt a bit better. My spare time was entirely taken up with schoolwork, skating, and trying to be invisible, so I didn't have a whole lot of time to worry about my new lack of friends, and besides, what else can I do? It's not my biggest problem, just my newest one.

At the end of the next week, when I got home from skating practice, my father wordlessly extended his hand and I passed over my Socials homework for inspection. Every night since the interim reports came out, he looks over all my Socials' work to make sure it's finished properly. It's always perfect now that half my waking hours are devoted to a single class, but only partly because the night Ms. Ganett sent our first mark home was a very bad night for me. It's become a matter of honour in the full-fledged war between Ms. Ganett and me, and I'm not going to give her any more ammunition.

I made a late dinner for us while he double-checked everything. When my mom left us, I became responsible for meals. Four years of practice and the desperate need to never mess up helped me get pretty good at it and I'd made a roast on the weekend, so all I had to do was make up a salad, cut some bread, and heat up gravy and slices of roast beef on the stove. He was just finishing his review as I brought the plates over to the table.

"At least you're good for something," he admitted grudgingly, tossing my work aside so that the pages got all mixed up before he picked up his fork and dug in to his gravy-slathered bread. Around the first mouthful, he started muttering about how he had better things to do with his time than look over some stupid kid's homework and how if I didn't have an A in my next report, being grounded would seem like a reward.

When you don't have friends, grounding's pretty meaningless, but I didn't point that out to him. I never point anything out to him. Instead, I waited to see if he needed anything else, made sure to put some water and a glass on the table near him, then sat down to eat my own food quickly and quietly. I try to spend as little time around my dad as possible, and when I asked to be excused, he grunted, "Other homework?"

I nodded back, which I do even on the rare occasions when I don't have any, and cleared the table quickly, putting the dirty dishes in the dishwasher and washing up the saucepan. I would have to go back later and clear up my dad's dishes, but for the moment I breathed a small sigh of relief as I quietly shut my bedroom door, then set up at my desk in the corner and did my Math homework first because I hate it the most.

This year, I've begun to solve every question in the book instead of just the ones they assign us, because it's the only way I can understand what I'm doing. Plus, that way I'm bound to have already done the questions they put on the tests. After a very painful hour of Math, I spent about two minutes memorizing all the parts of the eyeball for Science, then finally got to do what I'd been waiting for all day.

Oct. 6

Dear Amy,

Today at lunchtime, Stefan called me over to sit with him in the library. He's been in my class since kindergarten but I was one of the popular girls and he was one of the unpopular boys, so I never got to know him very well. Stef doesn't like sports or reading or school, so I never had a reason to spend time with him or even talk to him very much. He never gets angry or upset about anything, though, so I always kind of liked him. He's funny and nice and really talented at the violin. The kind of talented where he spends all his summers touring the world playing for people, even the Queen of England. He'd be popular at school just for that if he weren't so skinny and, frankly, dorky. The guys always make gay jokes around him, but none of us know, or even really care, if he is gay or not.

I guess it's just the most obvious thing to tease him about.

I wasn't sure why he was being nice to me because, although I never teased him myself, I also didn't make anyone else stop.

After a very short internal debate, I sat down with him even though he was sitting with the twins from our class whom everyone hates because if they're not whining about something, they're fighting with each other. Everyone calls them the Js because their names are Jeremy and Jeffery. As usual, I ignored them and they ignored me, but Stef handed me a drawing, asking me what I thought of it. He was trying to sound casual, but I think he actually cared.

It was weird for me to picture him caring about my opinion, especially about a drawing, because I might be the smartest person in the class, but I'm definitely the worst artist, permanently stuck at the stick-person phase of my artistic development. Plus, now that I'm a total outcast, what can I possibly offer him? His life at school is already kind of marginal. I mean, he has to hang out with the J's, and he hates them, too.

"Well?" he asked me expectantly, after I accepted the drawing of a tremendously, enormously, grotesquely fat man, looking content and well-dressed. He also looked powerful, but I'm not sure if it was the suit, the expression on his face, or his watch and ring that did that. I wasn't sure what he wanted me to do, but I had to say something, so I settled on the most obvious word.

"Corpulent," I said, handing it back, and Stef grinned. I relaxed a bit even though Jeffery immediately said, "That's not a word," making me roll my eyes.

"Stef," Jeremy pitched in, "you've never heard it before, have you?" Both J's sounded very smug, but Stefan just shook his head no, and kept smiling at me. "So what does it mean?" the J's challenged me in unison.

I didn't have to answer him because Stefan showed him the photo: "This," he said, with a smile that was deeper in his eyes than on his face.

After that, I did my homework while Stef doodled and the J's made stupid remarks. It was the best lunch break I've had in a long time, so how horrible was it that I still felt embarrassed about sitting with him, just because he gets picked on and people laugh at him? He's kind and funny and smart, and I was embarrassed to be seen with him.

There are a lot of things wrong with me, but that's the first one that made me really ashamed of myself.

Love, Caelie

I logged off my computer, shut it down, went back out to the kitchen to clean up my dad's dishes, then got into bed and stared at the ceiling for a while, wishing I were someone else. Also, some*where* else. I hate being at home, and now school and skating are hard because suddenly everyone is different, and I'm not.

My thoughts stubbornly dwelt on everything that's wrong about me, and every time I tried to visualize something good, my mind automatically turned it into a hideous disaster. I rolled over, closed my eyes, and concentrated on not thinking about anything at all.

School got a bit easier after that, because I at least had Stef to talk to and my grades were all back to normal, even in Socials. I was working a million times harder than last year thanks to our totally incompetent former teacher and the fact that nobody shared any work with me, but having no social life outside of school gave me more time to do it. Some lunchtimes, I had tutoring for Socials, but the rest of the time I sat with Stefan to find the perfect word for his latest drawing and then do homework. When he didn't have a drawing ready, he sent me secret messages written as music notes, which always took me forever to decode because I can never remember if the notes start at the bottom and go up, or start at the top and go down.

I have similar problems in Math.

I talked a bit with Stefan and even Doria sometimes, but I continued to ignore the J's and they were happy to reciprocate. It sort of felt okay, and things were going as well as I could reasonably hope. Maybe too well in English, which was so interesting that I worked on it every time I ran out of other things to do, and I ran out of other things to do a lot. Almost every night and several hours a day on weekends, to be exact.

"All right, class," Mr. Bowman greeted us on the day after Remembrance Day, "today is an individual review day, so you can tackle any assignment you like while I speak to you one at a time. There will, of course, be no one *else* talking," he added, his eyes sweeping the room even as he beckoned me over.

He always takes us alphabetically, so I was ready.

"I see that you've finished all of your assignments for this year except for public speaking," he said quietly, his blue eyes unreadable. My day for that was in February. "I've marked everything for you," he added, handing me back my essays and tests.

I skimmed through them briefly, and saw that my lowest mark was 97%, but most of them were perfect. Even with the extra Socials work and all my skating practices, I have a lot of time to work on English.

"What do you plan to do for the next seven months or so?" he asked me.

"I'll do more work, if you like," I offered. "I'm not done my letters yet, though." *Uh-oh.* The minute the words left my mouth I could have kicked myself. So much for being discreet and keeping a low profile.

"You do have to hand them in when you're done," he said, ignoring the fact that there was only supposed to be one.

"You said—" I began, but he interrupted me.

"You can hand them in sealed into an envelope already, Caelie, but you do have to hand them in so I can make sure you are completing the assignment. I will be checking the addresses and mailing them in for everyone," he told me firmly.

I bit my lip and nodded. Mr. Bowman reminds me of my Grade 3 teacher, who saw me a little more clearly than anyone else. I hoped he wasn't going to be too much like her.

"I understand that you're a competitive skater?" he asked, totally changing the subject.

I nodded back warily. That Grade 3 teacher is the reason my mom left us, I'm sure of it, and the reason I spent that entire summer inside my house, recovering from my dad's reaction. Telling the truth, even a tiny bit of it, can be hazardous to your health.

"Well, I'm sure you're quite busy, but if you have the time, here's a list of books and writing assignments you can work on to get some more experience," he said, handing me a packet of papers. "Keep up the good work."

I tried not to breathe an audible sigh of relief, and met his eyes more confidently before walking back to my desk.

Did I have to do the extra work or not? He seemed to be leaving it up to me. I skimmed the papers and discovered that I'd read a lot of the books already, although there were a few new ones in there. The writing assignments included poetry and short story work, and they looked pretty interesting. I wasn't ready to start anything new yet, though, and with an unexpected free block . . .

Nov. 12

Dear Amy,

I hope you read these, because there's nobody else I can tell, but you have to keep them a secret. It helps so much to know you're there. Writing to you is the only thing I have, so please don't tell, because then I'll lose you, too. Okay?

I'm kind of worried because Mr. Bowman just looked at me in a way that reminded me of my old Grade 3 teacher, who sicced the Ministry on me and took me to see the school counselor until my father found out and put an end to it. It's stupid that the laws are set up so that your parents get to decide whether you can talk to anyone or not, but it's even more stupid that people follow those rules. I didn't say very much, of course, because by Grade 3 I already knew how bad it would be if I told anyone.

The teacher got moved to a different school a few weeks after Social Services gave me a kindly lecture on how lucky I was and why I shouldn't be selfish and attention-seeking. They didn't use those words, of course, but they might as well have. It wasn't the first time I learned that my dad's rules are the only ones that matter, but it was the last reminder I needed.

I've been a lot more careful since then not to attract any attention, but today Stef asked me if I was okay. Nobody asks me that! It scared me because I don't want anyone to know that I'm not. Maybe I've let my guard down too much around Stef. He's nice, and I really like finding words to match his drawings. Sometimes they're easy, like the one of a soft, fat puppy with shining eyes, which was obviously 'innocence'. Last time, though, he drew a man who looked very normal except for his eyes. There was an expression in them that looked sad and calm and suppressed, like he knew something he couldn't say. It made me want to know more about him and the secrets he didn't want to keep, but had to. I said 'grave', and Stefan looked at me for longer than normal before taking it back. I look forward to our picture games, but if he can see that I'm not okay, I might have to ditch him after all.

I wouldn't say this to a normal person, but I know your life was just the same, so here's what was wrong that I didn't tell Stef: I forgot to leave the pet door open for my mini-retriever, Missy, on Friday morning and she scratched almost all the way through the door while I was at skating. My dad was going to lock me in my room for the weekend but he hit me too hard first and it broke my nose. I didn't even know I was screaming until he hit me again to get me to shut up. It really, really hurt, more than anything else I can remember. Plus, I've never seen that much blood at once before. It soaked through three bath towels—you'd have had lots of DNA to process. He had to take me to the hospital and pretend to be all concerned and everything, which was okay for him because everyone always sympathizes with him and admires him for taking such good care of me—what a great dad! And he's a single parent, too. How wonderful of him!

Watching it makes me want to scream. How can anyone believe him? Are they blind? I get that he's really powerful and popular and handsome and seems so charming to everyone that they instantly love him, but that part of him isn't real, and nobody else can tell. *Why can't anyone else tell?*

Amy? What's it like in foster care? I guess you wouldn't want to talk about it and overall my home's not that bad, really. Probably better than a foster home, anyway. You hear a lot of bad things about them. My dad's a jerk, but I know it's worse for other people. Besides, my dad's been the mayor for two terms, everyone expects him to move on to bigger and better things soon, and he's on TV all the time. It would be a nightmare if anyone knew the truth.

When my mom was around, she always said we had to be nice and patient with him and "make allowances" because he was under a lot of stress from work. I don't think that's a good enough reason for what he does. At least if he were an alcoholic or something, I could just avoid him when he was drunk. Sometimes I really do screw up, like today with Missy, but other times, it's just because he's mad, and it could be about anything or anyone at all. Or nothing, maybe. Who knows? That was a question the Social worker kept asking me. *Why would he hurt you?* As if there had to be a reason or it couldn't be true.

I wish I knew someone like you in real life. You understand that reasons, if there are any, don't change anything. Knowing why earthquakes happen doesn't change anything for the people who die in them.

Do you think you could tell me how to make things hurt less and not just pretend they don't exist?

Love, Caelie.

P.S. If you do read these . . . don't tell anyone, okay? No matter what I say. Please remember.

CHAPTER THREE

When I walked into homeroom the next morning, Aidan spoke to me for the first time in months.

"Hey, Caelie! Why does Janna want to see you?" he asked, not bothering to hide his smirk.

The whole class turned to look at me, but I ignored him, figuring he was teasing me.

"Scared?" Ethan added, laughing.

"Why should I be? She doesn't even know who I am," I sneered, getting my book out. We have silent reading in homeroom.

"Then why are you going to meet her at lunch today?" Aidan asked, automatically shoving at the one stray blond curl that always tumbles down over his right eye. He's the cutest person I've ever seen in real life, and I've had a crush on him since kindergarten. He and Ethan are best friends, Aidan blond and blue-eyed, Ethan with black hair and dark eyes, both of them good-looking, athletic, and popular.

I tried to ignore them, helped by the fact that the teacher was walking in and we all had to sit down, but a little pit opened up in my stomach and I decided that I liked it better when they weren't talking to me.

It was the first time they'd ever been mean to me, and even though I *know* it's just fun for them, it hurts. I wasn't stupid enough to let that show, though.

The words on the page in front of me just sat there dully, stubbornly refusing to mean anything at all. *Really Janna? What on earth could she want me for?*

Our Honours Program is incredibly small, but in the interests of making it accessible to the largest cross-section of kids possible, it's in a huge high school right downtown. That small fact, the simple location of my school, is both the reason I know who Janna is and the source of the huge part of my education that does not come from the curriculum, but from watching guys randomly grab the crotches of girls walking down the halls (okay, I only saw that happen once, but everyone, including the girl, pretended nothing happened so I wondered if it was a regular occurrence), add alcohol to their drink bottles right there in the school parking lot, flick lit cigarettes at their friends, sit in cars filled with so much skunk smoke you can't even see who's in them, and other things I think belong only in fiction, or possibly horror movies.

Janna, even though she went to my fairly sheltered elementary school, belongs to the horror movie category.

Until now, everyone in Honours has been pretty much immune to her because we only share PE and two electives per term with everyone else, and this year is the first time we've ever shared any classes. *What could I possibly have done to attract Janna's attention?* I kept my book open, one of the new ones from Mr. Bowman, but didn't take in a single word.

Ethan was right, I was scared, and I was going to have to wait until lunchtime to find out what I'd done wrong.

Nov. 27

Dear Amy,

Something very strange happened at school today. Not bad, just weird. There's this girl in my grade that totally rules the school and everyone is really scared of her (that's not the strange thing) but since I'm in such a small class and we've never mixed with any other students before this year, none of us have ever had anything to do with her until she summoned me at lunch today. I first heard about it in the morning when Aidan lowered himself enough to ask me why Janna wanted to see me. How was I supposed to know? I had no idea she even knew I existed.

My ex-friends made comments about it all morning, so I had a long time to worry about it until she sent her henchwomen to meet me outside my last class before lunch. I don't know if that's a word, but believe me, that's what they were. And how do people I've never even met know where my classes are? Seriously. They didn't say anything, just waited for me and then expected me to follow them, which of course I did. It would be suicide not to, and I mean the real kind, not the social kind. But here's the strange thing: all Janna did was ask me questions about myself and whether I liked school and stuff. We walked around the outside of the school with her henchwomen trailing behind us until someone else came up to her and she nodded at me to go away. Weird, huh?

Love, Caelie.

The next day, and all the days that followed, Janna nodded to me or said 'Hi' when she passed me in the halls at school.

I was teased a lot less and given a wider berth by people I didn't even know, and obviously it was because of Janna, but I didn't know how, or even why. Still, it made school a bit friendlier, knowing there were two people there who didn't hate me. Three, if you counted Mr. B.

I was making more of an effort in his class to appear normal, and he hadn't pulled me aside again, so maybe it was working. I wouldn't survive another call to the Ministry, so a lot of my efforts leading up to the Christmas break were in the area of appearing normal in front of adults. Homework was no longer a concern, even for Socials, and I was getting bored in everything except Math and English.

"You're making acceptable progress in this class," Ms. Ganett told me at lunchtime on the last day of the term. The only good thing about her was that she'd never be like my Grade 3 teacher. Well, and that she's predictably mean and petty. I can work with predictable.

She'd had me paged over the loudspeaker system for a last-minute meeting, and I think she did it on purpose so I would miss all the lunchtime activities, including Christmas cookie decorating, that the student council had arranged for the last day of school before the holidays.

There was no other point to the meeting that I could see, because I'd done all the extra reading she'd given me and shown up to five tutorial sessions with her over the last two months. My grade was a firm 98%, but she'd rather eat live toads than compliment me on anything, so she said nothing about that.

"Thank you, Ms. Ganett," I replied, keeping my tone polite but dully disinterested. It drives her insane, but she drives me insane, too, so I don't care.

"Make sure you don't fall behind next term," she warned me acidly, as the bell rang for us to leave.

"I won't, Ms. Ganett," I said, smiling meekly at her. She'd let me see how much I annoyed her, but I didn't let my pleasure at that show in my smile or in my voice. I now had the highest mark in the class, although she wouldn't admit it to me. "Thank you for all of your help," I added. I say it every time, and every time she gives me the most unbearably condescending smile. I absolutely hate her.

When she let me go, I got my lunch from my locker, ate it quickly as I walked through several halls and up four flights of stairs to the library, and then sat down by Stef, where we both pretended we didn't care about the student activities going on in the cafeteria. I was still trying to swallow my anger at Ms. Ganett when he slid over a picture of the two of us looking normal in the library, and a rush of gratitude swept through me.

"Together," I blurted out without thinking, and was interrupted by giggling from behind me. The J's and Doria had come to join us. I looked up at Stef, horrified, only to find him gazing skyward as we endured the onslaught of predictable teasing. When Stef finished conversing with the ceiling gods and met my eyes, he just shook his head slightly, letting me know they were being morons. Being friends with him definitely wasn't about that, and we knew it even if nobody else did.

I held his gaze and said very seriously, and loudly enough for everyone else to hear, "I wouldn't date you if you were the last guy on earth."

The J's and Doria shut up, and looked a bit taken aback, like they were wondering how Stef would take that. Did they think he actually liked me? He doesn't, but would anyone else think that?

Did they think it already? I really, really hoped not. Stef is nice and funny and smart. I'm not going to ditch him.

While the J's and Doria looked on, Stefan smiled back and reached out to shake my hand. "Ditto," he agreed fervently.

I grinned at him and he carefully wrote the word down on the back of the picture before putting it away. We both pulled out our homework, and the other three actually left us alone, in the pursuit of possible leftover cookies. *Dream on*, I thought, but kept my opinion to myself because I was so glad to get rid of them. It wasn't long before the bell rang and we headed off to a double block of Math. At least there, my brain was entirely taken up with the subject matter.

After the final bell, I walked down the hallway slowly. There was no skating today so I didn't have to rush. All I had to do was clean out my locker, take the bus home, and make dinner for tonight. My dad wanted a roast chicken with stuffing and everything, something I'd have to start as soon as I got home. It's a pretty easy meal, just mixing up bread bits with butter, onions, and poultry seasonings, stuffing it into the chicken and putting it in the oven with a bunch of peeled and chopped carrots and potatoes. There's nothing to do after that for an hour and a half, but the clean-up is awful.

Thinking about it helped me ignore all my friends exchanging gifts at our lockers.

I threw out some old papers so I'd pass the locker inspection, and packed everything else into my bag. There wasn't that much because I usually keep my locker neat and we'd handed in our texts already, which made my locker look even more bare than normal, especially compared to my old friends, who had pictures, posters, mirrors and notes stuck all over the insides of theirs.

As I walked away from the harassed-looking teacher on locker duty, who checked me off her list without looking at me or my neat, bare locker, the dull slamming of lockers and constant crumpling of paper couldn't mask the sound of Jill squealing over a new charm for her bracelet that Allie had given her.

For the first time all year, I trudged toward the school bus that goes by my house. Even when I'm injured, I go to the rink after school. Today, as I climbed on board, trying to leave the delighted squeals behind me, the bus driver tried to block me.

"Not just everyone can take this bus, you know, sweetie," he said, motioning me away. I hate people who call all girls 'sweetie'. I bet he calls all the boys 'buddy' or 'pal', too.

"I'm supposed to take this bus," I told him.

"I haven't seen you take it before," he challenged me. "What's your name?"

"Caelie Aimes. And I usually have skating after school," I said.

He frowned at me, but didn't bother to check his list. What was it about me and check-off lists today? "Well, what about the mornings?"

"I have skating in the mornings, too," I said. Skating is okay. I'm good at it, but it's not that much fun. The best thing about it is that it keeps me out of my house except for when I'm in bed or doing chores and homework. And it's good publicity for my dad when I win, of course.

The bus driver snorted like he didn't believe me, but couldn't be bothered to spend any more time dealing with me. "Get on, then."

I sat by myself in the empty seat right behind him and looked out the windows. It was wet but not snowy. We hardly ever get snow at Christmas, and rain's not that interesting to look at, especially after two solid months of it. I pulled out one of Mr. B's extra books to help me ignore the noise and jokes and teasing and cheer of everyone else on the bus.

Oscar Wilde was a much better distraction than the constant rain, the ugly and badly spelled black graffiti on the wall beside me, or the fact that every single boy on the bus was competing for the title of Loudest Human Being Ever.

When I got home, Missy jumped all over me. I normally don't get home before six o'clock because of skating, and it's bad for her because even though she's a little dog and doesn't need a ton of exercise, she still needs company. And play time. I petted her for a while and kissed her head until she stopped wagging her entire body, then I gave her the yellow ball that she loves and she ran out into the back yard to play and go pee while I made dinner. It took me almost half an hour to get the chicken in to the oven, what with all the stuffing prep, and then I called her back in again and gave her a duck treat so the chicken smell wouldn't drive her crazy.

My dad wasn't supposed to be home for another 3 hours, but you never know, so I opened a tin of apple pie filling and spooned it into a frozen crust because he has to have apple pie with a roast chicken dinner. I put the pie in the oven beside the roast and set the timer for half an hour. Then I let Missy in and she sat down with me while I finished reading *The Importance of Being Earnest*.

I liked it so much I was actually looking forward to doing the assignments.

My dad came home late and in a bad mood, but he didn't have anything to get mad about because I had everything ready, even the gravy, keeping warm in the oven, with foil over the chicken so it didn't dry out. He sat down and helped himself to a bunch of everything. When he was done, I put some on my plate and sat down with him.

"Your grades okay?" he grunted between bites.

"Yes, dad," I answered. I'd left my report card on the table beside his plate, and he looked it over briefly, just checking to make sure I didn't have anything lower than an A.

"Skating okay?"

"Yes, dad."

"What do you want for Christmas?" he asked.

I'd die before asking my dad for anything, but he didn't wait for an answer. "Guess you need a new dress."

"Yes, thank you, I'd like that."

I wouldn't really, but I have to go to all his work parties over Christmas, so I get my 'present' early and it's always something to make me look nice for his friends. Like my dad and I are a happy family.

It's the only lie I ever tell, but I tell it all day, every day, in a million different ways.

I didn't realize until I was clearing the table and setting out the pie that we didn't have cheese. He needs cheese to go with his pie. Cheddar.

"Where's the cheese?" he asked me, making my stomach go all queasy.

"I'm really sorry, Dad, I didn't notice we'd run out—" I bit my lip and backed away from him.

"I'll wait," he said grimly.

I grabbed some money from the jar in the cupboard and sprinted out to the corner store, even though it wouldn't make any difference. I was back in less than eight minutes, but I'd seen it in his eyes before I left, that awful hard shine that creeps over him when he thinks he has a good excuse, and needs an outlet for whatever happened to him that day. As I came in the door, he caught me on the back with the tip of his belt and didn't stop hitting me until blood was trickling down my legs.

It's mostly bruising, I reminded myself, as flames of pain ran up and down my back. I hate him so much that I'm usually able to deny him the pleasure of hearing me scream or seeing me cry, but I had to force myself to stay still as the blows rained down. The thick leather that whipped through the air and bit into my weeping skin and muscles, over and over, wasn't killing me. It just felt like it.

"Go clean that up!" he finally said. My legs had given in and I was now on my stomach on the floor. I pushed myself halfway up and handed him the cheese I'd had the presence of mind to hold onto gently, having learnt from earlier lessons, before I limped off to the shower, dropping my clothes in cold water in the sink as I took them off. When I checked in the mirror, I could only see five places where the skin was torn apart enough to be actively bleeding instead of just seeping a bit. I took four Advil before bracing myself to step into the spray of water, then used the brush to scrub my back with soap while gritting my teeth against the sting and the ache, and finally stood in cool water until I thought I might have stopped bleeding.

Every drop of water hurt when it touched me, but I didn't have time to give in to the pain yet. I gingerly put black clothes on so he wouldn't see any blood if it hadn't stopped, then put my clothes and towel in the washer and quickly checked for any stains in the front entrance. It makes him furious if he can see any blood afterwards, but my clothes had absorbed most of it and a few seconds of sponging off the floor and the walls near the door took care of it. I hate cleaning up the ceiling, especially the stupid crystal chandelier, so I was glad it didn't have anything on it.

When I walked back into the kitchen, he was still waiting for me to slice the cheese. He looked at me like nothing had happened and this was a normal father and daughter dinner, which it pretty much was, and I forced myself to keep the hate out of my eyes.

Letting him see how much I hate him is another mistake I will never, ever repeat, so I focused on his eyebrows instead of his eyes until he looked down pointedly at his plate, and we sat down and ate our pie together.

I couldn't lean back in my chair because even my shirt hurt incredibly badly when it shifted against the skin on my back, but showing that I was in pain would make him even angrier. Moving my hand to take a forkful of pie made my back scream out but I just moved as slowly as I dared, making every single movement deliberate.

"Nancy will get you something nice," he said as he left the table, referring to the personal assistant who despises me.

When he was gone I finally breathed out, and the tears came to my eyes. I didn't let them fall, though, knowing he could come back at any moment. With caution, I wiped them away, braced myself on the edge of the table and stood up gingerly to clean the kitchen. After a few minutes, the back of my shirt was sticking to me every time I moved, and the pain was incredible. I always forget how much pain there is until it comes back. I forced it away by screaming silently at myself about how stupid and weak I am, then took two more Advil and had another shower before I went to my room.

Dec. 21

Dear Amy,

I hate my dad so much. I have to skate in an exhibition tomorrow and my back won't stop bleeding. How am I supposed to make sure it doesn't seep through? I'm sure that it will have stopped by the morning, but what if some cuts open up while I'm skating? The costume is *white*. Why can't he ever *think* of things like that before he hits me? I don't see why it has to always be my fault. What'll happen if any blood does come through? How can I wrap my own back up in gauze? I wish I really knew you so you could help me cover this up.

Love, Caelie.

In the morning, I looked down at the smudges of blood on my sheets, and knew I'd have to wash them. Stripping my bed opened the cuts again, allowing warm blood to trickle down my back, but nothing as bad as last night. I grabbed another black shirt to wear and balled up my pyjamas and sheets together before tossing them into a cold wash. There would be time for the wash cycle to finish and for me to get them into the dryer before I had to leave for my skating exhibition.

When I got back to my room and looked at the thin, white skating dress hanging neatly in the closet, I decided I was in serious trouble. I glared at my reflection in the mirror, willing the very stupid girl inside to think logically and actually come up with a freaking answer. I only had forty minutes to figure it out and get into the car.

My dad spent the whole drive to the rink either ignoring me or advising me not to screw up. He was a charming companion, and I was glad he had to work today and couldn't stay to watch me try out some new combinations. If they worked, my coach was going to put them into my routine for the next competition, but if they didn't, nobody would be happy with me.

I was not in an ideal performance mood as I thanked him for the ride and headed into the ice rink.

"Caelie!"

I looked up to see my coach, on the other side of the rink, frantically gesturing to me.

"The programs were printed wrong, so we're changing the routines to match it," she called out. "Your short routine is now first."

Great. It was a good thing my dad dropped me off early. I quickly jogged around the arena a couple of times, then went in to the changeroom to get dressed, detouring by the bathroom to see if there was any blood seeping through. Luckily, my undersuit looked totally clean. I pulled on my white costume, quickly laced my skates and went out on to the ice, where my coach called out helpful comments.

"Twenty minutes, Caelie!"

"Your back leg is bent, Caelie!"

"Caelie, get your leg straight!"

"Ten minutes!"

"Watch your back leg!"

"It IS straight!" I finally called back in frustration. She called me over to show me the video she'd taken with her phone, where my leg wasn't actually bent, but it wasn't perfect either.

I skated back out and tried it again.

"Not bad," my coach called out, switching her attention to another of her skaters.

'Not bad' is the highest praise you can get in skating, unless you're at a competition where your coach wants to impress prospective parents and try to sway the judges. Then you are "perfect", "beautiful" and "wonderful."

I was only kind of glad when the exhibition was over because, even though I made all my combinations, it meant a break for Christmas and no excuse to avoid the billion parties my dad expected me to attend, or host, to help further his career. I planned to spend a lot of time with my laptop.

Dec. 27

Dear Amy,

I made it through the exhibition all right. It took me a while to figure it out, but finally I put some strips of tape on the bed, sticky side up, and covered them with a fat layer of gauze before I lay down on them carefully on my back and pulled the sticky ends of the tape around to my chest and stomach. I wore two undersuits, just to be sure. It worked, thank goodness.

I also survived an entire week at home with my dad. It probably helped that we were never alone together—we were always at a party or hosting one, and the media got some great shots of us as a family. They always do that at holidays, and then ignore me for the rest of the year unless I do well at a skating meet, which rates a mention in the local news as well as our newspapers on a slow day.

My entire reason for existence, in my dad's mind, is to make him seem like a normal guy with a normal family, but it's all unimportant background. I'm the exact right kind of boring to stay under the radar, with successful athletics and academics thrown in for good measure. Probably the media would like it better if I played hooky or smoked or drank or snuck out of the house to date a biker guy eight years older than me, but I don't.

I got through all my dad's parties, and was apparently an adequate daughter in front of all his friends. Or whatever they are, because I can't imagine anyone actually being friends with him. There was only one bad time when a girl my age showed up wearing a charm bracelet like the ones Jill and Allie and Vanessa have, and showing off her new charms. Her dad made some comment about how she 'had to have' a certain charm that all her friends were getting, and laughed about charm bracelets making such a huge comeback. I thought my dad was going to be really mad at me because he hates it when I don't look 'normal' but he didn't say anything at all. The next day, I found a charm bracelet with ten charms on it sitting on my bedside table.

I try to avoid him as much as I can, and I HATE that he was in my room when I was sleeping, but he'd have half-killed me for not thanking him. So I did. And it is a great bracelet. I just wish that it wasn't from him.

Next week is skating, all day every day before we head out to our international meet. I hope my dad isn't coming. He usually drives me when he can and I don't get to go on the bus with everyone else and it doesn't help me look less weird to the other kids. I hope you have a great Christmas!

Love, Caelie.

CHAPTER FOUR

Dec. 28

Dear Amy,

It's my birthday today, and the first day my back doesn't hurt. Being thirteen doesn't feel any different than being twelve, it just sounds weird when I say it to myself. I'm not sure I want to be a teenager.

Hey, I finally figured out how Janna knew who I was; her aunt teaches skating. Not to me, but at my rink. Janna's coming with us to the competition and my dad's busy so I get to travel on the bus with the rest of the team. I'm not totally sure about the bus trip, even though it can't possibly be worse than driving with my dad, but I don't know why Janna's coming. She doesn't even skate.

Everyone at skating is afraid of Janna, so it's not just the school that she rules, it's everyone. She's always nice to me, but I keep thinking of all the rumours at school about her being a prostitute and beating people up all the time. I can't figure out why the two things are related or whether either of them is really true.

I don't know why a twelve year old would want to be a prostitute, or whether you can be at that age. There are a lot of things I don't know. Of course, she's probably already 13 because I'm younger than most of the people in my grade, but . . . still. I heard those rumours when we were still in Grade 7, everyone *is* scared of her, and people do ask her questions about sex. Yesterday in the changeroom at skating, someone asked her how long it takes to have sex and she said you're usually finished in about 15 minutes. Is that true, Amy? You're grown up, so you must know. Why do you think anyone my age wants to have sex, anyway?

Love, Caelie.

The morning we had to leave for the skating meet was madness. I was there early, of course, because my dad does everything perfectly in public, including calling some of his media buddies out to document him being such a great dad while he wished me luck in my big competition. There was more media than normally turns up, and the coaches were running around like crazy and sending us all off on errands, like collecting a backup copy of all the music and getting extra tape and bandaids and laces and tights. Madness.

They finally herded us all together and got everyone's gear stowed under the bus, but we had to wait for Justina before boarding. She's always late and never gets in trouble because she's on the team to Worlds next year, but it didn't matter that much because even after she finally arrived, a whole bunch of parents were still fussing about letting their kids go off without them and checking to see that they had everything from toothbrushes to power cords.

Luckily, once my dad made his public appearance with me and got congratulated on doing such a great job as a parent, he left me alone and the media followed him. Janna beckoned me over a few minutes after he left, which meant that I had someone to stand with, but also that I was standing with Janna, and I'm still a bit scared of her.

Jan. 2

Dear Amy,

Whoa. I *have* to tell you about the competition. Well, actually nothing whatsoever about the competition itself (I came second in one event and first in another, which was better than they expected because it's my first year in a new level), but a LOT about the weekend. It started out okay—my dad dropped me off at the rink with my stuff and we all milled around after his media hounds left, loading our stuff onto the bus and comparing junk food. I had my standard apple juice, plain rice crackers and fruit leather, so I tried to keep my stuff concealed. So far, very normal.

When we finally got on the bus, I started to sit right up at the front by the driver, which is my favourite seat for about a million different reasons: you can see better, the air's fresher, you don't get as sick when you're reading or doing homework, you're not crowded by as many people, practically everyone ignores you, and you can get off first.

I was kind of annoyed that I'd barely stepped towards it when Janna motioned me to follow her to the back. The very back, where the older kids and the bad kids sit, so I didn't want to go, but it's not a good idea to ignore Janna. Besides, I was a bit curious, so I carried my stuff to the back and sat down beside her, right by the bathroom at the back where they have three seats together instead of two. Everyone wants to sit there, but obviously nobody at skating wanted to mess with Janna anymore than the people at school. She sat in the middle, I sat on the aisle, and a really mean girl named Deena sat by the window.

We'd only been driving for about ten minutes (the chaperones had made their rounds and assured themselves that we were all seated and suitably well-behaved) when we started playing Truth-Dare-Double-Dare. At first it was just the three of us, and it started when we all went into the bathroom together and Janna lit up a cigarette. I tried not to let my jaw actually hit the floor and, although Deena laughed at me, she kept telling Janna she would get caught, so Janna dared Deena to smoke it too. Of course she did, and was passing it to me (I'm not sure if I would have tried it or not) when Janna stopped her.

"Not Caelie," she said. Not Caelie. She said that a lot through the whole game, even when the 4 rows of kids closest to us were also playing. Nobody questioned her and nobody teased me then or afterwards. It was kind of weird.

She did let Deena dare me to have Jared, the cutest guy on the bus and two years older than us, French-kiss me after she asked what I'd done with guys and I said nothing. I mean really nothing. Not even holding hands nothing. I'm not allowed to date until I'm 16. So I went into the bathroom with Jared and Deena, who was making sure I went through with it, but I don't think he really wanted to, so it was kind of embarrassing. Also wet, and gross. Deena laughed at me.

It got worse after that, so I was pretty relieved when we finally got to the competition site because the game had totally gotten out of control by then and a girl got dared to go down on some guy and after that I really didn't want to play or even be around them playing. Apparently she did it, but I tried not to think about it. Who would *want* to do that *ever*, let alone on a bus filled with people you know? How could that not be hideously embarrassing for both of them? Gross, gross, gross.

The chaperones didn't notice anything, and why would they? As long as we weren't screaming or throwing things or getting out of our seats, they were happy.

It didn't get any better when we got to our dorms (we were staying at a college) and I was assigned to a room with Janna, Deena, and a girl 3 years older than me. Her pairs partner came over to our room after the post-dinner chaperone check, and they ordered the three of us out. I was refusing to go when Janna grabbed my arm and pulled me out, but I continued complaining until we found a stairwell to sit down in and Janna explained that I really didn't want to be in the room while they were having sex.

I just stared at her while Deena laughed at me again. It's not a nice laugh. We didn't get back to our room until after 10:00 and at one point I asked Janna about the 15 minutes thing and she said they could do it more than once. After that, I didn't want to ask anything else, and just sat there waiting.

There was no point telling anyone because it would just get me in trouble, and not just with Janna and Deena. Adults are happiest when you let them believe what they want but they get super aggressive when you make them deal with problems they'd rather not know about.

It was an educational weekend, but I think I prefer being boring and lonely. It's kind of scary to be with the 'bad' kids. You never know what anyone will do. Or have to do. Including yourself. I'm glad Janna likes me, but I have to wonder why. What if I do something to make her not like me anymore?

Love, Caelie.

It was not a relief to get home, because it meant more time with my dad, but the coaches had congratulated him on my performance, there'd been a nice write-up in the paper that mentioned him more than me, and he'd hit a new all-time high in the polls, so he was in kind of a good mood and I was able to lay low for the rest of the holidays.

I didn't see Janna or anyone else under the age of thirty for the rest of the holidays, but I did finish the extra English assignments that Mr. Bowman gave me. *The Importance of Being Earnest* is hilarious, but Oscar Wilde got in a lot of trouble when he was alive. It wasn't part of the assignment, but I read about his life anyway. I used the rest of my time off to play with Missy, help out at my dad's continuing parties and look after the house and meals and everything. Amy was my only real friend, and I looked forward to writing to her more than anything else I did, even when I didn't really have anything to say.

Jan. 5

> D'you believe in God, Amy? We had to go to church this weekend. And synagogue. And temple. When your dad's a politician, you learn early that to be successful in politics, you don't have to believe in anything. You just have to get other people to believe in you. The church places were all pretty much the same, I have to say, and everyone was really nice to us. I know you're into science and some people think science and God are mutually exclusive, but I don't see why. Do you?

> Love, Caelie.

When I got back to school after New Year's, everything was just the same. It felt good to hang out with Stef after the uncomfortable skating trip, even if we can never escape the J's. Doria's there too, but she never really says much, and Stef and I mostly do homework after the drawing game. He gave up on the music messages because I was so pathetic at them, and it was just as well because we still had all our academic classes plus new electives, and all my important skating meets were coming up. I needed my lunchtimes to study. Well, mostly study.

Jan. 22

Dear Amy,

> I have one really neat elective this term called Environmental Education. I thought that it would be a course about ecology and conservation and stuff, but

really it's about hunting. We've even gone to a rifle range to shoot at those clay things they fling into the air. The rifle hurts a lot more than I thought it would when you fire it. I'm used to getting hurt, but somehow it's different when you deliberately hurt yourself. I missed all of my clay targets on my turn to shoot, which made me feel really pathetic until the teacher pointed out that the rifle was taller than me, and probably weighed more, besides. I was the only one who actually fell over when we first tried firing them on the range. Mr. Jameson might make fun of me for being so tiny, but he doesn't actually blame me for it, so that's okay.

We've also done some orienteering in the woods to learn how to use a compass. Do you know you can make tea from pine needles? It's not bad. Yesterday, Mr. Jameson brought in a dead squirrel to show us how to skin an animal. It was actually kind of neat and the squirrel still looked very cute afterwards. I guess I expected it to sort of fall apart when the skin came off, but it stayed in a nice, compact squirrel shape.

At the end of the term, he's bringing in a bunch of meat from animals he's killed so we can try them all. I'm not sure how keen I am on that—he's bringing bear and moose and lynx. Isn't lynx an endangered animal? I don't think I could ever be a hunter, but I guess it's better than eating meat from some poor animal that's been kept in a cage its whole life and then terrified until it was its turn to get slaughtered on the conveyor belt or whatever.

Still, for a class called Environmental Ed, we sure don't learn very much about the environment except how not to get lost in it while we're out shooting things.

Love, Caelie.

Jan. 28

Dear Amy,

Janna doesn't come to school anymore. At first I thought she was just sick or something, but we've been back at school for almost a month now and she hasn't come back. Even though she'd only talk to me once a week or so, it was nice knowing that someone besides Stef might talk to me during the day. Not that she did very often, and it always made me a bit nervous, but it was at least a possibility. Maybe she moved away.

Last week, I helped the librarian unpack a new box of books, so I got to read them first. There was a new Gordon Korman that was okay, but the books he wrote as a kid are a lot better than his books now. He's not interesting or funny anymore.

We only have a week left to choose our courses for next year (I don't know why you have to do it so early) and I haven't decided on a career track yet. I don't want to give up sciences or language/history. You can always pick to do only academic subjects and not do any electives, so maybe I'll do that, but I can't think of any job that needs reading, history and dissection.

Love, Caelie.

Feb. 2

Dear Amy,

I hurt so badly, but I can't go to a doctor because it's too hard to explain this away as an accident. I guess my dad thought that hitting me in the back and stomach would at least not break anything or leave any bruises that people would see, but I'd rather have a broken arm or something because it hurts to breathe and there's blood when I go to the bathroom. What should I do? My dad will kill me if anyone finds out. Please, please, help me, Amy.

Love, Caelie.

Feb. 3

Dear Amy,

Please forget about my last letter. I was just being stupid.

Caelie.

I could barely move, let alone walk, and my dad called the school to say that I was sick. Mr. Bowman emailed me all my assignments for the week, which I freaked out about until I realized that it was just part of his job as the Honours program co-ordinator. I couldn't do any of the work at first, because it hurt too much to move at all. I barely managed to write a nice answer to his email so that he wouldn't start to think or worry about me.

As soon as my dad left the house for work the morning after it happened, I took 4 Advil and 2 Gravol so I could go back to sleep, then got up at lunch to let Missy out and take more Advil and Gravol to dull the pain from getting out of bed. I didn't wake up until just before he came home, after a dinner meeting that ended really late.

I pretended to be asleep.

The second and third days passed the same way, but when the house was finally quiet and dark on the night of the fourth day, I pulled out my laptop and stared at the opening of the letter I was writing to Amy, just reading and re-reading the first paragraph, thinking about how I lie to everyone. Everyone. All the time.

I can't lie to Amy. My secret reason for writing to her, one I didn't acknowledge to myself when I started the letters, was so I wouldn't start to believe my own lies. When it's down in black and white, I don't worry that I'm just dreaming all of it. I'll know I'm crazy when I start to think my dad is right, and there've been a few times lately that I have. Everyone listens to him. Everyone believes him. Nobody even sees me, not really, so it's like the things that happen at home only happen in my mind. Whole days go by when it's only the thought that this happened to Amy, too, that keeps me remembering it's real. It is real. Amy would believe me. Wouldn't she?

I re-read the first paragraph for the fourth time, then took a deep breath that made me gasp with pain, but I'd decided. I would not lie to Amy.

Feb. 5

Dear Amy,

Sorry about that. I was scared when I wrote to you and I probably exaggerated a bit. I only have to stay home for a few days and take some Tylenol and stuff. I'm still a little bit sore, but not too bad.

It's embarrassing and scary, but I leave the beginning because, somehow, deleting it would be like lying to her. My cheeks burn when I think of her reading it, but I go on.

Does this sound as stupid to you as it does to me? I'm lying about being okay, and to an imaginary person who will never see this! I never tell anyone the truth, but I tell you the truth and then it freaks me out and I want to take it back. I pretend that you're real a lot and I want to believe it so much that sometimes I do.

It's not the pain or fear that's really so bad, it's what happens when other people don't believe you—really don't believe you—and you begin to think you may be mistaken, even when you're not. Of course nobody's dad would do this to them, right? Especially not my dad, with his money and huge house and popularity. Not to me, who's in the right school and wears the right clothes and wins competitions in the right sports. It's ridiculous, isn't it? If no one else can believe it could happen, I must be wrong that it does. Only, I'm not. I'm not wrong.

It was really pretty bad. My dad came home late from work and I'd made salad and lasagna, so it kept pretty well, but I didn't know there were tomatoes he wanted used up and I hate tomatoes so I didn't put them in the salad. He hit me really hard in the stomach and, after I doubled over, he kept hitting and kicking me in the back. I haven't been to school or skating since then and it took two days for the bleeding to stop; hopefully whatever was bleeding inside me is actually healing. It was so scary, Amy, and I hate being scared.

Still, being scared about being hurt is better than being scared about being crazy. I need someone I don't have to lie to, and there isn't anyone else. It's not that I've never tried, it's just that it never works.

Love, Caelie

Feb 10

Dear Amy,

I feel a little better now, but I'm still very sore, especially in P.E. and at skating. I carry one of those little travel tubes of Tylenol around with me all the time, and it seems to help even if I am taking more than I should. I use ice packs at home, too, but not when my dad is around because it makes him angry. I wish I could make it stop, but no matter how careful I am or how hard I try to do everything right, he still gets mad at me. If I could just be better or smarter or . . . something. I don't know.

You used to be me and now you're okay, so there is an end, right? I mean, you're grown up and you don't really have friends, but at least you have people who respect you and are mostly nice to you and do care about you, even if they have no idea who you actually are. And you're safe. I can't imagine feeling safe.

Love, Caelie.

I walked pretty slowly everywhere at school when I got back, and Stef seemed to be watching me. Mr. Bowman was too, so I said that my stomach still hurt a bit from the flu, and I tried to be more lively when I was around them. On the third day at lunch, Stef handed me a picture. It was a drawing of me sitting across from him, doing my homework like always, but there was something strange about it. After a moment, I realized that everything around me was light, swirling into darkness as it got closer to me. "Homework," I said feelingly, rolling my eyes dramatically as I slid it back across the table.

He didn't take it at first, but I just smiled and turned back to my work. Finally, he slid it towards himself slowly, and I heard him writing on it like always, but this time he pushed it back. I didn't want to look at it, but I did. He'd written the word 'friend' on it instead.

"Thanks," I said, looking right at him and smiling. I'm good at lying, and not just with words. Being very, very normal in front of Stef was very important in that moment. I had to ignore the darkness in the drawing, pretending I hadn't seen it, or it didn't mean anything. Most of all, I had to make sure it didn't mean anything to him. "You're a good artist," I praised him. "I'm hopeless at drawing."

"I know," he grinned, but his grin fell away more quickly than normal. Luckily, Doria showed up with the J's in tow and I was spared having to do anything else to distract Stef. His drawing the next day was of a whole litter of kittens scrambling over each other to get their mom's milk. It was very cute, and a lot of the details he'd put in, like the wince on one kitten's face as its brother or sister stepped right on its head, made me smile. The fact that it wasn't about anything serious made me relieved.

"Life," I replied, and he wrote it down right away.

Feb. 16

Dear Amy,

Hey. I really do feel better now. And he's left me alone for a couple of weeks now, so that's good. Also, things may or may not get better for me at school (I'm reasonably confident they can't get worse)—Vanessa is moving away this weekend.

Love, Caelie.

It was Aidan who told me Vanessa was leaving, and I just looked at him as we pulled stuff out of our lockers and then stuffed our jackets in. If you put your jacket in first, there's no way to get anything else out.

"I know," I said back coolly, even though I didn't.

"Yeah, whatever," he snorted. "Where's she going?" he tested me.

I shrugged, annoyed to have been caught out in such a stupid lie. "I don't know," I decided to admit, "but it's not like I can avoid seeing Allie and Jill and Ness burst into tears every day after school. So?" I asked, returning the ball to his court. "Where is she going?"

"Montréal." Moh-ray-al, is how he said it, drawing each syllable out.

"Really?" I asked him, and it seemed almost like a normal conversation, the kind we used to have before Allie and Jill and Ness and I fell out, and I began hanging around with Stef instead of all of them.

"Yeah. Weird, huh?"

I nodded. She's terrible at French.

"Why?" I asked.

He shrugged and said, "Job, I guess."

Yeah. Hmmm. Well, no wonder Vanessa spent most of the day crying, although Ethan tried to cheer her up by telling her they had the greatest NHL team in the league, and she perked up a bit at the thought of rich, athletic guys and the teenagers who would admire them. New boys! Why didn't she think of that earlier? Good grief.

Feb. 21

Dear Amy,

Vanessa is gone and Allie was sick today, so Jill was here alone. Our lockers are close together and I was trying to find my English binder when she walked up, looking a bit nervous. I said hi and then looked back down again quickly in case she was still ignoring me, but she said hi back right away and sounded kind of relieved. So I risked looking up again and she was smiling. She started talking really quickly about how she and Allie had spent the whole weekend wondering if we would go back to "normal" with Vanessa gone.

I'm not sure that's possible, but Jill hung out with me in class and at breaks, and even though it felt a bit awkward and we tried to avoid talking about anything that's happened this year, it was still nice to have someone talking to me again. The guys are talking to me again now, too. Ethan and Aidan used to hang out with the four of us girls, and the other boys do whatever they do, so it was nicer at school today than it has been in a long time.

I kind of missed Stef at lunch, but Mr. Bowman looked pleased when he saw me with a whole group of kids, and I'm a bit nervous about the drawing game now, anyway.

Love, Caelie.

"Hey," Stef said to me, as we slid into place in English a few days later. Allie was back at school after a three day illness, and I was sitting with Stef again. It was nice to have everyone else 'like' me again, but it's not real. I don't actually like them anymore, and they only like the Caelie they think I should be, not the Caelie I really am.

"Hey," I smiled back.

"Are we still friends?" he asked me seriously.

I nodded. "Yeah." In my three days with the old crowd, I hadn't gone back to laughing when he got teased, or ignoring him when we had group work in class, and I always talked to him when he was near me. The others dealt with that by pretending it wasn't happening, or that he just didn't exist, which was a step up from them calling him names.

Halfway through the class, he slipped me another drawing. It was a picture of Allie on her cell phone, and I snuck a look over my shoulder to see that she was totally using it. In Mr. Bowman's class! I wrote 'suicidal' on the back of the drawing just as Mr. B stopped beside her and held out his hand for the cell phone. Like everyone else, I winced as he scrolled through the history of texts or whatever was on the screen before wordlessly pocketing it. There are other teachers who don't notice or don't care, but nobody has ever successfully gotten away with anything in Mr. B's class. He notices everything, but at least he doesn't read your screen or notes out loud like other teachers do.

Unfortunately, he stopped by our desks next.

"Mr. Barnes," he said, holding out his hand. Reluctantly, Stef handed over the drawing. Mr. B looked at it, then looked from Stef to me and back again.

"A remarkable talent," he commented mildly, and instead of putting the drawing in his pocket, he went into his office and taped it to his bookshelf, the one that's covered in quotes by famous people and also with Calvin & Hobbes comics. Nobody said anything when he walked calmly back into the class, but I could tell they all wanted to see it. They'd forget about it before ever getting the chance, though, because Mr. B only lets you in his office if he's specifically invited you, something that happens extremely rarely.

Mar. 2

Dear Amy,

I slept over at Jill's house for the first time ever, even though we've known each other since kindergarten. It was good but a bit weird. I guess new things always are. Weird, I mean. Not necessarily good. We spent until about 7:00 looking after her little brothers. She has six of them, which is even more horrible than it sounds, if you can believe it.

I know you had a brother, but he was older, right? I always wanted to have an older sister—you know, someone who could tell me things about growing up and teach me how to do girl things, and who would let me borrow her clothes and sneak into her room at night to talk. And, as long as I'm wishing, I'd like to have normal parents like kids in books have. Well . . . some books. Anyway, I would never want to have six younger brothers because they are incredibly annoying. They never shut up and they're always whining, shouting, whacking each other and tattling.

In the four hours we helped her mom take care of them, they weren't quiet for even one second. Also, they were always breaking stuff, making huge messes, or trying to kill themselves by riding down the stairs in a laundry basket. I think I'd go nuts if I were Jill. She says she used to hope for a sister but after the first four boys she stopped, figuring that no girl would want four older brothers. Especially her brothers. Plus, she'd have to share her room with a sister, and this way she's the only one with her own room. Thank goodness!

We hid out in her room as soon as her mom let us, which wasn't until after the three youngest were in bed, but I loved it at first sight. Jill has the smallest room in the house, and I think it used to be a crawl space. You can't stand up in it and there's this little tunnel that goes to a tiny window that doesn't open and has bars across it because it's barely above ground level. Her bed is just a mattress on the floor, and she has a little miniature door. She said she used to just have a curtain, but the boys would always get into her room and mess up her stuff, so her dad built her a little door. She can even lock it.

I've always wanted a lock on my bedroom door. Obviously. My dad says no, of course, like it's some kind of criminal request. 'Hey Dad, I don't want you to beat me up anymore, so can I have a lock on my door?' I've never said that to him, but I guess it's kind of implied because he gets mad when I bring it up, so I don't.

Anyway, Jill's room is pretty cool. She has it done up in a dungeon motif, and her aunt painted a really amazing mural window for her with a bunch of knights fighting to rescue her. She's got stone wallpaper, you know, those big stones that castles are made of? It looks so cool.

My room's still pink from when my mom did it for me ages ago. Walls, bedspread, carpet, curtains, everything is pink, so I think Jill's room is amazing, but she says she wishes she could have a regular room. We played board games for a while, then watched a high school movie that wasn't as bad as I thought it would be.

When even Jill's parents were asleep, we snuck upstairs to make ice cream sundaes from stuff Jill bought with her allowance and then hid so the boys wouldn't find it. Good thing, too! She had chocolate sauce, chocolate chips, whipped cream and gummy bears in her stash, and it wouldn't have lasted two seconds if the boys had known it was around.

We piled ice cream into our bowls and then topped it off with so much junk that the ice cream was completely buried. After that, we crept back to her room, sat down to eat, and started talking.

It was a pretty good night, and Jill's kind of normal on her own. I wonder if Allie still is, too?

Love, Caelie.

CHAPTER FIVE

Elections are coming up next year, and my dad's decided he wants to run this entire part of the country instead of just our city. It must have been in the works for a while before he called me back to the kitchen one night after dinner to let me know what my summer was going to be like.

"Nancy will be picking out your wardrobe and you will be wearing approved outfits for all public events, which means every day. Don't rip them or get them dirty, and waste all of her effort," he warned me. His assistant is about a thousand years old, and I've never seen her smile, certainly not at me, but I nodded anyway.

"We'll be on the road for several weeks to build up my recognition factor outside the city, and you will have to keep yourself busy, quiet, and out of the way unless we need you. I expect perfect manners and big smiles, so don't let me down."

"I won't," I promised, smiling at him to prove that I could do it well.

"Good," he said, not smiling back. "You still getting all As?"

"Yes, dad."

"I want that sticker for the car when we tour," he told me.

Oh, crap, I thought. A 'Proud Parent of an Honour Roll Student' sticker displayed on TV and in communities and cities all over our area is not what I need to stay under the radar at school. And to think, last week Jill was complaining about having to visit Disneyland with all of her brothers. The prospect of going on a road tour with my dad and his political advisors for two months made me a lot less sympathetic towards her. This will not be my best summer ever, although it can never touch the terrible one after Grade 3, no matter what happens.

"You'll have it, dad," is what I actually said.

"All right. Go on, then," he dismissed me.

"Thanks," I said, and went quietly back to my room, leaving the door open because he doesn't want to think I'm getting up to anything I shouldn't be. There must have been some parent awareness email or something recently, because I even have to turn my desk so that he can see the screen of my laptop when walking past my room, but I've discovered that as long as I do what he wants, he never looks closely enough to read the screen. Anyway, I can switch to a new tab super quickly and my letter file looks like what it is, a standard homework assignment. It's also password protected.

Why does he even care about Internet 'safety'? If I got abducted it would be bad publicity for him, but if he didn't have to deal with me anymore, I can't see why he'd care. Mom's been gone for five years now, and he's never cared about that. I guess, with all the publicity about the dangers of the Internet, he wouldn't want me to make him look stupid by going off with a total stranger.

Mar. 9

Dear Amy,

What's the best thing you remember about your childhood? Mine was summer camp. When my mom was around, she would drop me off at summer camp every year. It was a two hour drive from the city and it was usually a pretty quiet one because we didn't have that much to say to one another. When we got there, she would sign me in and help me carry my stuff to my cabin before saying goodbye. She was always anxious to get started on the long drive back home and I was desperate to run to the gym-barn (the outside looked like a barn and the floor was like a school gymnasium's, but the walls were really old and there were bats in the roof) to sign up for the good activities before they were gone. It was a quick goodbye; she just told me to have fun, gave me a hug and left. I would rush to toss my stuff onto a top bunk (I was there for 3 summers before I realized that some people actually *prefer* the bottom bunk, and I still can't imagine why) and sprint to the gym to sign up for activities.

I always wanted archery, canoeing, and gym, but one year we arrived too late for anything good and I had to take First Aid (soooo boring, especially since I did it in swimming lessons every year), swimming (okay, but you can swim every day anyway), and orienteering (which was basically going for hikes, and not very exciting).

I always wanted archery because where else do you have the chance to do that? Canoeing was pretty good, too. I really liked the quiet of the water and getting to explore around the lake. We saw birds and beavers and lots of fish. Once we were allowed to capsize so we'd learn how to right our canoe and get back to shore, but everyone looked at the leader like she was nuts. I talked my partner into it, but nobody else would do it (what is the point of going to camp, if you're not going to try anything new when you're there?). It wasn't that hard to get the canoe righted while treading water, but it was slow paddling back to shore with our canoe half-submerged, and then we had to change our clothes which made us late for lunch and all the good food (buns and oranges and cookies) was gone, so my partner was mad at me. I thought it was worth it, except that she stayed mad the whole week.

Gym was another good choice because we played lots of different games plus they had trampolines and two of those carnival rides that are like 3-D circles (just tethered to a beam, not attached to the actual ride) that you sit in facing someone and get strapped in before spinning you head over heels. I liked going backwards, but going forwards made me throw up. I wonder why? Some of the guys were really strong and they could spin you *fast*. You could use them in free time too, but only if you could persuade a counselor to take you, so it was good to be in gym because for sure you'd get a few turns.

After I signed up for my activities, I'd sprint back to the cabin to see who else was there and to arrange my stuff. That was pretty easy: unroll sleeping bag, toss pillow on bed, stow suitcase on shelf. Some people used to unpack their clothes and arrange them on their shelf, but my stuff was neat enough in my suitcase and besides, once I was 8, my mom made me bring pads "just in case" I got my first period while I was at camp, so I had to make sure nobody saw them. Now that I'm 13, I still don't have my period, thank God! Gross.

I read this book once where a girl and her friends actually *wanted* to get their periods and felt *left out* when someone else got it first. It was like peering into some alternate universe. How could you want to be inconvenienced and potentially embarrassed every single month? That may have been the stupidest book I've ever read, and I've read a lot of books. I did read this other book, though, about a residential school where the First Nations girl secretly got a cake and some gifts from her friends to celebrate her periods starting because it was an important rite of passage in her culture. I can sort of understand that, but the girls in the first book were just plain weird (a word I'm using now in favour of the more insulting "stupid"). Thanks, Mom, for giving me something to be paranoid about in my one free week a year!

At least she picked a great camp. The lake was at the bottom of a huge hill and they built a giant waterslide going all the way down the hill into the lake. There was also a rope that swung way out over the lake but you couldn't let go because the lake was too shallow there. It was tied to a high branch in a really old tree and you had to climb about 40 stairs to reach the platform and ride the swing. It was scary high, and creaked every time it swung back and forth, so we totally loved it.

Camp was awesome. They had the greatest porridge, which is kind of a weird thing to remember, but I love it and don't know how to make it, so camp is the only place I ever got it.

On the last night we always got to play Survival, and you had to bring dark clothes for Survival if you wanted to win what was basically a war game, where all the campers were soldiers who had to sneak into the enemy camp. If you made it to all the checkpoints without getting caught by the enemy (the counselors), you won, but if they caught you more than seven times (the counselors all had black markers and they would draw a line on the back of your hand each time they caught you), you were banished to prison (the campfire pit) until the game was over.

Once, we mounted a massive rescue with practically all the campers ambushing the counselors. We still lost in the end, but it was lots of fun. The little kids usually went to bed before it was over because the game lasted until midnight, but since we went home the next day, I guess they didn't really care if we were tired and cranky. I *was* always depressed on the last day, but not because I was tired.

All the stuff we did at camp was fun, even chapel and Bible study every day, but what I liked most about it was knowing how far away from my parents I was. I miss it; camp was the one time of the year I could feel normal, and Dad never sends me. This year we'll be campaigning all summer, which is the exact opposite of being far away from my dad. The

only good thing about an 8 week road trip with my
dad is that there'll be so many other people around
us and watching us that he probably won't be able to
hurt me that much.

Do you ever feel normal? I want to know if I will
when I get older.

Love, Caelie.

"We're going to the gym, Caelie," Jill told me before lunch, not
asking me to come. It just a polite heads-up that they weren't going
to hang around with me.

"Okay," I agreed. "See you later." Even if they wanted me to go
to the gym with them, I wouldn't. I ate my lunch really quickly
and then headed up to the library with my laptop. I still don't hang
out with them at school very much, and there've been no more
sleepovers, but at least everyone is nicer. I spend about half my
lunches in the library with Stef, who hasn't done any more weird
pictures. I'm happy about that, but also strangely disappointed, a
feeling I try to ignore.

Mar. 15

Dear Amy,

School is back to the way it always used to be,
sort of. Sometimes I go with Allie and Jill to get food
outside the school grounds at lunch, but I never hang
out in the gym with them. If one of them's sick, the
other one might come to the library at lunch with me,
but that's just because it's worse to be alone than to
be in the library.

We're all friends, but . . . careful ones, who try to
avoid anything contentious. They don't bug me about
not shaving my legs, which I really don't want to do,
and I don't call them stupid for going to watch guys.
We talk about school and sports and movies, although
I tend to walk away when they start talking about

movie stars they 'love.' It's bad enough going to the gym to watch guys who actually attend your school with you every day and whom you might have a remote chance of dating.

Maybe Allie and Jill are right and I am immature, but I can't help it.

Love, Caelie.

For the first time all year, I ran into Allie's mom on my way out of school. It was after spring break and I hadn't seen her since the last week in August. The sight of her put a huge, lead weight in my stomach, maybe because Allie's house was my favourite place in the world for most of my life.

"Hey, Caelie!" she said, smiling wide and looking very happy. I'd almost forgotten how nice and pretty she was, and I had to force back sudden tears when she absently tucked her dark hair behind her ear in an achingly familiar gesture. "You haven't been over in ages!"

I smiled brightly, blinking back tears and swallowing the lump in my throat.

"You must be so busy with skating," she said, before I had to think of something to say. "You'll have to come over soon, okay? Definitely in the summer. We miss you!"

"Thanks, Mrs. G," I said. "I'm going on the road with my dad this summer, though."

"Oh, that's right. Well, be sure to tell your dad that we'll be voting for him!" She grinned, and her attention was diverted as she spotted Allie and Jill coming out of the front doors together. She didn't hear me when I said goodbye.

Mar. 25

Dear Amy,

Hi. I miss you, which is kind of worrying, because I've never met you and I know you're not real. I dream about you a lot, though. Good dreams, where you're that big sister I always wanted and it's just the two of us together. It feels so nice to be around you. I hate waking up. Sometimes I think I'm silly for caring so much about you when you don't really exist, but then I watch an episode or read a book about you and I think about you constantly. I wish I really knew you.

I'm kind of scared that if I send these letters, your actress will read them and think I'm a freak, even though I found out that she might be nice.

I kind of imagined her as this totally normal (by which I mean clueless) person who is into her career and doesn't see or think much of what goes on outside her own world. Not that that's really bad, because I know acting's a very stressful and busy life, but then I looked at her website and she seems like a pretty decent person, so I don't know. Still, decent doesn't mean she'd understand me. On the other hand, to do such a good job of portraying you must mean that she understands you at least a bit, right?

Try to make sure she lets *you* read my letters. Especially this one. It's hard to explain that even though I know the writers create Amy Anderson, and Jane Allyson says what they tell her to say and does what the director tells her to do, you're still *real*. I mean, I'm real, and I'm a lot like you, so the idea of Amy is real. Right?

Sorry this is such a stupid letter.

Love, Caelie.

CHAPTER SIX

Apr. 2

Dear Amy,

Please PLEASE help me! I can't do this anymore. My dad locked me in the spare room downstairs while he dragged Missy into the laundry room down the hall. I don't know what she did, but he was really beating her. She was screaming and whimpering and I could hear thuds and thwacks as he hit her and . . . worse. I tried to protect her and that's why he locked me in here. He hates to miss, and I got between them and took some of the blows.

He came home in such a bad mood after work that I just laid low and stayed quiet and polite and obedient. We made it through dinner and I cleaned up the dishes and then took Missy out for a walk, partly to still be good, and partly to just get away from him. I hoped he could cool out a bit while we were gone, but when we got back, he opened the door like he was waiting for us and he was just furious. I knew he was out of control and that it would be bad, but I still freaked out when he grabbed her leash and started swinging her around with it.

A horrible noise came out as she tried to yelp, but couldn't manage it because her throat was being squeezed by the collar. I actually grabbed his arm to make him stop, but he flung me off and then let her fly. She smashed into the railings at the bottom of the stairs and broke through two of them. After that, he went incandescent, pounding on her as I screamed at him to stop. When I grabbed at his arms again, he picked me up and threw me in here and locked the door so I couldn't get out. I couldn't see him. I could only hear him, and imagine what was going on.

Her sounds got weaker and sometimes a whole minute went by when I couldn't hear her at all, but he never stopped. I couldn't do anything. I don't think I can stand it. At first I pounded on the door and screamed and flung myself at the door to try to get out, but I couldn't. I was frantic to get out and help her. It was so awful to listen to. My fingers are bleeding from scraping at the door. I couldn't get out. I couldn't help her.

Even when I couldn't hear her anymore, he was still grunting and pounding. I feel like I am going to explode, but also like I'm freezing. I couldn't help, but I had to listen. I can't be here anymore.

Caelie

I stared at the wall, even though it was so dark I couldn't see it. I had no idea what time it was, or how long I'd been in here, and I didn't care. I hated him before, but now there's so much hate, and it's not just at him. I'll never be able to see the good in anything anymore, because who cares? There's nothing good enough to erase this.

Apr. 3

Dear Amy,

He made me clean it up. He left me locked in overnight and when he opened the door to let me out, all I saw was blood everywhere. He used one of the broken railings on her and there were . . . bits. All over. She didn't even have a face anymore.

The teeth made a tiny, screeching, scraping sound when I mopped them up. I tried to spot them before I wiped, but there was just too much of her and I couldn't always see them. It took me two hours to clean up the blood and find all the bits and then I buried her in the garden with all of the paper towels. Neatly. You can't even tell now.

When I saw her body, I was kind of mad at *her*, but then I felt guilty for it. Maybe this is how my mom felt. She couldn't protect me and it made her feel desperate and hopeless so she got mad at me instead. For being weak. Or stupid. Or careless.

Something inside me got turned off when I was in that room last night. I think it might be an important bit, but I don't care anymore. You know when I said I couldn't be there anymore? Part of me left. I feel cold. And hard, inside. I didn't help her. I failed. As much as I hate him, I hate myself more.

Caelie.

CHAPTER SEVEN

"Caelie!" A wide, surface grin, and hands momentarily outstretched as if the tall, bulky man were both surprised and delighted to see me.

Automatically, I smiled at him and held the door open wider. An old football pal of my dad turned city official, he comes to all of my dad's parties and is often in my dad's office, too. "Hi," I greeted him politely as he stepped back to get a better look at me. He does it all the time, for show, because I've looked the same for years.

"Well, aren't you becoming a looker," he said, like he says every time. "You'll have to watch out for her pretty soon, Rich," he warned my dad laughingly.

My dad didn't even glance at me, just clapped him on the shoulder and pulled him inside. "She's on duty tonight," he told his friend. It was true. After I greeted the first eight arrivals, I had to make sure that everyone's bowls of chips, pretzels, and mixed nuts were filled. This was supposed to be an informal gathering, so we had caterers for the meal but not for anything else. Just an evening at home with me and my dad, his closest supporters and the money behind them.

"Pretty and useful," the guy joked as they walked away together. "I've got to get me one of those."

I had to keep smiling pleasantly because the next couple was already walking up to the door, and it was Nancy, who'd picked out my blouse and slacks for the evening, and advised me to wear my hair pulled back. She hates my hair.

"Hi, sweetie!" she said loudly and with a lot of artificiality. "Now, aren't you just a chip off the old block!"

I smiled at her even though she wasn't really looking at me. "Thanks, Nancy. It's great to see you here!" Again. I kept smiling as she told her husband what a credit I was to my dad, frowningly tried to smooth down my hair, and then headed out happily to the patio area. Once they were gone, I returned to the door for the next five arrivals.

This was going to be a long night.

Apr 18

Dear Amy,

My dad had a party last night. Everyone was outside, drinking and talking and having a swell time with their great buddy, my dad. I had to keep refilling the snack bowls and everything, and I ended up sitting outside with them. They were laughing and admiring my dad, and all I could do was smile back. I felt like I was going to scream.

When someone at our table dropped a bottle, I quickly moved to clean up the glass on the ground, and one of the pieces fell onto the floor as I was walking to the garbage can. I bent down to pick it up, and something about how cool and smooth and sharp it felt made me keep it in my hand when I threw out the rest. It was separate from my dad and party, separate from me, separate from everything, and it just sat there in my hand.

I gently touched the smooth and sharp sides of it, while a darkness and a power stirred inside me and the music and conversation of the whole party pressed heavily and swirled thickly around me. It seemed impossible to stay there, to stay me, and in a moment that required no thought at all, I sliced the sharpest edge of the broken glass across the soft skin on the inside of my forearm, over and over. It was the only bright, clear feeling in the room, and the black hatred inside me disappeared in its light. There was more blood than I expected, but I was wearing long sleeves so I politely excused myself (not that anyone was paying attention to me anyway) and went to the washroom to check out the damage.

The long, angry lines made me feel even better, and I'd never realized what a bright, powerful colour blood was. The drips and streams swirled into the water, and I regarded them with satisfaction and a dark delight. Only a few moments earlier, I'd been so full of anger and hatred that I couldn't stand it anymore, and now that was gone.

I walked out of the bathroom feeling powerful and calm, arms bandaged but bleeding, and a new shirt on to hide the evidence. The feeling of being in control, of being able to separate myself from the biting, clawing darkness lasted the whole night.

Unfortunately, the marks turned into a problem. It's super hot out and they go along the inside of my arm from my wrist to my elbow. Long, red, scabby lines. My dad hasn't noticed or doesn't care, and I wore long sleeves to school of course, but our gym uniforms are short-sleeved, and they're, you know, uniform, so my gym teacher noticed the cuts and pulled me aside to ask me what had happened.

A lot of people had already asked me in the changeroom, giving me a chance to practice the delivery of my response before talking to the teacher, and I told her the same thing I'd told everyone else: when I tried to grab a wild rabbit in our yard, its hind feet scratched me as it jumped out of my grip.

There are wild rabbits all over, even on the school fields before classes start, and I did a great job of seeming chagrined and embarrassed at trying to catch a wild rabbit in the first place. My voice was self-deprecating because I should be old enough to know better, of course. She looked like she thought it was possible and didn't really want to pursue it (what could she really do, anyway, I could see her thinking) but I made a mental note to be more careful in the future.

We were having gym outside with the guys and it was a major topic of discussion with everyone for at least five minutes, so I had to talk about it a lot. Stefan didn't ask me about it, but he heard me explaining to other people and then looked at me with no expression at all on his face. I had to look away. My heart raced when he stopped me later on at my locker, but he only asked if I was okay. I didn't pretend I had no idea what he was talking about, which I felt would be insulting him, but just nodded and thanked him.

So . . . there is at least one person who doesn't believe my plausible lies. I find that disconcerting, hopeful, and inconvenient. It's kind of nice, but too late.

Love, Caelie.

I stared at my screen for a moment. Was I telling her too much? There's a difference between not lying and being that needy, clingy kid that embarrasses everyone, even herself, without noticing.

"Hey, Caelie, can I have some Tylenol?"

Startled, I turned around, completely freaked that Jill might have seen part of my screen and trying hard to hide it.

"Sorry," I said, forcing myself to smile ruefully. "I don't have any."

Jill pouted, and I relaxed. There was nothing in her eyes but slight annoyance at being turned down. "But you always have Tylenol!" she argued. "Isn't that it right there?" Totally uninterested in me or my laptop screen, she was pointing into my bag, where you could see the corner of a travel Tylenol container.

"My skating partner used it up last night," I told her, shrugging. "Sorry."

She frowned and turned to Allie, and I let out a breath of relief. I wasn't carrying Tylenol in that bottle, and I didn't want anyone else opening it. I made a mental note to get some real Tylenol on my way home.

Apr. 26

Dear Amy,

Hi. I don't know if I want you to help me anymore. It hurts too much to care. There's nothing to rescue me from anymore, because wherever else I am, I'll still be myself. It makes me angry when my teachers and coaches praise me for being smart (which I can't help), talented (which I also can't help) and having such a great work ethic (which is the only possible option for me).

I used to keep all my medals, ribbons, awards, and trophies on my walls but I can't even pretend to be proud of them anymore. No matter how well I do at everything, I can't erase that time in the spare room from my mind, and that's the only thing that matters. Who cares if I use punctuation correctly and can memorize a science textbook? Who cares if I skate well enough to compete internationally? I can't stop hearing Missy die, and I don't think I can stand it much longer.

I continue to do well at everything, but I don't know if it's a matter of habit, or if I just don't know how to do badly. Maybe it would just be more of a hassle to deal with everyone if I didn't keep doing well. Anyway, working keeps my body busy and sometimes occupies my mind. That's a good thing, because when I'm tired and busy, I don't get angry. And *that's* good, because when I'm not angry, I don't hurt myself.

That time with the glass was just the first time, not the only time. Afterwards, I smashed some disposable razors apart and took the blades. They fit perfectly into a travel Tylenol container, so I carry them around with me everywhere. It's sort of like having my laptop with me so I can always write to you if I need to. Writing to you makes me feel human instead of hard, though, and I think that's a bad thing.

I'd rather be cold and separate and apart. I haven't used my razor blades yet, but carrying them makes me feel stronger. Safer. In control. Like if something unbearable happens again, I'll have a way out. It's not like writing to you.

When I write to you, I wish for things. I wish I could talk to you. I wish I could help you. I wish you could help me. I wish that I didn't feel so alone and separate and desperate. It would be nice to have someone know who I really am and understand me and still like me, but that's just silly and weak.

I'm different now. Sometimes you really can't go back. Now when I wish for you, it only lasts for a second before this nasty voice reminds me that I don't deserve anything. I know better than anyone that wishes don't come true.

Love, Caelie.

I closed my file but left my laptop open. It was English class, nobody could sneak up behind me, and I was making a minimal effort to pretend to be working. I didn't pretend well enough, because Mr. Bowman invited me into his office for a meeting after class.

"How are you doing?" he asked me, once I'd walked into his office and he'd shut the door behind me. That wasn't normal, a policy I know has more to do with protecting teachers from students than students from teachers. It's a messed up world.

I'd finished all of the extra work he gave me, mostly during Christmas break, and he'd given me another list of novels, plays and short stories to read. I was finished those, too.

"Fine," I said, smiling a bit. I never say anything extra, because I might slip up. I'd like to talk to him about English, but the more I say, the greater the risk. Mr. B's pretty sharp, for all his greyness.

"You're a bit ahead," he commented, and I couldn't tell if he was happy or worried about that.

"I like English," I told him.

"And your marks in Socials have improved," he added, looking down at his marks book even though I got the feeling he knew exactly what my marks were.

I said nothing. It wasn't a question.

"How's skating?" he asked me.

I smiled again. "Fine, thank you."

"I saw in the paper that you won your last competition."

I nodded. I'd won, but I was starting to hate skating, maybe because I'm good at it and it's public, so it's just like standing downtown and shouting out to everyone that my dad is doing a fabulous job and we're the perfect single parent family. It makes me want to slice into my skin so deeply that all the blood and lies and life pour out and disappear forever.

Thinking about that wouldn't help me here, though, and I willed the enticing image away, holding Mr. Bowman's eyes as if nothing were wrong, but remaining silent.

He had some chalk dust on one of his eyebrows, because he doesn't think old is the same as obsolete, so we use all kinds of technology in English. He makes us write with charred sticks sometimes, and one whole wall of the class is whiteboard, which he uses for projections as well as writing, while another wall is chalkboard. The rest is windows or bookshelves.

Mr. Bowman looked like he was going to say something else, but changed his mind.

"Do you have any problems, or any questions you'd like to ask me?" he offered, after a moment.

I shook my head. The lie stuck in my throat so that I couldn't speak, but I smiled again, and he let me go.

May 3

Dear Amy,

My dad got called into school yesterday to talk about how quiet I've become and how maybe I'm working too hard or could something else be wrong? Were there any problems in the family the school could help with? He must be very busy now with preparations for the elections, after all. He had no trouble dealing with it, of course, and everyone was smiling and relaxed by the time he left the office, except for Mr. Bowman, whose grey eyes had stayed on me the whole meeting. I pretended I didn't notice, but I had to hold my hands together in my lap so they didn't tremble.

None of them had any idea how absolutely furious and insulted my dad felt, and when the last bell rang, he was waiting at my locker. I knew right away that it would be bad, and after he smiled at me and greeted Allie by name, he didn't look at me or speak the whole drive home. As soon as we got inside, he backhanded me across the face and then held me up against the wall by my hair.

I didn't catch everything he screamed at me because he was hitting me too, but it was clear that he thought I was an idiot and that I'd embarrassed him and wasted his whole afternoon. He yelled about how many things he'd had to reschedule and how bad I had made him look with my retarded behaviour and if I *ever* called attention to myself again . . . I lost track after that, because all the yelling kind of blends together after a while. When I started throwing up, he dropped me in disgust and then kicked me for a while. I prayed very hard to be one of those people who passes out when they're in a lot of pain, but it didn't work.

He finally stopped because he had to go to a televised meeting and needed to clean himself up a bit. I just lay there and waited for him to leave. When he was gone, I crawled into the bathroom to clean myself up. It was the same bathroom I used when I had to clean up after Missy, but even the spike of rage and self-hatred that comes every time I think of her didn't dull the pain. After I showered off the vomit and blood, I cleaned up the front hallway and made my way slowly and carefully upstairs into bed. I fell asleep holding my Tylenol bottle.

This morning I got up and iced my legs and arms and back before taking a bunch of Advil and getting dressed in long sleeves and pants to cover my bruises, punctures and scrapes. I had to ask my dad for a note excusing me from gym. He looked like he wanted to hit me again when I asked him, but I was quiet and polite and kept my eyes down as I mentioned that our gym strip is a sleeveless shirt and knee-length shorts. He wrote the note.

My right leg hurt really badly all day and I'm worried that it might be fractured, but I can't do anything about it. I even have to pretend to be happier and more energetic than normal so he doesn't get called back to school. One of my fingers is definitely broken, but it's a baby finger, so I can get away with not using it very much until it heals. I hurt way too much to want to use my razor blades. I guess that's a good thing.

For some reason, hurting myself is satisfying and distracting in a way that getting hurt by someone else is not. I can do it right in class and at lunch and everything, and nobody notices. I just keep smiling and talking (or working, in class) and I look people in the eye when I'm doing it and even if they're right beside me, they don't see anything.

I used to have the outside part of me, which everyone thinks is nice and smart and pretty and . . . normal, and the inside part of me that would be screaming, "PLEASE HELP ME!" but now I have a third voice that reminds me that I *am* stupid and useless and a failure and that I don't deserve help. Then the inside part feels sad and ashamed and doesn't ask for help anymore, but just accepts the pins or glass or razor blades as necessary and right. I deserve them, after all. And they help me to keep acting normal. Maybe that's the help I was screaming for all along.

Caelie.

I could barely walk this morning, so my dad let me stay home from school. Normally he doesn't, because too many absences make teachers ask questions, but he really didn't want to take me to the hospital, so he called in and said that I had a cold. Schools are kind of freaked about pandemics now, and eager to confirm that keeping the kid home is the right decision. I don't know what to do about my leg. What about gym? It hurts to move my leg at all, even when there's no weight on it. I'm almost out of Tylenol and Advil, too.

May 5

Dear Amy,

We had gym at school yesterday, and it was both fortunate and unfortunate. It was field hockey, which I love, and I was taking four times the normal adult dose of Advil so I could at least walk without screaming, but I wasn't sure how I'd be able to run. All the Advil in the world wouldn't completely dull the pain.

Luckily, within the first ten minutes, the strongest girl in our class accidentally slashed me really hard with her stick, right on my sore leg. It hurt so much that I screamed, and then I couldn't stop the tears from coming. The secretaries couldn't get in touch with my dad, but the first aid attendant called an ambulance anyway. You could tell from looking at my leg that it was broken—one piece of bone was pushing up against my skin from the inside, but it hadn't broken through, at least. So, fortunately, my leg got taken care of without my dad having to take me in, but unfortunately, it hurt like crazy. Not as bad as the broken nose, but still so much.

It took 3 hours to get my dad on the phone and by then they didn't need him to show up, but were just letting him know what had happened. Thank God. The school has my health number and everything, and there were plenty of witnesses to say that I'd been hit really hard with a field hockey stick. I wanted to tell the girl who hit me that it wasn't her fault because she actually threw up on the field after she saw my leg, but all of my gasping, "It's okay," between screams didn't help. I couldn't tell her the truth.

They took X-rays of my leg and were wheeling me in to surgery before my dad showed up, and I liked that, too. It was a huge hassle getting pins put in my leg and having a cast on, but my dad seems kind of pleased that I managed to get it really broken when he was nowhere near me. I think he already knew it was, but what could he do? He was happier than normal to get away with it, and maybe if he's happy, he'll leave me alone for a while.

Love, Caelie.

"Aren't you sick of those things?" Jill asked me, annoyed after my crutches had fallen across her locker for the third time in a single day.

It wasn't my first time with them, and I was sick of them before the cast was dry.

"Yeah, sorry. I can't wait to get rid of them," is what I said, knowing Jill didn't care—or even think—about how it felt to have to use them. Why should she?

To Jill's obvious disgust, Stef stepped up from out of nowhere to hold them for me. He's been pretty quiet around me for the last few weeks, and it makes me a bit uncomfortable.

"Here," he said.

"Thanks."

Jill made an impatient noise, shut her locker door, and walked away. Having crutches and a cast had made me interesting and exciting for the first two or three days, especially since the whole thing had actually happened at school, but now it just made me tiresome, and most of my friends acted slightly annoyed with me all the time.

"Want help with your books?" Stef asked me. He asks every day.

"No, thanks." I smiled back, just like I always do. I carry everything around in my backpack so my hands are free for the crutches.

"Okay," he agreed, passing them back to me without further comment. We headed in separate directions for our electives, but I felt his eyes on me for several long seconds after I turned around and began to swing myself along the hallway.

June 10

Dear Amy,

I can't wait to get my cast off. At first it's helping you not to be in so much pain, but after a bit it's really annoying because you need so much more space to maneuver around the halls at school and if it's wet out, your crutches slip on the floors and you have to try not to fall down, plus people are always tripping over them in class and it's hard to move around with them and still carry all your stuff for classes. Also, it really starts to smell and itch after a couple of weeks. I can't wait to be able to walk around. And shower. Everyone at skating really hates me now, though, especially my pairs partner. They assigned someone else to him, but she's a bit bigger than me so he can't do all the lifts he wants to do. I'm tired of people hating me for things that aren't my fault. After all, there are so many *good* reasons to hate me. It seems such a waste to be hated for a lie.

Love, Caelie.

P.S.—I only have two days left to write to you and then I have to hand my letters in, so I guess this is almost it.

"Settle down," Ms. Ganett told the class warningly, on the day after my cast finally came off. It had created a very tiny stir in the class, but I was the one creating the disturbance, so she hated it.

She wasn't even in the class when everyone crowded around to see what my leg looked like. They were grossed out by how skinny my leg was, but they thought the scars from the pins were cool, even though they're really tiny.

At the first pinched syllable, everyone scattered, and Ms. Ganett glared at me. Our war had become a draw because neither of us was willing to give an inch, and she couldn't fail me on my work. I was polite but distant to her every day, and she was cold and sarcastic back. Sometimes I wonder if we might have liked each other if I'd been on time to that first class, but mostly I think she's just a jerk who needs someone to pick on.

June 11

Dear Amy,

I could barely keep a straight face in homeroom today. You will never guess what our homeroom time is being used for this week: informational seminars on abuse. You know, how to avoid it, how to recognize it, how to report it. We watched a nice, friendly, helpful video about nice, friendly, helpful people who can make your life oh-so-wonderful if you'll just ask them for help.

Who *makes* these videos? What, are they designed to be as inoffensive and unalarming as possible to people who never experience abuse so that way their parents won't complain that their children got traumatized from watching it or something? Heaven forbid some poor little normal kid should get upset by finding out what life is really like.

I alternated between wanting to throw something through the screen and walk out, or just laugh at the idiots who were making us watch it. I compromised by reading a book under my desk. Anyway, this is my last letter to you because we have to hand them in today. They'll already be in a sealed and addressed envelope when I give them to Mr. Bowman. He promised not to read them, but I'm not taking any chances. Good luck, and thanks for being there. It was good to talk to you.

Love, Caelie.

CHAPTER EIGHT

I handed my package of letters to Mr. Bowman after class so that nobody else would notice that I didn't have just one.

"Caelie," he said hesitantly, "Can I . . . ?" He paused for a minute without finishing his sentence. "Is there anything you want to talk about?"

I wish he would stop asking me that. "No," I said, looking down at my shoes. Lime green is just ugly. I don't know why it's popular.

"I've checked with your other teachers." That got me to look up at him, but neither his voice nor his expression changed. "And your marks are incredibly good in all of your classes."

I nodded, sensing a 'but' coming up.

"You seem to have more friends than you did at the beginning of the year," he commented.

Well, what do you know, teachers do notice some things.

"But you look a lot more . . . distant. Strained."

I didn't say anything. This was too dangerous a conversation to have. Even if I told Mr. Bowman the truth, and if he miraculously believed me, it wouldn't matter. All it could do was hurt his credibility, get me another Ministry lecture that would make me believe I'm crazy, and give my dad some bad press, which would probably make him kill me for real and then tell everyone he'd sent me off to boarding school.

Adults like to think they can help, but they can't.

"You're sure there's nothing you want to tell me? Or someone else, maybe?" he added.

My stack of letters sat conspicuously on the corner of his desk, but I didn't look at them. Amy was the only person who might understand, and she doesn't really exist.

"I'm fine," I said reassuringly, in what was probably the single greatest lie of my life. "Thanks, Mr. Bowman," I added for good measure.

He didn't look convinced, but let me go anyway. As I left, he turned to his computer, a comfortingly familiar action that alleviated my sudden stab of worry.

Exactly two weeks later, he asked me to see him after school. For a minute, I was terrified that he'd read my Amy letters instead of mailing them, but he sounded calm and low-key when he asked me. I decided it had to be something else. Still, I spent my final two classes worrying about why he wanted me. It's never good when a teacher asks to speak with you, so I didn't take much in when they were describing the final exams for us. Luckily, we also had handouts. I stuffed them in my bag, quickly grabbed my after-school snack out of my locker, and headed to his classroom.

Get bad stuff over with quickly, I reminded myself, because it's going to happen anyway and delaying does not make it better. It definitely doesn't make it go away.

His door was open when I got there, and he was inside his office, waiting. When I obeyed his beckoning finger and walked into his inner sanctum, he nodded acknowledgment of my presence, finished marking the paper he was reading, and then pulled a bulky envelope and a glossy photo of Amy from the top drawer of his desk. He passed them over without comment, and my heart almost stopped when I saw that it was signed by Amy Anderson. One of her team members, Jock, calls her signature chickenscratch, and this was the same. Real. On the back of it was a note, which said:

Dear Caelie,

Please do what they ask you to do. Trust me.

Love, Amy

A kind of warmth I've never felt before began to spread through me.

"Ready to go?" Mr. Bowman asked me, standing up.

It took me a second to focus back on him, and I saw that he was shaking his head. Without a conscious thought, I'd backed away from him, and not towards the open door.

"Not with me, Caelie," he explained gently, staying behind his desk. "Amy has sent some people to meet you. They're outside in the staff parking lot. Will you come?"

My mind spinning, I barely registered that it was a question as I followed him out in a daze. There were people and noises in the hallways, the everyday slamming of lockers and everyone shouting to be heard above everyone else, but I was oblivious to all of it. *Amy wrote back to me.* The thought filled my mind from edge to edge as Mr. Bowman led me to the parking lot, where the sharp edge of panic returned as I spotted two women waiting there, lounging against a dull beige car.

"This is Caelie." Mr. Bowman said formally, when we got close enough to be heard, gesturing to me as if there were a bunch of girls standing around clutching photos of Amy and he had to point out the right one.

"Hi Caelie. I'm Morgan, and this is Charlotte," the closest one said matter-of-factly as they stopped leaning against the car. Both women were tall and lean, and the word 'languid' popped unbidden into my mind at the sight of them. I'd never seen anyone before that I could apply it to, but they seemed to have it down pat, at least until they moved. When they shifted to a standing position, the image of cats rushed into my head, and I realized that both 'languid' and 'graceful' apply to large, wild predators. Unless you are the prey, of course, in which case 'imminent death' is the only relevant description.

I took a moment to study them. The one who'd spoken had hair just like mine—long and curly and red, except that hers was a light strawberry blonde, with loose curls that fell to just below her shoulders. Morgan was a good name for her. The other one looked just like a Charlotte. Her soft brown hair was tied back neatly, she had warm hazel eyes and freckles, and she was also bit taller than Morgan. Both of them were strikingly beautiful.

"Hi," I said nervously, glancing sideways at Mr. Bowman.

"Here's where I leave, Caelie," he nodded briskly. "Good luck." He gave me a bit of a smile, and when he winked at me, his eyes were as pale and clear as always, if a bit softer than usual. "By the way," he grinned over his shoulder when he was a couple of paces away, "you got your whole 15% on the letter writing assignment." I automatically smiled back at him, even though grades were the last thing on my mind.

The sound of the parking lot gravel crunching under his scuffed, sturdy leather shoes seemed ominous in the sudden silence as he walked away.

"Charlotte is a police officer," Morgan said, drawing my attention back to her and tilting her head towards Charlotte as my stomach instantly filled with ice. "I help her out in the lab." Even though I was concentrating hard on concealing my panic, I noticed that Charlotte's eyes flickered toward Morgan when she said that.

Morgan noticed Charlotte's quick glance, but her gaze never veered from mine. I shook my head a bit and tried to back away, but Morgan's gaze held me where I was.

"I'm fine!" I protested, without thinking. I can't have anything to do with a police officer. Was Amy trying to get me killed?

"Well, I'd like to take your word for it," Morgan said lightly, "but I've known Amy for a long time, and she disagrees."

Oh, God.

"She got your letters," the tall redhead added unnecessarily, "and called me. We'd like you to come for a ride with us."

A ride? Where? They both looked at me as I stood there, the ice spreading from my stomach into my chest. With nowhere else that was safe, I looked down at Amy's solemn expression in the photo and, without consciously deciding anything, turned it over. My fingers traced the words on the back.

Do what they ask you to do. Trust me. Love, Amy

Visions of my dad descending on me after the Grade 3 incident stabbed viciously through my mind, and a dark Stygian smoke obscured Amy's words. I couldn't live through that again.

"Why?" I choked the word out, and lifted my eyes.

Morgan studied me for a moment, her head tilted to one side. Charlotte seemed content to let Morgan lead, even though there was something in her stance that made me think she was used to giving orders and being in charge. She reminded me of someone, but I couldn't think who. I wondered if she could be a friend of my dad's, but Amy would be more careful than that. Right?

I almost shook my head to dislodge the thought. Amy doesn't make mistakes like that, and Charlotte didn't look the type. He only likes people who need something from him, and she couldn't possibly need anything from anyone. Perfect hair and nails, beautifully tailored, flattering clothes in soft orange, smooth beige and a hint of jade, discreetly perfect makeup, and the sort of poise and grace very few people are born with, with a deep, easy power moving fluidly beneath it all.

Morgan shrugged, and the movement snapped my attention back to her. She smiled slightly. "Well," she answered, "I'd say she called me because it was the only thing she could think of that would work. And she was right." She let the statement hang in the air for a few minutes, but I didn't argue. How would I know?

"As to why we want you to come for a ride, well, think of it this way: is it likely to make anything worse?"

Uh, yes. That's not exactly a tough question. On the other hand, Amy never makes anything worse. Ever. I looked back towards the school, but Mr. Bowman had disappeared inside, and the after-school hub was dying down now that the buses and student cars had left. Slowly, I turned my body back to the women but kept my eyes on the ground. I could not see how it would help me to go with them, but their jobs would obviously be simpler.

"It'll be easier for you if I get in the car," I said, with a bitter hint of accusation.

"Oh, yeah," Morgan agreed readily. Pleasantly. She paused briefly before looking right at me, ignoring Charlotte's disapprovingly rigid stance. "For example, it will have a pretty unfortunate effect on my career and social life if I have to kidnap you to save your life."

She sounded completely serious, and I almost smiled in surprise. Charlotte opened her mouth to interject, but Morgan merely lifted her fingers slightly and Charlotte subsided. Huh. Morgan's eyebrows went up and stayed there, her gaze steady on mine until I looked away.

I looked past them at the trees that lined the school property, moving in a perpetually soft, swaying dance in the breeze that never quite died down. A hundred shades of green wavered and shimmered in the distance as branches bowed and leaves twirled. Here by the car, there was no wind at all, just still air and dusty gravel that I nudged absently with the toe of my shoe.

So far, Morgan was like nobody I'd dealt with in Grade 3, but *was* there any other possible outcome? My dad in counseling? A social worker visiting every few days? I couldn't see either of those working. And where was the social worker? I was pretty sure there should be one, but I'd have already run away if there were.

"Granted," Morgan went on reflectively, "you're facing a choice between the devil and the deep, blue sea. On the plus side, though," her voice lifted and I risked meeting her eyes, "we're the sea."

My dad is the devil, all right. I looked away again.

"Worse things happen at sea," I returned, speaking to my shoes. I've read that in books, and wondered why it became a saying. I guess it comes from the time when ships were small, cramped and leaky, voyages insanely long and nearly suicidal, and it was still okay to kidnap or buy your entire, unskilled crew. What sort of worse things could happen at sea, though, I don't know, because life on land seemed pretty awful then, too.

"Sometimes they do," she agreed, in a quiet, even voice.

The devil and the deep, blue sea. And I was supposed to choose.

"This time?" I asked.

She thought about it for several seconds, long enough to interest me. Finally, she shrugged. "If I thought so, I wouldn't be here, but you're the only one who'll really be able to answer that."

Adults always tell kids that everything will be fine, even when they have no idea, but she didn't. She also said 'Amy', not 'Jane', without acting weird about it. I looked back down at the photograph Mr. B had given me. Amy's dark hair is straight and frames her heart-shaped face perfectly. You could barely see her freckles in the picture, and her mouth was held in a straight line. There were no lines or expression on her face at all, but her eyes showed the real Amy. Inside that still mask, she was smiling, just waiting for someone else to see through it. I can see her. I have always been able to see her.

Trust me.

I have to believe that she can see me, too, because if she can't, nobody ever will. I'll be invisible forever, until I finally fade away completely, even to myself.

I reached out gingerly and touched the door handle of the police women's car. The one named Charlotte moved slightly and then seemed to check herself. For someone who was probably supposed to be keeping me calm, she was doing a terrible job.

"Do you know Amy?" I asked, keeping my fingers on the door handle but not opening the door. Morgan waited for me to look up at her, but when I did, she didn't say anything. I looked into her eyes, which were not the same shape or shade of blue as Amy's, and held her gaze. *Yes.* The word was right there in my head, solid and certain, exactly as if she'd spoken it aloud. I looked back down to the image of Amy I held in my hand.

The photo was genuine, the signature and message in the same writing, writing that I know as well as my own, or Stef's, Allie's or Jill's. Writing that belongs to Amy.

Amy was keeping her word to me, and that was why Morgan was here. Could I keep mine to her? Could I trust her in real life?

A seagull flapped away from the garbage bins at the end of the visitor's lot and I watched it gain height and disappear over the trees.

Love, Amy

Looking back down at the photo, keeping my eyes on hers, I got into the car.

CHAPTER NINE

They talked to me in the car, and it sounded pretty official, but I barely heard any of the actual words. Two women I don't know, both of whom work for the police, and me, alone with them in a space they controlled. My dad was going to kill me. For real this time.

I felt trapped and out of control, like someone had locked me into a car on that horrible Ferris wheel in California Land. It looks so carefree and innocent with the hugest, happiest Mickey Mouse ever blithely smiling out from it at the whole world, but shortly after it begins to move, you become certain you are going to die. In Disneyland. I was out of control like that now, and with just as little chance of escape.

When I realized we were driving to my house, I started to grab for the door to escape, but my darting movement meant that I dropped the photo of Amy on the floor. Amy. Finally, I started to focus again. I'd made a choice. I would make it again. *Trust me. Love, Amy.* I looked up at Morgan, but I'm not sure why. I trust Amy, but I don't even know Morgan.

"We'll be fine at your house, I promise," she said, and I felt the reassurance spread through my muscles and bones as her voice washed over me, the words becoming more than just incomprehensible sounds in the background. "Your father has a televised rally this afternoon, Caelie. Remember?"

It wasn't the fake calm-and-friendly voice people use when they're impatiently trying to help someone annoying, and the rally part was true. Morgan spoke as if this happened every day and was no big deal, and not in a dismissive way, either. It was important to her, but not worrisome.

"And we won't be at your house when he gets home," she assured me gently. When I was able to get past the fear enough to concentrate on her, I could see competence, certainty and something more in her eyes. Fury, but not fuelled by fear like my father's anger. It was fury fuelled by acceptance, and shaped by relentless compassion. I was looking into Amy's eyes, but they were in Morgan's face.

"Have you heard anything that we've said?" Charlotte put in, as Morgan turned her attention back to the road. She didn't say it meanly, but I was starting to dislike her, and not just because she was a police officer. She was nervous, and trying to conceal it. How could I trust her if she was scared?

I shook my head numbly in response.

"Okay," Morgan said. "Are you with us now?"

I swallowed hard, took a very deep breath, and nodded once, warily. Starting to imagine that Morgan was Amy, no matter what I saw in her eyes, was scary.

"Don't think too far ahead right now," she told me calmly, in the kind of voice that makes you automatically do what the speaker is asking. "Try to put everything outside of your mind for a bit. Your dad, skating, homework . . . everything. There's only one job you have to do right now, and that is to help us out for a bit. It won't take very long, and the next step will be just that. One step."

Morgan spoke slowly and confidently, like she didn't doubt me for a minute.

"Consider this a mini-break for you. You don't have to think or worry or work." She looked over at me and I met her eyes for just a moment. They weren't sharp and grey like Mr. B's, and they weren't Amy's deep, dark blue like the sky at twilight, but I saw both Mr. B and Amy flash through my vision in that one small second.

My mind worked furiously, thoughts flying and whirling in all directions. Morgan seemed smart. Really smart. I got the feeling that, whatever I saw in her, she could see right through me. Normally, people take care not to see me too well because it's so uncomfortable for them, but maybe this Morgan sees kids like me all the time. If Charlotte wasn't here, I might ask her. But no. That wasn't safe. *She's not Amy*, I reminded myself. The eyes thing had unsettled me, that was all, and I needed to regroup.

"I need you to do two things for me," Morgan continued, assuming that my silence meant co-operation. We'd just pulled into my driveway and I'd stopped breathing, but she did not seem to think that was a cause for concern. "And then we'll talk about what happens next."

I didn't want this, let alone any 'next', but I bit my lip, looked down at my photo of Amy and slowly let out my breath. I had no choice now, so what was the point in answering?

The modern cement monstrosity of my house loomed over us, the concrete pillars in a row at the front seeming like the bars in a giant's jail, and I tried to keep my eyes down so I couldn't see anything beyond the interior of the car I was in. From the outside, it was a nondescript beige car that nobody would look at twice, but the inside of it was weird. There were no clock, no buttons that seemed to do anything, and no glove box. The whole front was covered with smooth, dark glass, or maybe some kind of plastic. I wanted to reach out and touch it, but I didn't.

Morgan was still looking at me, and Charlotte probably was, too, and nothing inside the car—however strange—could distract me for long. The darkness inside the house reached out to fill me as I realized that my father could never let me escape and Amy could never let me stay. I was going to fail someone.

Maybe it would be okay, I tried to convince myself. Amy knows everything about me, even the things I wish weren't true. *Especially* the things I wish weren't true. What did Morgan and Charlotte know? I was starting to like Morgan even if I did think it was stupid of me, so I'd have to be careful.

It was Charlotte who spoke next, and what she had to say didn't make me start to like her. "First," she said, "we need you to show Morgan where Missy is."

For one mad moment, I thought about the best ways of pretending I didn't know what she was talking about. Showing her what was left of Missy would be the beginning of the end. Telling someone real. It wasn't real when I wrote to Amy. Not sitting-beside-me-with-a-badge real.

I started fingering the Tylenol bottle in my pocket, rolling it back and forth from my fingers to my palm, thinking about what to do next. I couldn't run away because my dad has so many cop friends. They would find me and, worst of all, it would embarrass him. Could I lie?

I'm sitting in a cop car with a cop and someone who analyzes evidence, sent by Amy, and they know about Missy. It's way too late to lie. I looked back at both Morgan and Charlotte, who were waiting. Charlotte couldn't hide her uneasiness and I tried to pretend she wasn't there. Morgan looked cool, which I found calming, and even though they looked nothing alike, she reminded me of Amy so much that it made me want to be stupid and trust her.

Do what they ask you to do.

What if she can't help me? *I'll still die,* I thought. *He will kill me anyway.* But if she can? Whatever I chose, my father would blame me, and it would take more than a few punches for him to vent his anger. He'd held back with me lately, but he wouldn't hold back after this. I'd forgotten, in my stupid, childish daydreams about Amy, that it could get worse. And now it was. I wanted to slide the blades out of the Tylenol bottle so badly it hurt.

I concentrated on my breathing so I could stop thinking about everything else.

If Amy really existed, she should be here. The wish drifted into my thoughts, and I imagined what I'd do if she were.

The certain terror of my father slowly drained away as a kind of switch flipped in my brain. There's nothing I can do about him, but I can make sure I die as the Caelie I like, not the one I hate. The Caelie who's not crazy, and would do anything for Amy. The Caelie who wants to stop being alone. I breathed in again deeply, squeezed the bottle one more time, then took it out of my pocket.

The worst he can do is kill me, and that's always been true. It's not any more true now than it was before.

I risked looking at up at Morgan, who was still calm and still waiting. Slowly, I held the bottle out, offering it face up in the palm of my hand.

Morgan waited until I met her eyes, shocking me again with a depth of feeling I've never seen before in anyone but Amy, before she took the small cylindrical container. She twisted the cap open and tipped the blades into her hand, and it felt like a long time before anyone spoke again.

"Thank you, Caelie," she said gravely. She didn't look surprised or worried or concerned or anything that a normal person should feel when a kid hands over a bunch of razor blades she's been carrying around in her pocket. Morgan let the blades slide back in the bottle and tucked it into her own pocket before she and Charlotte shared a look, reminding me that it was the two of them against me.

"After that, we'll take you inside for a bit and talk about the next step," Charlotte said more confidently. "It won't take very long."

Morgan smiled slightly and nodded to me. She feels so safe, but she belongs to the police, so she can't really be safe. She can't, but Amy sent her.

"Okay." Not knowing what else to say, I agreed.

"It's best not to think too far ahead, Caelie," Charlotte said. "Let's just do what needs to be done before we worry about what happens next, all right?"

"Best for you, or best for me?" I couldn't help asking nastily. Did she think I had no idea what all of this meant? It meant I was going to die. On my own terms now, which was something, but my death was both closer and more inevitable than it had been this morning. Nothing I did from this point on would change that at all.

Charlotte didn't look away from my accusatory gaze, and she didn't pretend not to see it either. She just looked steadily back at me, and it was Morgan who answered.

"Best for all of us," she said gently, and reached over to hold my hand. Startled, I looked away from Charlotte and stared down at Morgan's hand. And mine. Her hand felt nice and warm and smooth. She had nails cut as short as they could be with no nail polish. Just like mine. For a minute, I wondered if she'd ever played violin because the way your nails bend when you press the strings feels horrible if they're even the tiniest bit too long. It seemed a stupid thing to focus on, but nails and violin lessons are much safer things to think about than what I was really here for. What they were really here for.

We sat there for a few minutes before I looked up at Charlotte and smiled a little apology. It would be stupid of me to trust her but I couldn't shake the feeling that it would be just as stupid not to trust Amy. More than stupid, even—a betrayal.

Charlotte smiled back and shook her head a little, as if to say that it was okay, but I didn't care.

"Why didn't you bring a social worker?" I asked her suddenly. Last time, I'd barely been allowed to breathe without a child advocate and parent present.

"Do you want one?" Morgan offered, and it was not concern I saw in her eyes before I quickly shook my head. It was something much more interesting: nothing at all. She could go as blank as I could, and as blank as I'd ever seen Amy when she was hiding who she really was.

I would never have gone with them if they'd brought someone from the Ministry. "The rules are set up to protect him, not me," I said defiantly.

"True," Morgan agreed lightly, "but if you know *all* of them, you can generally find a way to get them to work for you, even if it's under protest."

"You know," I said accusingly, "last time all anyone would talk about was how advanced our laws and systems were, and how everything was designed to protect me."

"How shocking," Morgan said mockingly, instantly defusing my anger. I really could have done with having had her around last time.

"Your father's very influential and powerful," Charlotte commented.

Oh, God. I'd been working so hard to pretend he didn't exist. Why did she have to say that? I desperately tried to force the image and scent of him away, but the fear rose anyway, almost choking me. His broad shoulders and solid muscles flashed into my mind. The glint of light from his ring as his fist rose in the air.

"I imagine you would rather be safe than examined or questioned or lectured," Morgan said, pulling me back into the present. She spoke as if that was a normal thing to want, instead of the exact opposite of how the system was designed to work. "It's Charlotte's job to keep you safe," she added.

For now, I thought, and the words passed through my mind in Morgan's voice. Had she said them out loud?

"I'm good at my job," Charlotte told me mildly, but the strength behind the words was palpable, leaving no doubt whatsoever that she was exceptional at her job. That was good news, because so was my dad.

I closed my eyes and stepped out of the car. The decision was made, and whatever happened now, I was out of options. I walked away without looking at either one of them again, although I could hear their doors open and close, and knew they were following me. When I got to the gate that led to the backyard, I pulled the latch quickly, pushed open the gate, and walked over to where I'd buried Missy.

"Here," I said to Morgan, sweeping my arm quickly over a two foot square area near the back of the garden. I hadn't come into the yard since Missy died, and the low-hanging tree in the most concealed part of the yard brought up images of the muddy earth, blood and fur that had stuck to my hands that morning. I swallowed hard several times as I forced my mind to focus on the fence instead.

Raspberry bushes grew along the entire fence, and chickweed was already thick on the ground in front of them. By examining in detail the tiny green leaves and plump, red berries, I pushed out the remembrance of how I had felt that day.

My clothes snagged briefly on the gooseberry bush I knew was there, but couldn't see through the thick tears that threatened to spill from my eyes as I strode towards the house as fast as I could without actually running. Now that I was doing this, I wanted to get it over with, and with as little thinking as possible. Charlotte was right behind me, but Morgan didn't come until I'd gotten the back door unlocked and was pushing it open. I didn't walk up the stairs closest to my room, but went through the laundry room to get to the front stairs.

"Storage room," I said, as we walked past it. They were both behind me now, following closely but silently. If they knew about Missy, they would know that was where my dad had locked me in when he'd been killing her. Morgan didn't stop or say anything to me but I did feel her look at it, sizing it up at a glance. When we started up the front stairs, I said, "He glued them back together," gesturing to the second and third railings from the bottom. As I heard the sentence come out, the room disappeared. The sound

Missy made when they'd snapped under her frantic, tumbling body echoed inside me, and then everything went dark.

I stumbled blindly, gasping for air and flailing ineffectually for support from the wall I couldn't see before firm arms encircled me from behind and pulled me down to rest on the stairs. I'm not sure how I knew it was Morgan and not Charlotte, but I did. I sat there, blind, until the sound of her regular breathing helped me breathe again on my own. For long minutes, her calm, even heartbeats thudded softly and reassuringly through the swirling darkness that surrounded me.

As it receded, allowing first a dim greyness and then the beginning of shapes and colours, I focused on her pale, smooth arms and tried to keep my mind from thinking about anything at all. There was nothing outside her arms that was safe for me to think about, so I didn't.

Morgan's arms had tiny, soft, red-blonde hairs on them, and some freckles. I learned long ago how to fill my mind with nothing, and worked desperately to do it now. It helped me stop panicking. She, at least, was real, and if I could convince myself that nothing else was, I would be okay. After a few minutes of desperate concentration, it worked and I stood up stiffly, moving away from her to stand by myself.

Morgan acted like it was totally normal for me to practically pass out on the stairs and then sit in her lap. While she sat there comfortably, not radiating any concern or worry or fear, I believed for a moment that I might not be a freak.

How could she get me to believe that, even for a second? An insistent desire to find out about her arose somewhere in the midst of my growing fear and embarrassment and I immediately looked away. *She is not Amy.* Charlotte was waiting at the bottom of the stairs, looking out through the clear glass windows that framed the front door. Gratitude rushed through me unexpectedly, and I started to like her a little bit for not watching me at my very worst. I don't want pity. Then I looked back at Morgan, who *was* watching me. With Amy's eyes.

"Okay?" she asked quietly. There was no trace of pity in her voice or movements, and it looked like she was having some kind of debate with herself, but I didn't know what it was. Of course I wasn't okay, but she wasn't really asking me that anyway.

"What next?" I asked. I'm not weak.

Morgan paused so briefly I wasn't sure she hesitated at all, then stood up, smoothing imaginary crinkles out of her soft cream blouse and moss green slacks. "I need you to go with Charlotte for a little while, but first you can come to your room and pick out some things you'd really like to keep with you. Things that remind you of stuff outside your life, and outside yourself. You know, the things that help you survive. Everyone has them," she stated matter-of-factly, with a slight shrug of her shoulder that caused the soft material in her sleeve to move like a waterfall.

"With Charlotte?" I asked, hating myself for the weakness even as the words escaped my mouth.

Morgan didn't say anything for a minute, and I regretted not controlling myself more. There were a lot of stupid things I could do, and wanting to be rescued by Morgan was way at the top of the list. Thinking it was bad enough, but actually saying it out loud was unforgivable. When people know how to hurt you, they do. I was already turning away when she spoke again.

"Caelie, do you remember the episode where Amy was in charge of those twin boys and she had to leave them for a bit so she could do her job? It was Amy doing her job that really helped them, right? But she came back," Morgan said. "So will I." She didn't say it patronizingly or as if it were really important; she just said it.

I looked at her steadily for a minute, trying to figure out if she was telling the truth. If she wasn't, she was a very good liar with her eyes and face as well as her voice. She waited, letting me look at her all I wanted, and didn't seem uncomfortable at all. That was kind of cool, but it was not a good idea for me to care if I ever saw her again or not.

I shrugged as if it didn't matter to me, and headed for my room, but once I got there, I just stood in the doorway. How many times had I been in here imagining that I was somewhere else? The dull brown carpet held no happy memories, and neither did the pink frills or dark brown walnut furniture. The single, overhead light cast a pale, sickly yellow over the room, and I felt the darkness pressing in on me again, slowly this time.

"Caelie?" Morgan prompted me gently. Her sudden presence at my side startled me back to the present.

Right. Packing. There was nothing in the room of me except my books, and I was grabbing handfuls of them off the shelves before Morgan stopped me. She didn't say anything, just shook her head seriously.

"I need my books, Morgan." I was not joking.

"I know, Caelie. I know." She looked concerned for a few seconds but then brightened up. "You won't lose them forever. Pick the most important ones, okay?"

They're all important, or I wouldn't have them. I looked at her incredulously for a few seconds, to no avail, then turned away to the dark, wooden shelves I've always hated. The wood makes the night blacker and the day more forbidding, and feels like a black vortex constantly trying to swallow the neatly lined up titles.

I turned to my favourite author first, forcing my mind to engage. Terry Pratchett's books have come out in new covers that are much better than the originals, so if I have to replace them, I won't mind that much. I picked the best guards one and the best witches one, plus all the Tiffany ones and *Nation,* and stuffed them into the cloth bag Morgan held out to me. His books keep me alive in ways I don't know how to explain.

I moved on, and Agatha Christies, Nancy Drews and Trixie Beldens are everywhere, so I left all of those. The modern series could stay, too, because they're so easy to find. That left me with . . . a lot. It's hard to find Cynthia Voigt sometimes, so I picked *Homecoming, Dicey's Song,* and *Come a Stranger.*

Ballet Shoes was the only Noel Streatfeild one I had to keep with me, but what about *Bruno and Boots,* or *Emily of New Moon,* or *Freckles?* How could I possibly leave them behind? In an agony of indecision and loss, I looked up at Morgan.

"I swear you'll get them all back, Caelie," she told me. "I'll take care of them myself."

I bit my lip as I turned back to my shelf. I'd had to special order *Daddy Long-legs* and wait six months for it to arrive. It went into the bag, but the well-known classics are in every bookshop and library, and they're free on lots of eReaders, so I left them on the shelf. It was very hard to abandon *Jane Eyre* and *Pride and Prejudice.*

"We have to get going, Caelie," Charlotte warned, glancing at her watch. She hadn't entered my room with Morgan, who'd sat down companionably on my bed, but was still standing in my doorway. She wasn't talking to me, either, even though she was looking at me and had used my name.

With a defiant glare, I swept all of my Famous Fives and Malory Towers into the bag, getting ready to argue for them even though the bag could barely hold them. They've been out of print for over 50 years and are practically impossible to find. They used to be my grandma's.

"Okay, let's go," Charlotte said abruptly to Morgan.

I was having a lot of trouble believing that Amy had sent Charlotte, who acts like I'm not even here. Morgan winked at me, which I ignored, then she nodded to Charlotte and took my bag of books from me. I kept my face blank but Morgan just smiled, turned away, carried the bag out into the hall where Charlotte was waiting for her and then started talking, leaving me alone in my room. I took one last look around at the pink walls, curtains, rug and bedspread that I've had for as long as I could remember.

I don't remember a time when my room wasn't pink, but I've seen baby pictures of me in a room with clown wallpaper. Both types of decoration, I imagine, served the purpose of publicly presenting me as a normal and even lucky girl. *Sugar and spice and everything nice*, I thought bitterly, and felt an overwhelming hatred rising inside me. In a desperate attempt to force it away, I dug my nails into my wrist until all I had to think about was the pain. It made me feel a bit more under control, and the welling blood got me the rest of the way.

Blood is a bit of my life, and its red is so brilliant and vital. Killing it feels powerful and righteous when the hatred rises, because what I hate so much is myself. A lot of the time I wouldn't even care if my dad killed me, as long as it was fast. If I could only be sure that God wouldn't be mad, or that I wouldn't be failing some cosmic responsibility, I wouldn't even have to feel guilty about it, or stop at just hurting myself.

I let the blood soak into a Kleenex until it wasn't flowing any more, then balled the Kleenex up and was about to toss it in the trash when I remembered Morgan's job. Would she be able to tell how old the blood was? I stuffed it into my pocket instead, then pulled my watchstrap down over the marks to cover them.

As I turned to leave, I saw the one item besides my books that was out of place, and impulsively grabbed the yarn doll that my great-aunt made me when I was a baby. I'm too old for dolls, but I like this one because it makes me think someone wanted to do something just for me and thought nice things about me even before I was born.

She died before I was one, but there's a hand-embroidered heart on Sara's chest, with the thread still a deep, bright red because it's always protected from dirt and sunshine by her clothes. I carried that doll everywhere with me when I was little. Remembering, I squeezed her limp body in the crook of my arm as I walked away from my room, then stood in front of Morgan and looked at her until she opened the book bag.

I dropped Sara on the top of the books and followed Morgan and Charlotte to the car, catching a bit of their muffled conversation while they were stowing my bags in the trunk.

Of course, they were talking about me

CHAPTER TEN

I heard Charlotte say, "I should have . . ." and then Morgan interrupted her with, "We knew she'd be better with a . . ." before I got into the front seat and slammed the door shut. I hate it when people talk about me.

As soon as I shut the door, though, Morgan appeared at it.

"Caelie, I'm sorry," she started to say, as if it mattered. As if I mattered. I turned away from her and would have locked the door if I could have figured out how to, but the inside of the door was as smooth as the dash. She walked around to the driver's side and climbed in. Her soft curls spilled over her shoulder and almost touched my arm as she leaned in towards me.

"We don't have a lot of time, Caelie. I'm sorry." She spoke matter-of-factly, but seemed sincerely apologetic. "You shouldn't have to hear us talking about you. We're concerned because you seem more comfortable with me than with Charlotte and we want this to be as easy for you as possible."

I snorted, and she thought back over what she'd said and almost laughed, which made me think she was probably fun. In normal circumstances, which these definitely weren't. Against my will, I warmed to her a bit more, although I wasn't idiotic enough to let her see it. I remembered how it had felt to sit with her on the stairs and, so secretly that I didn't even admit it to myself, wished she would reach out to me again. I felt something in her arms that I've never felt before in my life.

Policemen are not safe, I said silently to myself, forcing the words to line up and march around inside my head.

"Right. Sorry. As non-threatening as possible," she amended. "But I need to stay here. I will be helping you by staying here, and I trust Charlotte," she said seriously. "She'll move heaven and earth to keep you safe."

When I stayed staring stubbornly away from her, she put her hand on mine briefly and then climbed back out of the car. The warmth of her hand burned through me, bringing a measure of peace and comfort that made me long to stay with her. I shook it off, but my anger had drained away.

As Charlotte got in and started to back us out the driveway, I rolled down my window and called out, "I'd be better with a what?!"

Charlotte stopped the car so that Morgan could come back to my window, but I was certain she did it for Morgan and not me. Impatience and worry were coming off her in waves.

"We figured you'd be more comfortable with someone who works in a lab, Caelie. Right?" Morgan asked.

I shrugged, pretending it didn't matter. "Was that even true?" I asked, remembering the look on Charlotte's face when Morgan had introduced herself. I had to give Morgan credit. Again. She didn't even look at Charlotte, but answered me matter-of-factly and with no hesitation.

"I do help Charlotte in the lab," she confirmed. "I help a lot of other people as well. I'm Darian here." Darian is Amy's boss on *Last Line of Defence*. He runs the lab, is scary smart, and is responsible for everything and everyone. Morgan held my gaze evenly, unhurriedly.

Working with evidence doesn't make her Amy any more than learning to skate would make Stefan into me, but I like that she told me the truth, and I do care that she isn't a police officer.

From deep within me came the certainty that I could trust her. You know, in some parallel universe. I could not trust Charlotte, and not just because she's both normal and a cop. The shimmer of uncertainty that surrounds her whenever she has to talk to me makes me edgy and resentful. Worse, the feeling that Charlotte was a bit familiar persisted. I bet she knows my dad. Most of the police here do, so it would be a pretty safe bet. Knowing that my dad runs the city, and the city controls the police, did not increase my confidence.

"When am I coming back?" I couldn't help asking the question, even though it immediately made me feel like a baby. You'd think I would have better self-control by now, but Charlotte's obvious nervousness was infecting me.

"I don't know yet," Morgan said, shaking her head a bit and not looking like it was a stupid question. She gazed at me steadily, waiting until I accepted her answer as the best one she could give me at the moment.

I nodded and pretended I didn't care. Liking her would only get me hurt. Still, I looked back as we drove away. She stood in the driveway, and it looked like she was waiting for something more than for us to get away safely.

By the time we got to the end of our street, I knew what it was. Two marked police cars had passed us, driving in the direction of my house, followed closely by three other dark, business-like SUVs. No wonder Charlotte had been trying to get me out of there. I pushed them out of my mind and concentrated on the car's interior. Not being able to figure it out was starting to feel like a personal failure, a thought that faded too slowly for me to hide it from Charlotte.

Obligingly, her fingertip swiped the glass and she entered a voice identity code, after which an intricate and detailed display came up which she immediately deleted, and all the normal things appeared instead—speed, temperature, direction, time, gas tank reading, even Sirius.

I'd seen enough, though, and I looked over at her and touched the spot where my name had so briefly appeared, followed by some number, then paragraphs of text which had seemed to be writing themselves, new words coming in as quickly as the old ones disappeared. It didn't do anything when I touched it, of course, and she said nothing, so I sat back in my seat and ignored her. The entire interior of the car was like Allie's iPhone, only much bigger and with more personal security.

We drove through a Wendy's right away, after which I picked at my salad and fruit. Lunch seemed like it had happened in a completely different lifetime instead of three or four hours ago, but I had no interest in food and finally shut my salad container up and put it back into the takeout bag. No matter how crisp the lettuce was or how colourful the fruit and nut garnishes, I couldn't eat it. I had no intention of eating my baked potato either, but I kept it against my stomach for the warmth.

We drove for a long, long time, leaving the city behind so there was nothing left outside but a blur of trees, a steady rush of air and the hum of our tires as we sped down the highway. Hours passed before I worked up the courage to ask Charlotte the question that had been nagging at me ever since I'd dropped Sara on the jumbled bag of books.

"Am I going to a foster home?" a tiny voice that sounded nothing like me asked. Where had my perfect control gone, and why would it abandon me when I needed it the most? I had to pull myself together, and fast.

"Not yet, Caelie," Charlotte answered. I didn't relax, knowing that if she didn't hurt me now, it would just be worse later on when she did. I did, however, stop acting like I cared about the answers.

"Why not?" I persisted. Where could we possibly be going?

"Maybe later."

I stewed in silence for a few minutes and then thought of a new tactic.

"Morgan would tell me what was going on!" I accused her. Somehow I knew it was true, even though I'd been trying to put Morgan out of my mind. Charlotte had taken her cues from Morgan, and Morgan hadn't lied to me. *And how did I know that?*

When I was really little, I believed that somebody would eventually help me, but no one ever did. All that happened was I made them uncomfortable and they went away. If I was lucky, that was all that happened. Sometimes they talked to my dad out of concern for me, and then things got very bad, very quickly.

Don't hope, that was the first rule I learned, followed closely by: don't let anyone know anything about you because it'll just be used to hurt you. The third and final rule of survival is not to feel anything, or at least give no signs when you do.

At my outburst, Charlotte's eyes tightened and her lips pressed together. I immediately shrank away from her, but before she even noticed that I was scared, she started laughing. She laughed until there were tears running down her face and I managed to relax my muscles, one by one, so that by the time she could focus on me, the sick feeling in my stomach had faded and I was back to at least looking normal.

"Oh, Caelie," was all she said at first and I stared at her, keeping my face carefully blank. Why should I care why she was laughing? And why did her voice sound familiar to me? Maybe I really was going crazy.

"I'm sorry," she apologized, sounding a bit more distant. I realized it was the nervousness creeping back in. For one second there, she hadn't been scared of me at all, and I could imagine what it would be like to get to know her.

"I'm not laughing at you," she explained, glancing appraisingly at me. "Honestly. It's just that Morgan knows how to talk to you, Caelie, and I don't, and I didn't expect—well, it's not just because her job is different that we chose for her to talk to you first," she explained, looking over at me.

A few things fought for dominance in my thoughts. They'd planned who was going to talk to me first? What else had they planned? Was she saying that Morgan understood me, for the only possible reason? How could Charlotte know that?

The last question bothered me the most. You never tell normal people about your life because they can only make bad things happen to you, even if it is inadvertently, and it upsets them for nothing. Charlotte seemed entirely normal to me, aside from the car, so how would she know about Morgan? If there was anything to know, that is. I sat and thought about all of that for a while, watching trees and road signs whiz by.

The lack of a social worker was still preying on my mind. Cops have to follow rules, or at least pretend to, and the game those rules follow is one my dad always wins. He owns the rules, the gameboard, the pieces and even the dice. Did Morgan and Charlotte know that, and was that why they weren't playing it?

"I still think I should know where I'm going," I stated.

"For now, you're just going on vacation, okay?" Charlotte asked, some weariness entering her voice.

"But what about school? We have finals this week," I protested. It was a relief to argue about things that didn't matter to me. At least it kept my mind off what was happening at my house. I hoped my dad didn't get home early. It was better—necessary—to think of him experiencing a normal day.

"You'll have access to your finals," she said, glancing at the schoolbag that held my laptop. "If you want to, you can write them and submit them electronically. If you don't feel like doing them, your final marks will be your current accumulated marks. The school is being very co-operative," she said.

The school. Mr. Bowman.

"Did he—" I faltered.

"No," Charlotte said quickly. She looked over at me to make sure I knew she was telling the truth. "Mr. Bowman has not read your letters."

Immediately, I knew that she had. I could see it in her eyes, that combination of pity and horror I knew would be there if anyone saw me for who I really was, and I realized I'd been seeing it right from the moment I met her after school. Her, but not Morgan. I should have known then what it meant, and at some level, I think I had.

There was something else in Charlotte's eyes, though. Something I hadn't expected, which looked like determination, or control. I wasn't sure how I felt about that, but I put it aside for the time being. Nobody I'd had to actually see in person had ever known anything real about me. And now a total stranger knew everything.

"Ms. Al—Amy read them and sent them on to us. They've been friends since Morgan's first visit to the set as an expert consultant—" Charlotte stopped again, and reddened.

"I *know* Amy's not real," I muttered tightly. Amy is played by someone called Jane Allyson, and who knows if that's her real name? "I'm not stupid."

"She's real to you," Charlotte said sharply. "That's real enough."

I'd written those letters to Amy Anderson in the full expectation that nobody would ever read them and it took a minute for Charlotte's words to sink in. Expert consultant?

Morgan not only knew Amy, she'd helped make her. I tried to wonder if that meant she'd helped with Amy's character or just her job, but I kept circling back to the thought that Charlotte read my letters. Morgan read my letters. Amy read my letters. I don't mind about Amy, even thought it's real now, but I don't want to think about anyone else seeing them. *Everything* is in them—all the things I think and feel and went through. I don't want strangers knowing my most despicable thoughts and my most awful fears and actions. Especially a stranger I'm stuck sharing a car with.

I sat in silence as the light faded from the sky and complete darkness slowly replaced it. It was important to keep my mind blank, which I did first by making my mind dwell on every single physical detail of the car's interior. As night fell, the display became paler until it was only a faint glow, and Charlotte did not seem to do anything at all to make that happen, something I only noticed in the back of my mind as I silently recited all the poetry I could remember, which was quite a lot because our Grade 6 teacher loved both Shakespeare and recitation. I'd memorized *The Lady of Shalott* as well, one day in the fall when it was beautiful and crisp and colourful outside, and I managed to get the whole thing word-perfect after nearly an hour of concentration. Anything to keep myself from thinking.

Finally, we pulled into a hotel and I had some other things to keep my mind off my letters. Was I relieved to find out that she wasn't passing me off to a new stranger? I couldn't think clearly. Charlotte checked us in and I grabbed my schoolbag and followed her, ignoring the panic that was rising inside me. If I could only keep from thinking about anything except what I could see right at this exact second, it would be okay. None of this would really be true when I woke up. It didn't feel real, and I wanted to keep it that way.

When we walked into the room, I found two pairs of jeans, two pairs of shorts, six shirts, a pair of pyjamas and some underwear and socks on one of the beds. They looked new.

"I'm sorry we couldn't let you bring any of your own clothes, Caelie," Charlotte apologized, setting her own small suitcase by the side of the bed closest to the door. She looked a lot paler than she had this afternoon, and when I checked the clock in the hotel room, I saw that it was after midnight.

"That's okay," I told her. I don't care about clothes. "Thank you."

She asked me if I wanted to eat, but I wasn't hungry so we just took turns using the bathroom to get ready for bed. On my turn I almost laughed when I saw that the pyjamas they'd picked for me had Strawberry Shortcake on them. This entire day felt so surreal that I barely had to pretend it was a weird dream, but the effect was a bit spoiled when Charlotte winced as I walked out of the bathroom.

"What?" I asked in a bored voice, deliberately ignoring her reaction to me.

"I'm sorry," she said again, this time in a tone of voice that made me think she was angry, but not at me. I quickly realized she was talking about Strawberry Shortcake. I shrugged, wondering why she would even care, but then I met her eyes and the look in them made me think someone else was going to be sorry, too. I found it kind of interesting, but it also made me remember she was a police officer. How could I have forgotten that, even for a second?

Her pyjamas were Lululemon, dark grey and morning blue, and she could easily have gone to work in them instead of using them to sleep.

I started to wonder if I'd passed out at school and this was all some kind of bizarre dream. Vaguely, I hoped not, because my dad would be very angry. There had been enough attention called to me this year and he had been holding back his rage lately, but it was still there, just waiting for a chance to get out.

I concentrated on the strange scenario Charlotte and I were enacting. If this was a dream, it was a pretty good one. Normally, my dreams are about trying to save someone who's already been caught by a serial killer. They are not at all fun and I never save the person. Or me, for that matter. When you die in a dream, you don't die in real life. At least, I don't.

"I don't care," I told her, about the clothes. It's hard to find clothes in my size that are appropriate for a teenager. Toddler clothes, while feeling tight on me at last, still fit.

I climbed into the bed beside the window, pushing the blanket all the way to the bottom and just tucking the sheet back up around me. Charlotte asked me if I wanted a light on, and I said no, but I don't like people being able to see me when I sleep, so I just pretended to sleep until her breathing had been regular for a long time, and then I crept back into the bathroom with my arms full of pillows from my bed. There were six pillows on my bed, which I thought was a bit excessive, but they would come in handy to make my bathtub-bed more comfortable. I locked the door so I could sleep in the tub without worrying about her coming in, and even stuffed some towels at the bottom of the door so that I could turn the light on without waking her up.

Once I flipped on the light, I saw my backpack hanging on the hook behind the door and remembered the envelope from Amy, which she'd told me not to open until I was alone. Even if this was only some kind of weird dream or hallucination, I wanted to see what she'd sent me. I pulled it out of my bag and settled into the tub, pillows cushioning the hard plastic frame, to open it.

What spilled out were all the seasons of her television show, signed by all the cast members in their characters' names. I flipped through them for a little while, just to see all the pictures of Amy. There was also a smaller envelope, and when I peeled it open, I found two passes to the set and another note from Amy.

Dear Caelie,

> *Wishes do come true, but sometimes you have to work insanely hard for them. No, strike that, you <u>always</u> have to work insanely hard. So what? Now, I'm not going to lie to you, this is really going to suck. If you can, focus on your finals; I found that it helped me a lot to concentrate on schoolwork. At least I knew that I was good at school and that it was bringing me closer to what I wanted. Memorizing all that stuff kept things I didn't want to remember from flashing through my head every few minutes. Do your best to get through this, even though at times it will be impossible, painful, unbearable . . . There are no words, really, for how bad it will be. I know, and I will never leave you alone in it. Keep going. Always keep going. Also—here are some passes for the set. I know you can't make it out for a while, but I can't wait to meet you when you do.*

> > *Love, Amy.*

P.S. Please call me whenever you want.

At the bottom was a phone number with Amy's initials beside it, but my eyes skipped over them without really taking them in. It was somehow reassuring that she said it would get worse, and it was very definitely from her. Nobody else talks to kids like that. I smiled as I re-read it, and thought that I might never stop.

Finally, my eyes traced the numbers at the bottom of the letter, over and over. Her writing was scrawling but bold, and the numbers were clear. I stared at them for a few moments, wondering. I would never actually call her, but it was nice to pretend, and a much better thing to think about than the darker thoughts that were trying to smash through the barriers I had set up.

CHAPTER ELEVEN

I woke up abruptly, with the light still on overhead, to Charlotte hammering on the door. Any pleasant daydreams and wishful thinking were gone, and my heart was pounding. All I could see were images of my dad. His hands, balled up into fists. The hard light flashing off the cold, white gold that encircled his finger as it sailed through the air. His face, mobile in rage around his cold, dismissive eyes. His muscles, moving inexorably beneath his dark silk clothing.

"Caelie! CAELIE! Open the door!" Charlotte was shouting.

I managed to unlock the door and still lean over the toilet in time to throw up. The warm jungle scent of blood filled my mouth and nose, and I choked on it. I was used to having nightmares where someone was trying to kill me and I had to outwit them, but this was different. It was also a lot worse. The last images of my father coming for me faded away as I finished throwing up, rinsed out my mouth, picked up my backpack, and told Charlotte I had to leave.

"I have to go back," I stated, walking towards the door. How stupid could I have been, to think I could just walk away from my life like that? Knowing that he would kill me, I had let people get between us. People who would try to protect me. People he would destroy just to get to me. I'm not worth that. A flash of Amy's lifeless eyes looking out at me from behind her shattered face made me stumble, and Charlotte reached out to steady me. I backed away.

"Caelie, sit down for a minute, please," Charlotte asked, dropping her hand. I couldn't bear the thought of her touching me, and she could see that. She held her ground, but kept her arms by her sides.

"No, I have to go back," I insisted. "I lied. I have to go back." The sounds Missy had made as he beat her to death still rang in my ears, but it had not been Missy's body in my dreams, and my father hadn't stopped with Amy. I couldn't look at Charlotte's face, even though she stood between me and the door I had to get through. She would die to protect me. *She had died to protect me.*

When I realized that she wouldn't let me pass, I started screaming. *I had to go back.* I won't let anyone else die for me. I was only dimly aware that I was screaming and crying and hitting her, but I wouldn't stop. Couldn't stop. I had to go back! I tried so hard to get to the door, but she was immovable, even when people started pounding on the door, and the phone began ringing shrilly, over and over and over. I kept screaming even when my voice gave out and they were silent screams. I *had* to go back! How could she not understand that? I had to go back.

Finally, the door opened, but I still couldn't get out because the room filled with people, swarming around us and pulling Charlotte away from me. After a flurry of movement and argument, I felt a sharp prick and then everything around me went black as I fell backwards, ever so slowly, onto something flat and yielding.

It was a nice black that held me, not a scary one. A deep, soft, welcoming black where I knew that there was something important I had to do, but I couldn't quite remember what it was. Pretty soon, it stopped seeming important at all. In fact, everything stopped feeling important. I had no energy to move at all, or even to open my eyes, but I could still hear voices, louder or quieter. Sometimes it was Charlotte, arguing with new voices. I didn't care about any of them, a thought which filled me with peace.

There was movement around me, swirling movement like dark dancers against a shadowy backdrop, and gentle pressure against my skin as objects were placed on it and then taken away, but it felt so far away it was like it was happening to someone else. I had no trouble dismissing all of it from my thoughts. I could hear Charlotte's voice, less easily dismissed, answering questions that were obviously about me, and her words edged themselves inside the soft mists swirling around my thoughts.

". . . so sudden. I'm pretty sure she was asleep when she started screaming," was what Charlotte said, before there was another long pause.

"Tranquilized her. She isn't awake enough to listen, let alone resp—" Charlotte was cut off.

"Don't you think we can give her some time?" she asked after a few seconds.

Granted, I haven't known Charlotte for very long, but I've only ever heard her defer to one person. *Morgan.* The name sounded in my mind before the mists enclosed it, hiding it, and anything it might mean, from me completely. Almost immediately, the phone was pressed against my ear. It was warm, and I wondered why for a moment, until I figured out that it was warm because of Charlotte. Only then did I realize how cold I was, a realization that was immediately followed by the knowledge that I preferred feeling nothing. I tried briefly to pull away from the phone, but it was pressed firmly against my ear, and I couldn't be bothered trying to move.

"Cael? You're going to have to answer me, okay?"

I didn't want to recognize the speaker, too afraid I would see what my dad had turned her into instead of who she really was. The voice whose face I refused to remember sounded normal, but there was an edge of desperation, even of panic, that she was trying hard to conceal. I could remember feeling like that, and I didn't want to anymore. I let my thoughts bounce away to summer. Boating. I like boats, when you can get away from everyone and just float aimlessly, with nothing but the warmth of the sun, the gentle cooling of a breeze and the small lapping of waves around you.

The voice broke into my daydream of lying down in a gently rocking boat just looking up at the sky, and made me mildly annoyed, but feelings were a bad thing, so the annoyance just washed over me and only the voice was left in its wake.

"I *know* you feel responsible, but you're not."

Responsible. Yes, I was responsible for all of it, did she have to remind me? I veered off in another direction. Woods. Woods are nice, with the sunlight filtering through the branches and between the tree trunks, falling on the forest floor in little patches of illumination, and all the leaves a different shade of green when you look up at the endlessly soft, blue sky above them.

The voice kept going but I managed to block out any sense of the words themselves. No more words. No more people. No more . . . anything.

Her voice sounded quite far away now, and I was mildly pleased before it was replaced by a different voice, a voice that instantly pierced through all the protective layers surrounding my brain.

"Caelie."

"Amy," I whispered. It was Amy's voice, and I answered automatically. Amy.

"You can like it or not," she said, in her typical no-nonsense voice, "but the only place your dad can beat you now is inside your head, and I'll be seriously pissed off if you let that happen. We're in charge of everything else, and he's going to have to deal with us."

I couldn't let that happen. So much blood, and all of it because of me.

"Oh, please," she continued, as if I'd answered out loud, "I'm insulted that you'd even consider the possibility I might not win. Have I ever lost? At anything?"

Well. No.

"We're not going to lose our battle with him, and that's exactly what it is," she stated, "*our* battle. You're out. Penalty, red card, injury, someone else is skinnier, they preferred to cast a blonde, whatever. You're out of the game, and your dad no longer controls the board. I do," she said with such certainty that I almost believed her. "And so do you. Dreams are not real. It's your head. You control it," she ordered.

I felt a bit of resentment at the last part. *Dreams feel real. They come from what is real.*

"You can't control them when you're sleeping, but you're not sleeping anymore," she reminded me somewhat coolly. "Get a grip. Now."

"Okay," I managed. Having Amy threaten me was deeply reassuring, even comforting.

"You will have a time to look back or across or whatever you want, but it's not today, so stop messing around."

"I'm not messing around!"

"So you are in there somewhere," she said, sounding pleased but no more patient. "Good. You know, if you disappear into your head, it's no better than running away and leaving us to deal with your crap. Is that what you want? Is that what you want us to think of you?"

No, I thought, and didn't need to say it out loud. She didn't ask me anything else, and she didn't say anything either. She just let me think about it.

"Amy?"

"Yep," came her voice, solid and tight and . . . Amy.

"I won't give up," I forced the words out.

"No shit," she agreed, and then I did smile. Parts of me I didn't even know were tense, relaxed. Amy's only nice to people she thinks are weak, and I crave Amy's respect more than anything else in the world. *She wasn't nice to me. I was going to make it!*

"Thank you," I said, more sincerely than politely. The words felt thick in my mouth, and I could barely force them out. My arms and legs would not respond to me, and my voice was going, too. She didn't seem to mind.

"Anytime," she answered seriously. "Oh, and Caelie? Morgan sent you with Charlotte for a reason. Actually, several reasons," she added reflectively. "But the only one you need to care about right now is that you're safe with Charlotte. She's far more powerful than Morgan or me," she said, and there was genuine awe in her voice, something she seemed to be trying to downplay.

"Or your father," she added as an afterthought, and I realized through my genuine exhaustion that she didn't care about him at all. He was nothing to her, even though he was everything to me. What a horrible thought that was. I didn't want him to be anything, and he really was winning if I let him become so huge in my mind. The fear shrunk even more as my hatred of him rose. I would *not* let him win.

"Try not to be too hard on her, okay?" Amy said dryly, talking about Charlotte once more. Her voice sounded fainter but I could still hear her smiling, and I smiled back as whatever drugs were now in my system threatened to overwhelm me with sleep.

"I love you, kid," Amy's voice said, but I wasn't sure if it was real or if I'd just imagined it. The echoes reverberated in my mind, filling it with her.

The last thing I heard before I drifted out of consciousness was Charlotte's voice, talking to someone on the phone.

"Don't worry, we'll be there tomorrow," Charlotte said firmly.

I had enough time for that thought to settle in my mind before I fell asleep for good.

CHAPTER TWELVE

When I woke up, the sun was streaming onto the bed. A strange bed. Hadn't I gone to sleep in the bathtub last night? For about two seconds, I wondered how I'd gotten here, and then pieces of last night swam hazily into my mind. I began to concentrate hard on my breathing, hoping that I could stop the panic from rising. My eyes fell on the photo of Amy that was propped up against the lamp on my bedside table, facing me. *You're out of the game.*

My breathing slowed down and I made a conscious effort to bring back all the details of last night, and not just the scary ones that crashed over me a few seconds ago. I drew my mind away from thoughts of my dad, the taste of blood and vomit, and the raw pain in my throat before I went into the bathroom as quietly as possible. Charlotte was still asleep in her bed, and I didn't want to wake her up.

I turned on the shower as hot as I could stand before stepping under the steady spray, then I closed my eyes and let the water sting me as the steam rose all around. Amy had taken me out of the game. Bloody visions from my nightmare tried to force their way in to my thoughts and my stomach clenched painfully in response, but I held on to the memory of Amy's voice. *It's your head. You control it.*

I remembered hearing Charlotte's voice very faintly last night, the last thing I heard as I'd fallen asleep. We would be somewhere today, but I didn't know where. *Had I really promised Amy that I'd be nice to Charlotte?* I wondered, knowing the answer. I sighed. Even though it would be hard to trust someone who was afraid of me, Amy's confidence in her had been crystal clear.

Trying hard not to think about my dad, because that would just make me crazy again, I toweled off, combed out my hair, and packed all my stuff into my backpack. I swallowed once by accident and tears welled up in my eyes because the simple act of swallowing was like someone had taken a very jagged saw to my throat.

I stood very still and breathed tiny little breaths in and out until the pain subsided, then gently brushed my teeth, being careful to spit gingerly and not swallow anything by accident. The picture of Amy, I tucked into the clear plastic pocket of my backpack so that I could always see it and it wouldn't get wrecked. When I was done, I walked out of the bathroom to where Charlotte was waiting anxiously. She looked awful, which made me feel a bit more cheerful. I'm not proud of that, but it's true.

"Sorry," I began, deliberately not wincing at the pain in my throat, but she interrupted me. My voice had come out as a whisper, and even that sent flames of pain raging through my throat.

"Here," she said, holding out a glass of water with a spoon in it.

I frowned questioningly at her, not wanting to risk speaking again.

"Salt water," she elaborated. "Go gargle with it for at least 30 seconds. It's better than any sore throat spray you can find in a store."

I reached out tentatively, and she pressed it into my hand. "Go on," she said.

I went back into the bathroom, shut the door behind me, and studied myself in the mirror for a moment. How did she know about my throat? Not from personal experience, I imagined. I'm pretty sure that Charlotte, who looks more serene and put-together than the top twenty models, actors and world leaders all rolled into one, even when she's exhausted and worried, has never screamed like that in her life.

Holding the glass up, I dipped a finger in and touched the tip of my tongue to it. It was definitely salt water. I shrugged, tipped the liquid into my mouth, and gagged. The fear of swallowing that much salt combined with the fear of throwing up, and I kept my mind firmly focused on blowing air continuously through the salt water in my throat and not letting any of it escape down to my stomach.

The first ten seconds of gargling were agony and I almost gave up, but I'd promised Amy, so I kept at it for the full thirty seconds and by the time I spit the water out, my throat was nearly numb. Huh. It worked. I stepped back out of the bathroom and met Charlotte's eyes. I was grateful, but I still didn't want to risk speaking again.

"Try this, too," she said, holding out some packets of honey and a glass full of ice cubes. When I took them, she pulled some cough lozenges out of her pocket and placed them in an outside pocket of my backpack. She's definitely organized, I have to give her that. I nodded my thanks to her.

"It's a lot to have to deal with, Caelie," she said, as though the words had escaped some sort of dam, "and Morgan told me some of the behaviours to expect, and you're doing really well, considering," she said brightly.

This is why I don't really like Charlotte. Why does she need Morgan to tell her things? This is her job, after all. *I* am her job. I tried to block the thought of Morgan out of my mind, but treacherous speculation about exactly what Morgan had told her arose. I squashed it, and thought about how Charlotte uses horrible words like 'behaviours.' I'm not a lab rat.

"No, I'm not," I stated. That should be perfectly obvious to even the most regular, mundane, normal person available, but I still tried to keep the sarcasm out of my voice. She'd made me angry enough to start speaking again, and I was glad the salt water solution was holding.

Charlotte looked undecided for a minute. *Why* do I make her so nervous? Nobody else does.

"Well," she said, finally ending up with, "you will be."

I rolled my eyes and shook my head. *After a lobotomy, maybe,* were the words I thought, but did not speak aloud. The hoarse whisper that came out whenever I tried to speak sounded weird. She just looked at me, and I was the one who broke the silence.

"Where are we?" I still had confused memories of last night and being confused always makes me afraid and defensive. I remembered voices and people and feelings, but there was a white haze obscuring a lot of it. "Was Morgan here?" I'd heard her voice last night but I could see no evidence of her.

"She's still at . . ." Charlotte broke off, apparently afraid of upsetting me again.

"Work," I finished her sentence for her. I could feel the pain lurking behind the numbness that the salt water had provided. She nodded, avoiding my eyes.

"She's at my house still, right, Charlotte?" I pushed. What was so wrong that she was always trying to keep things from me? Should I be more worried than I actually was, assuming that was even possible? Or did she just think that not talking about anything bad would make me forget it existed? It was a good thing I could so vividly remember what Amy had said to me last night, because Charlotte was really starting to get on my nerves.

"Caelie," Charlotte began, in a nervously lecturing tone of voice. I *hate* that she's nervous of me.

"Look," I said, faintly but firmly, deciding to set her straight. "You don't get me. Be happy that you don't. I can act normal and then you'd be more comfortable, but I'm not going to. I'm sorry about last night. I can't control anything he did, but I can control what I do. Thank you for getting Amy on the phone. That was really the only thing you could do for me. Inside. Because I don't care what happens to the outside still, even though I know that's really your job. Keeping the outside of me safe. Maybe that's why I don't care about you, I don't know. You're doing your job, so thanks, but I know people are over there, in my house, in my room, in my life, looking at my blood, finding all my X-rays and medical records, doing *their* jobs. I know. I'm going outside for a bit, okay? I need some time by myself."

I slung my backpack over my shoulder in one easy motion and said, "Don't worry. I'm just going to study. I have finals this week."

As I was walking towards the door to the little balcony, she stopped me.

"Caelie, there's something you should know," she began, but I turned my back to her and kept walking. The pain had come back full force about two thirds of the way through my speech, but that was only one of the reasons I didn't want to talk any more.

"Okay, Caelie," she called after me. The woman just does not give up. "You can have a break from me for a bit, but then we have to go. There are two chairs and a table out there and it should be pretty quiet right now. After I have a shower and get dressed, I'll order some breakfast and you can eat that out there, too. Then we have to get started. We have a long drive today," she finished, before walking into the bathroom.

I wondered again where we were going, but pushed it out of my mind as I stepped outside and positioned myself so that I was facing the door. Once I was safely seated, I booted up my laptop and started to review my Science notes, slipping a honey-dipped ice cube into my mouth. It was good, and it did help. I could have used Charlotte's knowledge of simple pain remedies earlier in my life.

After several minutes and about four more honeyed ice cubes, I discovered that Amy had been right. Underneath the layer of facts I tried to push directly from the textbook pages into my brain was a constant, pulsing current of panic and jostling memories, but I could force them down by concentrating hard on my work, even when that work consisted of trying to memorize the periodic table, all the parts of a sheep's eye and a bunch of incredibly boring stuff about electrons, which are going to keep on doing whatever they're doing whether I know about them or not.

I was word perfect in two Science units before Charlotte brought out my breakfast. She knocked first, then set the tray down and went back inside, which made me feel a little better about her. Also, she'd apparently had no trouble getting breakfast food delivered at one in the afternoon.

I finished one more unit while I was eating, then she knocked again and I assumed it was time for us to go, but when the door opened I found that it wasn't her at all. Some tiny, older guy with a grey goatee, tiny spectacles and almost no hair on his head at all opened the door and walked out on to the balcony.

"Where's Charlotte?" I asked immediately. He held the door open wide so I could see her. She just nodded at me, and I turned my attention back to the man.

"Hi, Caelie. I'm Dr. Ungel," he said.

I nodded back at him, warily.

"I'm a psychiatrist," he continued, undaunted. "You know what that is, right?"

"Because of last night," I said matter-of-factly, then surprised both of us when I started to laugh. There's a great line in a Cynthia Voigt book, *Dicey's Song*, and the words came back to me suddenly: Dicey admits to her littlest brother that she's in trouble, but she doesn't mind because it's her own trouble that she made herself. This was my own trouble that I made myself, and the first time I've ever made trouble in my life. For some reason, that struck me as hilarious, and I laughed louder and louder. The laughing hurt my throat, plus I had the urge to keep laughing until there was no me and only laughter, which was the same way I'd felt last night when I was screaming, so I stopped abruptly.

"Right now, yes, it's because of last night," he said, looking slightly concerned now that the initial surprise was over. I couldn't blame him for that. "What's so funny?" he asked me, when it was clear I had a grip on myself again.

Figuring I owed him an explanation, I told him the quote. It didn't sound as funny when I said it out loud, and I immediately forgave Charlotte for not explaining why she was laughing in the car yesterday.

"Do you want to talk to me about last night, or anything that happened before?" he asked me bluntly.

"No," I shook my head politely. I could afford to be polite because I could tell that he wasn't going to make me.

"Okay," he answered agreeably. "I just have to check your blood pressure and a few other things before I let you go. You had to be sedated last night, you know."

I nodded and let him get on with it. I didn't remember that, but was willing to take his word for it. He must have been what Charlotte wanted to prepare me for, but it wasn't too bad. He just asked me questions about school and stuff while he was checking me, so that was okay. Then he tilted his head towards the ice cubes and honey packages.

"That's a good remedy," he told me.

When he went in to talk to Charlotte, I followed him.

"She's okay to go," he said to Charlotte. Then he turned to me, "It could help you a lot to work with a therapist, but there's no point in doing it before you're ready. When you want to—*if* you want to," he corrected himself, "just ask Charlotte and she'll make sure you find someone."

Not in this lifetime, I thought, smiling noncommittally, but he smiled back for real, so I think he could tell what I was thinking. He waved to both of us, and Charlotte turned to me once he was gone.

"All set?"

I nodded. She was the same person she'd been before Dr. Ungel came in, and so was I, but for some reason I no longer felt as annoyed with her. I went out on the balcony, turned off my laptop and put all my stuff back in my backpack, then checked the whole room quickly to make sure I wasn't missing anything before I followed Charlotte back out, down the long checkered-carpet hallway I hadn't paid any attention to last night, into the glossy beige and bronze elevator, through the lobby and out the revolving glass doors to the car.

"So," I began as I buckled myself in, "where are we going?" I was getting used to the weird glass interior that responded only to her.

In response, Charlotte looked at me and grinned. It was a challenging, rather than friendly, grin and that was okay with me.

"Fine." I actually smiled back, surprising both of us. It was our first non-confrontational interaction, and neither one of us wanted to push our luck.

Charlotte turned the radio on to an oldies station while I slid my laptop out of my bag and onto my lap. We drove in silence, except for the radio, and I finished Science and then moved on to Math. I can't stand Math, but it kept the flickering images of last night and the rest of my past from taking over, at least for a few hours, at which point Charlotte decided we had to talk.

Once she started, I could tell she'd been thinking about me. About us.

"Caelie, we don't have to be the same to get along," she announced cautiously, when I was so thoroughly sick of Math that I'd slid my laptop back into my bag in disgust. "You're right, my job is to make sure you stay in one piece. Even if you don't care about that, Amy and Morgan do, and aside from not being someone who fails at anything very often, I have no desire to explain to them that I failed them in this."

Amy's impressed by Charlotte, but Charlotte feels actual dread about Amy. Interesting. I said nothing, just nudged my backpack towards the door so I could move my feet.

"You're also right that I don't know what's going on in your head," she acknowledged, ignoring my silence, "but we're stuck with each other, so let's figure out something we have in common."

She sounded real for only the second time since I'd met her, so I considered it and she waited while I thought it over.

"Smarties or M&Ms," I asked her, sucking water through the Camelback water bottle that was waiting for me in the car when we left the hotel. As long as I keep swallowing things, my throat feels okay. Not good, but bearable. Maybe Charlotte knew that because she revealed a tiny cooler, stocked with ice cubes, built into the space between our two seats. I couldn't swear it had been there yesterday, but it must have been. It would be tricky to open packages of honey in her car, even though I still had some. It's unbelievably clean and I was concentrating on not spilling anything.

"M&Ms," she replied, instantly picking up on the game. That was a point in her favour, but I still shook my head sadly. M&Ms taste burnt compared to Smarties.

"Okay." She quickly countered with, "Coke or Pepsi."

"Coke," I said instantly. It was her turn to shake her head at me. I smiled a little.

"Ereaders or books," I tried.

"Books or iPad," she said decisively, making me smile.

"Outdoors or indoors," she said.

"Outdoors," we chorused.

"Well, that's something, anyway," Charlotte said. "What kind of outdoors?"

"Someplace with trees and water. And not a lot of bugs," I added. "Or people."

"Ocean or lake?" she asked.

"Doesn't matter. Well, ocean, I guess. I hate leeches more than barnacles," I volunteered, breaking my rule about giving only the shortest, most relevant information in response to a direct question. It was a bit late for that with Charlotte, so I just kept going. It felt kind of good. "And oceans have more sand, usually. I don't know. Either one. What about you?"

"I like mountains. Hiking," she elaborated. "I pack in what I need and just get away from everyone for a few days."

"That sounds nice," I commented. There was silence for a bit, then, because it was more comfortable to be friendly than hostile and I was in no danger of ever trusting Charlotte, I spoke again.

"I can read, you know, so it doesn't make a lot of sense to not tell me where we're going."

She looked over at me and grinned. "Well, here's the thing. You wouldn't take off on Amy, but I'm not Amy." She raised her eyebrows at me and then turned back to the road.

That's for sure. "Smart," I commented, shrugging so she wouldn't think that I was impressed. "But . . . it would make her worry. Besides, she told me not to give you too hard a time. I guess that precludes me running away from you."

She studied me for a moment and seemed to come to a decision. "Precludes, hey?" She didn't give me time to decide if she was making fun of me or not before she kept talking. "Well, we're off to an apartment that my family rents out sometimes in the winter, and uses for vacations in the summer. You will be close to the beach. But the real reason we're going is that it's close to a very good Children's Hospital. You're having a complete check-up, full body X-rays, everything."

"What kind of 'everything'?" I asked her suspiciously. The ice cubes were doing a great job of dulling the pain in my throat, although my voice was still hoarse.

"The kind you don't want," she replied evenly.

"He didn't do anything like that, you know," I protested. "I would have told Amy."

Charlotte had nothing to say to that, even though I kept looking at her for a while.

"Doesn't a parent have to sign for medical treatment?" I tried.

She gave me a *look*, but decided to answer me anyway. "Short answer, no," she told me. "You're thirteen, and doctor-patient confidentiality exists for you, up to a point. Long answer, no. You're now a temporary ward of the state, and I'm a slightly less temporary agent of the state."

Those answers were the same length, but I didn't point it out to her because the whole agent of the state thing was kind of intimidating. "I hate being a girl," I finally muttered, staring back at the road. "And then what?"

"I don't know," she admitted cheerfully. "We'll be there for a week, you'll go to the hospital, you'll study and write your finals, you can go swimming."

"With you," I added.

"Yep," she agreed. "You're stuck with me for the next week."

"Why? Why do I need a police officer? Where is . . . he?" What was going to happen at the end of the week? *I don't want to know, I don't want to know, I don't want to know.*

"You don't need to worry about him, Caelie," she said.

"Oh, yeah, that's *your* job," I said pointedly. Fear really does bring out the worst in people.

"Morgan works fast," was her only comment.

"And then?" I reminded her, not wanting to think about Morgan or what she was doing.

"We'll see," she said. "There's no point in thinking too far ahead."

"Right," I challenged. "Like you don't know what's going to happen to me in a week. You have a job, right? Besides me? It's not your job to watch over me forever. Are you sending me to foster care? Trying to find my mom?" My rapidly-becoming-a-tirade was interrupted as the dashboard slowly rippled with a pale blue, liquid light.

The radio had stopped, and she glanced over at me uncomfortably. What had I done now? I turned to look out the window, and her voice came clearly to my ears.

CHAPTER THIRTEEN

"Hi," said Charlotte, attempting to be quiet, and I realized the rippling light must indicate a phone call coming in. She'd put on her headset and touched a part of the dashboard that looked no different from any other part, but instantly made the light stop and the radio come back on. Obviously, she didn't want me to overhear her; I rolled my eyes, but she just looked steadily back at me before returning her attention to her conversation.

I got the hint and took out my laptop again, even though I couldn't help hearing her. It's not like there was anywhere for me to go except the backseat, and I was pretty sure a cop would frown on me taking off my seatbelt and climbing over the seats while we were zipping down a highway.

"In the car," she answered.

"She seems pretty normal to me," she said, glancing over at me. I stopped pretending that I wasn't listening to her.

"Smarties. Carbonated beverages. Being stranded on a desert island," she replied glibly. I rolled my eyes again, and there was a long pause during which Charlotte's face lost all of its animation and most of its colour.

"I'll ask her," she said. I shook my head because I didn't want to answer anyone's questions, especially not anyone who made Charlotte look ill, but she wasn't paying attention to me. She listened to the phone for another minute and stipulated, "On speaker then. And I need to record it. Give me a second."

Her fingers swept across the glass, moving as gracefully and as surely as a concert pianist's. Writing temporarily covered the dashboard, but if it was in any Latin-based language, I couldn't tell. Just as quickly, Charlotte said, "Record and display incoming call," and Morgan's face shimmered into view. Wow. Could she see me, too?

"You understand that I'm recording this conversation, right?" Charlotte asked me, completely unnecessarily. She was all cop now, and I was glad I'd never been tempted to trust her. I nodded. *Uh, yeah.*

"Hi, Caelie," Morgan said, and from the way her eyes met mine, she could see me as clearly as I could see her.

"Hi, Morgan," I answered. I was pretty sure I'd smiled when I first saw her face and was trying to make up for it now, keeping my face neutral and my voice carefully but distantly polite. "I'm sorry for disturbing everyone last night." I mostly meant Amy.

"She was glad to talk to you," she assured me, smiling slightly back at me. "So was I."

Her eyes looked deeply into mine and I smiled back before I could stop myself. I'd missed her. How stupid was that? I don't even *know* her! Besides, even though she sounded both calm and nice, I knew this conversation was not going to be easy and I wanted to be ready for what was coming. I couldn't let her trick me into relaxing.

What else could there be? I didn't leave anything out of my letters that Morgan could find evidence of around my house. I didn't leave anything out of my letters at all. Would they tell me if my dad was free? My mind raced to cover all the possibilities, but the only thing I knew for sure was that whatever it was, I didn't want to hear it.

"Is it him?" I ventured. I could see why Charlotte and I were spending two days driving and she wouldn't tell me where we were going if they'd lost him.

"No," Morgan was quick to reassure me. "You never have to worry about that again," she said, so dismissively that I actually did stop worrying for a moment. "I just have a few questions about your family. Things you didn't write to Amy about."

"Amy told me to study. I don't want to talk about anything!" I said desperately.

"Cael, let me ask," she said calmly, "and if you don't want to answer, we'll talk about something else for a minute until you're ready to go on with Charlotte, okay?"

I still didn't say anything. Did she know she'd just called me Cael instead of Caelie?

"I'm sorry, Caelie." She did sound like she was sorry, but not sorry enough to stop asking.

"Okay, fine. But I'm not answering if I don't want to," I said stubbornly.

"It's about your mom," she said. "You wrote that she was gone, but not why or where."

"I don't want to live with her, either," I said quickly. "She never helped me."

"No," Morgan said slowly, "don't worry about that."

I breathed a little easier. "Why and where?" I repeated, then shrugged. "I don't know. She was just gone one morning when I woke up. After the whole Grade 3 thing. My dad got angry when I asked about it, so I didn't ask him anymore."

I don't want to remember how furious he was after the Ministry visits, but I know that's why she left. "I figure she got fed up with him and took off. If I don't have to go with her, why does it matter?" I asked.

"Did he ever hit her?" she asked me.

"I guess. Not much when I was around," I said bitterly.

"Any injuries stand out for you?"

"Well, she broke her leg skiing once," I shrugged.

"What happened to all of her personal belongings?" she continued. "Did she take everything with her?"

"No. He made me sort through it, keep the clothes I could wear and give the rest away."

"Did you notice if anything was missing?" she probed.

"Not really. Most of her stuff seemed to be there," I answered, getting curious.

"Which leg was it?" Morgan circled back. Her tone was light and indicated only a mildly polite interest but I suddenly saw where she was going with these questions. And why. She saw the understanding in my eyes, and her own grew darker.

I looked out the window to try and refocus. My mother hadn't left us; he'd killed her. Morgan waited for me silently, but I had nothing to say.

Charlotte had pulled into a rest area, and I motioned to both of them that I was all right as I climbed out of the car and headed towards the nearest picnic table. I sat on the table part and rested my feet on the bench, breathing slowly. It smelled nice, not like the city where it only smells nice for a little while after it rains. Of course, it rains all the time in our city, but this air smelled like earth.

I breathed it in and watched Charlotte talk to Morgan, or at least listen to Morgan. I was deliberately not thinking about anything except the smell of earth and the coolness of the wood underneath me until I realized that Charlotte was looking at me anxiously and I nodded back to reassure her. She left the car and started to come towards me, so I hopped down off the table and went to meet her.

"I'm okay. Is Morgan still there?" I asked. Charlotte nodded at me and we walked back to the car. I sat down before looking at Morgan's life-size face on the dash.

"Her right leg. It was broken several centimeters above her ankle. Both bones were broken." I remember because she couldn't walk for weeks. Couldn't even stand up. "The only things I noticed missing were the clothes she was wearing the day before and the locket she always wore."

"Oval," stated Morgan.

"With a picture of me as a baby in one side," I said.

"And herself as a baby on the other side," Morgan finished. "I'm really sorry."

"So he would have killed me anyway." It shouldn't have, but the certainty surprised me so much that I said aloud what I only meant to think.

"He's never going to get near you again," Morgan answered. I noticed that she didn't disagree.

"You don't know him," I told her flatly.

"You don't know Charlotte," Morgan replied, just as evenly, although I think her calm might have been real. It was definitely tinged with pride instead of the bone-deep fear I felt about my father.

"Where did you find her?" I asked, veering away from a pointless argument. It couldn't be a coincidence that my mother's body had been discovered now.

"We found some human bones while exhuming Missy's remains," she explained. The most sheltered corner of the garden, with the softest dirt. I closed my eyes and tried to think of anything but Morgan while she kept speaking.

"It may not be her," she added, more out of a sense of duty than out of any desire to provide me with false hope. I could tell she didn't believe it.

I opened my eyes. *Really?* I thought, sarcastically.

"That's fine, Caelie," she said, as if I'd spoken out loud, "but the clothes aren't in good shape, and neither is the body. It will be difficult to tell for sure."

"A positive identification." That was how they always described it on television.

"Right," she said.

"Like there could be a lot of bodies that my dad buried in the backyard." I was sarcastic, although, hey, with my dad, you never know.

"What can I say? We have to work with the laws, even when they're not perfect. Or anything close to perfect," she added.

Why, if she doesn't like them, does she work to protect them?

"Caelie, I really am sorry about your mom. And that you had to find out this way."

I shrugged. "It's not your fault. I should have known, but she was never that great a mother so it didn't surprise me when she took off. Or when I thought she did, I guess."

"Well, it could have been worse." There was some light in Morgan's eyes now, which made me realize that she'd been eclipsed in darkness before, something I only noticed once it was gone. The darkness became her, but the light intrigued me.

Did Morgan know me because of my letters or because of who she is? I decided to find out.

"Yeah, I could have been born to nice, normal people who liked spending time with me and lived on a farm where I could have my own horse," I agreed. "That would have been really awful."

Charlotte was taken aback, but Morgan laughed out loud, confirming what I was already beginning to believe about both of them. I was glad it wasn't Morgan here with me because it would be way harder to prevent myself from liking her.

"Hang in there, okay?" she told me, and the darkness I saw in her—the darkness that matched my own—disappeared entirely for one shining moment as the memory of her laughter lingered.

"No problem."

Morgan's image went still, capturing an appreciative but almost-concealed smile, and I looked away as Charlotte reached for the glass to erase Morgan's image. I like Morgan. A lot. She's funny and nice and doesn't seem to hate me or be scared of me. It's weird, comforting and alluring, and I have to stop. If I start to like her too much, it will hurt so much more when she walks away. I am, after all, a job she has to finish.

About my mom, well, I was so mad at her before she left that I didn't really care when she was gone. I would never stand by and watch while someone hurt a little kid, even if it wasn't *my* little kid. I've hated my mom for a really long time. Why should I hate her any less because she's dead?

I didn't notice I was crying until Charlotte gently laid her hand on my shoulder.

"Don't touch me!" I screamed, jerking away from her. Well, I tried to scream, but it came out as a hoarse and scratchy whisper that rasped through my throat like a blade.

"Sorry," I immediately apologized, a lot more calmly, holding my hands up to placate her and distance myself so I could calm down for real. It hurt terribly, but it had to be done. "Sorry, just . . . please don't touch me, okay? I don't like being touched very much," I added.

"Okay," Charlotte agreed, not pointing out that I let Morgan touch me. I liked it, even. She handed me a plain water bottle and pointed outside. "I salted it this morning."

Gratefully, I stepped out of the car again. My throat was burning with pain, and I hated crying in front of her. I walked away, gargled twice in a row with the salty water that made me want to throw up everything I've ever eaten in my life, then walked back to the car and sat back down.

"I'm sorry about your mom, even if you weren't close to her," she said, taking the water bottle back and tucking it into a holder between us.

I nodded. I could see that she really was sorry. It wasn't her fault that she couldn't understand.

As she turned back to the wheel and pulled back onto the road, she said, "You know, your father may be dealt with for the murder of your mother, if that can be proved, and you would never have to go to court at all. Nothing that he did to you would be brought up," she explained.

She sounds confident when she talks about the law, and Morgan can't keep the sarcasm out of her voice when she does. Yet another reason to think that Morgan is like Amy, because laws are designed by and for normal people, which Amy is not.

"Besides, the penalties for murder are a lot harsher than those for child abuse," Charlotte added, and the bitterness she'd kept out of her voice and body still stung the air. Even her eyes, when she glanced at me quickly, betrayed no hint of the pain I *knew* she felt about that last statement. Living with my dad had taught me to listen to what people didn't say or show.

Charlotte is a good liar. That would be important to remember, and I filed it away as my mind dwelled on what she'd actually said.

My mom never protected me when she was alive, but it looked like she might be able to do it dead. The part about me going to court was obviously ridiculous, because Amy had said I was out of the game. Court was definitely for active players of the game, and besides, going to court and testifying against my father was ludicrous. As I dismissed the idea, an awful thought entered my mind, making me dizzy. The blackness swam in front of my eyes again and I blinked it away with difficulty.

"Charlotte, where are my letters? Will . . . he . . . get them?" I asked, so horrified that I could barely ask the question. I could see the answer in her face before she said anything, and my stomach turned over. She pulled over on to the shoulder right away and I almost fell out the door in my haste to throw up outside and not in her immaculate car.

When I finished, she handed me a cup of iced water that did not have salt in it along with what I knew had to be a handkerchief, although I've never seen one that nice before in real life. I rinsed my mouth out, spat the water onto the gravel, buried my face in the handkerchief, and hunched over. This could not be happening. *Make this not be happening.*

I needed my razor blades back; they are the only things that make me feel better when I just can't take any more. As urgently as last night, I had to get out, now. The need was so strong that it nearly overtook me until I remembered that we were on the side of a highway; running would not allow me to escape Charlotte, but I could still get what I needed.

"Can you pull forward a bit?" I asked her, acting like I had to throw up again. She moved the car forward a few meters and I leaned out, coughing a few times as if I were going to throw up, and grabbed the first piece of broken glass I saw. The immediate relief I felt was worth the agonizing pain in my throat from the coughing.

There's always broken glass on the side of a road, and the curved green class calmed me down immediately, while the pain in my throat kept me distracted. Pain is something real to hold on to, a way to remind myself that I am nothing and no one, and everything that happens to me is equally irrelevant.

"Thanks," I said, concealing the glass in my palm and taking another sip of water. She'd mixed honey in with it this time, but I was in no mood to appreciate taking care of myself. I drank a bit anyway, because it made me look more normal.

Charlotte looked at me speculatively for a few long moments, long enough for me to remember my promise to Amy, then spoke quickly, as if that would make it better.

"They are, I'm sure you know, evidence right now and as such, yes . . . yes he will get to see them if he goes to trial for abusing you. The defense is entitled to access the evidence being used by the prosecution." Her voice got stronger as she took refuge in the overused, meaningless legal terms, but this time I could summon up neither anger nor disdain.

"No. No, no, no. Not possible," I shook my head and clenched the glass harder, feeling it pressing against my skin. If I squeezed any harder or moved my hand even slightly over it, it would cut me, and the desire rose up in me so sharply I could hardly contain it, even with Amy's voice ringing in my ears. I had promised her I would make it through. "They're *my* letters!"

"I know, Caelie, I know." Charlotte was trying to calm me down, a task she didn't realize was impossible. "If the trial is about your mother's death, that won't happen."

"What if they can't prove it?" I wanted to know.

"Then he can still be tried for the abuse," she stated. I thought about that for a while. He couldn't *ever* see the letters. I could not get up in court and talk about them or him, but he shouldn't get away with everything. Am I such a useless coward that I can't stand up for myself, even with all these people helping me and keeping him away from me? Yes. Yes, I am. I have always been useless and stupid and worthless.

Charlotte's voice, heavy and sharp, broke into my thoughts. "Caelie, you have enough to deal with right now. *If* it's your mother, and *if* he killed her, and *if* he gets convicted for it, he won't be getting away with anything. And he'll get a much longer sentence for murder than for child abuse."

So what he did to me or Missy will never matter? I'd gone from fearing my dad to hating him in less than three seconds. "I want Morgan, please," I said quietly. I hadn't meant to say that aloud, or even at all, but her only reply was to move her fingers over the instantly responsive dashboard again. The rippling light returned, but this time it moved towards the centre of the car instead of originating there.

"Javers," came Morgan's voice, brisk and professional. There were other voices in the background, but no image.

"Morgan?" Now that she was on the phone, I began to think I'd made a mistake. I glanced over at Charlotte, and heard her mutter something about caller ID.

"Caelie, hi," Morgan said quickly. She switched to a softer voice, and moved to a quieter area, but no image came up. "What's up?"

"I'm sorry to bug you at work," I whispered.

"You're not bugging me."

"I don't want him to see my letters, Morgan."

"Oh." She took a deep breath and sighed loudly. "Oh, Caelie. I'm so sorry. I know you don't. Maybe he won't have to. But even if he does, he still won't know you. He still can't touch you," she assured me.

I started to cry. I couldn't help it. This was so much worse than anything I'd imagined. For my entire life I hadn't thought much beyond 'Please let this stop happening,' and now that it had, it was horrible. I really didn't think I could do this, and I desperately wanted to not have to. I buried my face in my knees so that Charlotte couldn't see me crying.

"Caelie, honey, you have done your job."

Did she understand? I hadn't told either of them what I was thinking.

"You stood up to him by writing those letters and sending them to Amy. You keep standing up to him by going on with your life and staying safe. By doing well in school and being successful and still caring. You're winning, Caelie."

"I'm scared!" I sobbed. She understood, but she was wrong. "I'm *not* winning. I'm useless and stupid and failing." The only thought in my head now was, *Please don't make me have to do this!* I can't do it, I can't. I can't let him read my letters. I would rather die.

"Listen to me, Caelie," Morgan said fiercely, "you don't have to stand up there in court and look at him and tell him what he did! He already knows. It's not going to be a shock to him. Having other people know about it doesn't make it any more real, and not charging him with it doesn't make it any less real. The only thing that telling us has accomplished is getting you safe," she finished more quietly, making an effort at controlling her voice.

The anger was still there, but it was as if she'd reminded herself that anger terrified me and then made a deliberate effort to control a fathomless rage. She was stronger than her emotions, and stronger than her instincts. *Just like Amy.*

"You've shown incredible courage and strength by telling Amy and getting through the last twenty-four hours," Morgan said, her calm voice now tinged with pride. In me? "You will never be as manipulative or as physically strong as he is right now, that's a fact. But there are more important ways of being strong, and you are, and always have been, stronger than him."

I had nothing to say to that. I was still thinking about the first part, about how my dad did already know. It was obvious, but something I hadn't thought of before. I'd imagined this whole thing as a terrible blow to my dad, but that couldn't be true. He knew. He always knew.

"Nobody expects you to stop being scared," she continued more gently. "It's scary enough when a normal person's entire life gets totally changed in an instant, and you didn't get to start with a normal life."

There was another pause. I would like to stop being scared, actually. I hate being scared, and I've never had a single hour in my life when I wasn't afraid. Will I have to be afraid forever?

"Caelie," she added, as if she'd just thought of something and was quite pleased about it, "do you ever watch a movie and the main character does a whole bunch of stupid things because they didn't trust someone else, or wanted more information than the other person was willing to provide, or some other reason that's barely plausible, but if they'd just believed the person in the first place, nothing bad would have happened?"

"Are you asking me if I've ever *been* to a movie?" I managed, through my tears. I wasn't less scared, but I was listening.

Morgan's voice changed, as if she were still serious, but smiling now. "Okay, well, trust us. *Really* trust us."

"I do trust you," I sniffled. It was true, although part of me was raging. It's not safe to trust her! What am I doing?!

"It wasn't easy for me. It's not easy for Amy. It won't be easy for you."

"But I *want* it to be easy! I'm tired of *everything* being hard!" I tried to shout, before being consumed by wracking sobs. I *hate* crying and I tried to fight it but I couldn't. After a bit, it felt good. The pain inside me subsided, and even my throat didn't hurt too badly. I relaxed my grip on the glass, but kept it in my hand.

Morgan just let me cry for a while. When I finally petered out, she was still there.

"No doubt," she said, wearily but with humour.

"Just tell me it gets easier later," I pleaded half-heartedly. After all, she'd just admitted that she was like me, hadn't she? So she must know what it's like later. Right?

"It helps to focus on very small good things, like acing your finals. Break everything into manageable chunks, and don't think too far ahead."

So it doesn't get easier. "I'm sorry," I apologized.

"For what?" she replied. "You're not doing great."

Like Amy, she doesn't lie to me, or pretend that things are different than they really are.

"Why should you be?" she asked reasonably. "But, Cael? There's one really important thing for you to remember here. When you were living with your dad, you had only one job to do—just one thing you were responsible for—and that was telling someone who could help you. You did that, and you did a great job of it. It's our turn to do a great job now."

I thought about that as she hung up, and wondered if it was possible. I handed the phone back to Charlotte and just sat looking out the window for a while. She only waited a moment before she turned the car back on, put the radio on low and then pulled back onto the highway. We drove quietly for a while. Finally, I turned to her, deadpan.

"Are we there yet?"

She rewarded me with some semi-hysterical laughter and I had to say, "It wasn't *that* funny," before she calmed down.

"No," she replied, wiping tears away, "but stress is stress. Are we good?"

I shrugged my shoulders at her and held out my fist, palm side down. She frowned at it and finally held her hand out beneath mine. When she did, I spread my fingers out and let the piece of glass fall into her hand.

She stared at it for a moment, then closed her own hand around it and continued to drive. We were both silent for quite some time. Finally, she said, "I don't know what to do about this."

I almost smiled at the unexpected admission, and I could think of a lot of things. I decided to share them, counting them out on my fingers as I went.

"One," I listed, starting with my thumb, "you can take me to a psych ward, where they'll probably release me less than an hour after asking me if I plan on killing myself and I say no." I snuck a glance at her, and she seemed a little more tired, and a little bit sadder. It's true, but hearing it said out loud hurt her in a way that I didn't understand. Against my will, I felt sorry for her, and tried to suppress it.

"Two," I continued, index finger up, "you can call Morgan or Amy and have one of them talk to me. Morgan will tell both of us that we handled it really well and then tell you to keep a closer eye on me. Amy will tell me that it's part of my past, and a part I should leave in the past. That it was a useful and effective tool when I needed it, but that I no longer need it." I glanced sideways again. Was she almost smiling? Maybe.

"Three, you can throw it out your window and pretend this never happened." She gave me a withering look, although I got the feeling that she was tempted by that one.

"Four, you can write it up in your report, but you have to do something about it so you can write down what that was. Five, you can give it back to me because it makes me feel better." The look on her face told me that one was not going to be an option.

"Six, you can ask me why I did it."

The last option surprised both of us, and I wasn't sure I wanted to answer if she did ask me. I lowered my hands to my lap, fingers curled back in.

"How about we ask Morgan why you did it?" she countered, and I began to turn away before I realized that she wasn't being mean or threatening. In fact, what she'd just said worried her, and I figured out what she was telling me.

"Morgan used to cut herself?" I asked.

She didn't answer me. Maybe she couldn't. "When you need help," was all she said, "open your mouth and ask for it. Do you know how many people have the number to Amy's private cell?" When I didn't say anything, she answered, "Eight. You, Morgan, her agent, and five members of her immediate family."

I thought about that. Amy doesn't have six people in her family; she doesn't have any family at all, except for an older foster brother she never sees anymore. Jane probably has a family, though. The idea of it freaked me out a bit because there's no cover of a magazine in any store anywhere in the country that does not feature Jane every week of the year. She's always on TV, there are constant updates about her on the radio, and don't even get me started about online sites and forums.

All of that, and I'm one of eight people in the entire world who can get through to her private line? After mere seconds of deliberation, I decided that it was easier to think of her as Amy, and I was going to continue to do so. I know Amy, and Amy knows me. It was Amy who'd called me, not Jane.

"Wait. How do you know that?" I asked. Amy's number was inside the envelope I had not shared with Charlotte.

"Do you think I would hand a sealed envelope to a minor in my care without checking to see what was in it?" she asked me.

"Mr. Bowman gave me that envelope."

"And I gave it to him. Or, actually, Morgan did. She picked it up from Amy yesterday morning, and told me that you're to be put through to Amy whenever you want."

"So you did give me a sealed envelope without checking through it yourself?"

She sighed.

"You'd better toss that," I advised her, because she was still holding the glass in her hand. "It makes me want to use it when I can see it." There's something addictive about the sight of your own blood, the power that comes when you draw blood out of your own body, and the rush of endorphins that accompanies it. Plus, I wanted to annoy her.

The look she gave me was more than a little displeased, but she did roll her window down enough to throw it out. I relaxed a bit with the temptation gone, but the tension in the car remained, and I wondered what she would put in her report.

CHAPTER FOURTEEN

We ended up at a beachfront condo complex, and I was getting worried about Charlotte by the time we got upstairs. It was dark, past midnight for the second night in a row when we finally parked.

"You should go to bed, Charlotte," I commented, once we were inside the apartment, which was huge.

She just looked at me.

"I'll be good," I said, in a long-suffering voice. "I promise," I added, because she definitely takes her responsibilities seriously, and I was that responsibility for now. She was exhausted, though, and needed sleep. I'd slept in the car and felt way better than last night, which I was trying hard to block from my memory, but it was probably right in the front of her mind.

"I'll be fine," I told her, unwilling to say the rest of it, which was that I actually did feel okay. The dream-hallucination had turned out to be real and I was somewhere strange and new and far away. The fear was still there, but being this far from him, in a strange city, let me push it down.

She studied me for a few seconds longer before nodding her acceptance of my promise. "Feel free to explore," she offered, then went into one of the rooms and fell full-length on the bed. "Inside," she specified. "The door in the other bedroom locks, but leave mine open, please," came the muffled request from somewhere in the mattress. "And for heaven's sake, open your door if I knock, okay?" she lifted her head up for that and gazed directly at me.

"Okay," I agreed.

"Ummf," she mumbled, and was asleep about two seconds later.

I put my stuff in the other room and looked around a little bit. There was a bedside table, some paperback novels in a little bookshelf along one side, and an ugly picture of a dog and a child that somebody probably wanted to get out of their own house and figured they could dump here and pretend it was art. From what I could see by the light from the living room, the books were all true crime stuff and romance novels, so I wasn't interested. However, I'd be very glad I made Charlotte help me drag my own books up here if I ever found the light switch in my room.

I wandered around the mostly dark apartment and found some DVDs (normal popular stuff like *Star Wars* and *Indiana Jones* along with what looked like every John Candy movie ever made), but nothing to watch them on, an imposing stainless steel and glass room that should have been the kitchen but actually looked completely empty except for the table and chairs, and a bathroom with the biggest shower I've ever seen.

An entire wall in the living room was made of pearly glass, and then I noticed that all the counters and tables in the kitchen were glass, too, reminding me of Charlotte's car, and I went to check my room. Yep, a glass wall there, too. I reached out and touched the glass, but nothing happened. Nothing happened when I touched the glass in the other rooms, either. Big surprise.

I took a shower just for the fun of it, and discovered that I could make the whole thing fill up with steam, dump an entire raincloud's worth of water on my head, and spray water from the sides. I let the steam rise and the hot water pound me from all directions for a while before I dried off in the most enormous, fluffy yellow towel ever, and headed into my room, stumbling into the wall in the dark. The only lights on were the ones Charlotte had turned on in the bathroom and the living room, and I couldn't find any lamps or light switches anywhere.

Giving up, I lay down on the bed and tried to sleep.

In the morning, I awoke to the sound of the shower running. I never did figure out how to lock my bedroom door, and I wasn't all that happy about the lights situation either. I knew they could be accessed. Just not by me. I quickly got dressed and tried to comb out my hair, which was a futile exercise; I can only get a comb through it when it's just been washed and conditioned and is soaking wet, so I ended up pulling it back into what I hoped looked like a casual ponytail but probably looked like what it actually was: a desperate attempt to get all the masses of intractable curls away from my face. It did not improve my mood.

When Charlotte finally emerged from the bathroom, she was completely dressed and ready to go. She marched to the kitchen and started opening cupboards and drawers, finally peering into the fridge and freezer.

"So," I called over loudly, annoyed that both she and the apartment itself were ignoring me, "what's for breakfast?"

"Eggos," she replied.

"Eggos?" I asked. Coming from Charlotte, who'd so far only consumed vegetables that were as unprocessed as our situation allowed, it was more than a bit surprising.

"Eggos," she repeated.

I shrugged and walked all the way in to the kitchen. The fridge that she held open was completely empty, which was kind of weird because most people always have mustard or *something* in there, and the freezer contained exactly one ice cube tray (empty) and half a box of Eggos.

"We'll go shopping today," Charlotte announced.

"You think so?" I asked sarcastically, noticing that all the cupboards and drawers were devoid of food, although dishes, cutlery, pots and pans did exist. And a toaster, which rose out of the centre of the shimmering countertop. I did not see a stove, and didn't try the glass.

"Am I a prisoner in here?" I asked her.

"Why?" she frowned at me.

"Um . . ." I gestured expressively towards the glass surfaces in every room, including the giant wall of glass that clearly led out to the deck even though I couldn't make it open.

"Oh," she said, wincing. "Sorry about that." Handing me the first two Eggos and putting two more in for herself, she began to speak. "Provide level 3 access for Caelie." Her fingers swept over the glass, entering information I couldn't even guess at.

"What does that mean?" I asked her.

"It means you can access internal entertainment and subsistence functions," she said absently, running water into two glasses for us.

"What?" Now that it was gone, I was beginning to miss her nervousness. And, you know, basic English.

"You can turn on the lights, use the phone, watch TV, open windows and the deck doors, use the stove," she listed, half-motioning with a glass of water towards the stove area. She then handed the glass to me and sat back to sip her own. "Obviously, you can't access the outside locks, disable security, or engage in research functions, and the computer will keep a record of everything you do."

Like magic, my face appeared on the glass in front of me as soon as she stopped speaking, and Charlotte guided me through the process of being recognized by her computer system. I had to press my hands to the glass, have my eyes scanned, and read a series of words and numbers out loud.

"Level 3 provides menus, so when you touch the glass somewhere, it will list everything you can do."

"Your family owns this?" I asked. The place looked like it was ready for a TED talk to begin filming.

"Can you cook?" Charlotte asked me in return, her face composed but blank. Either her family or her technology was off-limits to me, that was very clear.

"No, my dad was a gourmet chef," I answered sarcastically, stung by her blanking me out.

"Good," she said calmly. "We'll share. You pick dinner one night, I'll do the next. But we'll cook together. It's more fun that way and we can each learn to make new things."

"What if you pick something really gross?" I prodded.

"You can fire me," she said wearily. She didn't look very happy, but kind of like she was trying to pretend it didn't matter.

"All right. We'll cook," I agreed. "Who gets to pick tonight?"

"I'll flip you for it," she offered, the first indication that her newfound bossiness was somewhat negotiable.

"If I weren't your job, what level access would I have?" I asked her.

"You are my job," she replied. "And it's not my job to trust you, Caelie, it's my job to keep you safe. Your access is limited for that reason, and every second that we are not in here, I will be with you, including at the hospital."

I was disposable to my dad, a weirdo to my friends, and a job to everyone else. How was that better than being invisible? Her words, and the evenness with which she delivered them, made me feel hollow.

Charlotte was oblivious. "Your first appointment's in half an hour, so we'd better get going," she said, swallowing her last bit of Eggo, putting both our glasses in the sink, and grabbing her bag. "Come on, Caelie," she prompted me, and I stood up. For a moment, she reached out her hand as if to squeeze my arm, but then pulled it back without touching me. "It'll be okay," she said instead, then moved off to the front door.

Everything will always be okay for her. I don't think she really gets how that's not true for me, but I grabbed my school backpack so I could study if I had any free time, and followed her.

"Whose job is it to trust me?" I wondered, once we were underway. I kept my eyes on the dash, which Charlotte had not engaged.

I don't think it's anyone's job," she finally answered. "Which kind of sucks for you," she decided. "Or it would, if you didn't have Amy."

It would be far too babyish to ask Charlotte if Amy really trusts me, but the thought did keep my mind off the upcoming doctors, and I was pretty quiet the rest of the way.

All my previous hospital experiences involved lots and lots of waiting, followed by a few minutes with the doctor where I felt bad for taking up his time and worried about what he was going to think. This visit was actually not that bad, partly because we never had to wait more than five minutes, and also because I felt pretty anonymous.

It was just as busy and linoleum-filled as every other hospital I'd ever been in, with colours painted in lines on the walls to direct you to different departments, and everything else a kind of grey, plastery colour that reminded me of papier-mâché without the lumps. It smelled like every other hospital too, of a fathomless, untouchable sweet and sour staleness under the sharp antiseptic.

Nobody made a fuss over me or exchanged significant looks with someone else over my head. Nobody even knew who I was, so I didn't have to be 'The Mayor's Daughter'. Charlotte marched me to the various different departments, checked me in, and somehow made everything go very smoothly. Even the internal exam wasn't unbearable. It was kind of cold and a bit painful, but pretty quick and not overwhelmingly humiliating.

It was a woman doctor who did it, and she was very chatty. She spent the whole exam telling me all about toilet training her two year old, so I didn't really have a lot of time to be embarrassed or self-conscious that I was naked with my legs apart for a strange woman with fairly non-threatening plastic tongs and a very long Q-tip. Apparently, toilet training a toddler is difficult.

All in all, I was only in the hospital for about 5 hours, one of my shortest visits ever. I wondered if it had anything to do with the police requesting the tests, or the fact that everyone who saw Charlotte immediately started to look very busy and competent, but either way I hoped I never had to have another X-ray, ever. As it was, I'd probably be deformed for life. In addition to blood tests, scans, swabs, soft tissue testing, and a urine sample, every single part of my body had been X-rayed from at least three angles today. How much radiation can one person stand?

"Are you ready to go for groceries?" Charlotte asked as the doors to the outside whooshed open and the first fresh air we'd had all day rushed over our skin. She looked cheerful, which was an improvement on this morning.

I shrugged and followed her out. First, she drove us to this really small restaurant featuring organic vegan food and, after two days of drive-through and a couple of dry Eggos, it looked pretty good. I picked a tofu vegetable stir-fry and a bun made with approximately a thousand different grains and seeds. Charlotte had some kind of squash soup and a salad sandwich.

That's not what it was officially called, but believe me, that's what it was. She seemed to enjoy it, and my stir-fry was great although there really were too many nuts and seeds and who knows what else in my bun. We didn't talk that much over lunch because what was she going to ask me? 'Hey, how was the probing?' I didn't volunteer any information, either, so it was pretty quiet.

Once we got to the grocery store, though, it was different. We discussed the relative merits of skim milk, which I hate because it tastes like plastic, versus chocolate milk, which Charlotte refuses to put on her cereal. I don't see why we can't have two different kinds of milk and I don't even understand her sugar argument because I'm the one who picked Shredded Wheat while Charlotte made a push for Froot Loops.

Shopping with Charlotte was kind of fun. I didn't tell her that, but maybe she could tell. I don't know.

We made dinner together and I studied some more while it was cooking. Charlotte messed around in the kitchen, putting stuff away and setting the table until the timer buzzed, and then we sat down across from one another at the big glass table, steaming plates of lasagna sending up clouds of yummy cheesy tomato steam.

I could tell she was going to talk to me again and I took a giant bite of garlic bread so I wouldn't have to reply to whatever she planned on saying. It didn't deter her.

"So," said Charlotte, forking up a gooey bite of lasagna with more class and competence than I've ever managed, "I guess you're at a bit of a disadvantage, since I've read your letters and you don't know that much about me. Anything you want to know?"

I thought for a while, chewing on my bread. It tasted a lot better than store-bought. She'd made it like it was important, with fresh garlic, parmesan and pepper, and I enjoyed how real she seemed when we were cooking together.

Finally, I swallowed and took a sip of my iced tea. There was nothing wrong with it, but there was a bitter taste in my mouth nonetheless. Did she have to remind me about the letters? I'd almost managed to submerge them under all my schoolwork and food-related thoughts.

There was one thing I wanted to know.

"How do you know Morgan?"

CHAPTER FIFTEEN

"Ah, the million dollar question," she said lightly, so I could tell there were lots of things for me to know about that, and she wasn't going to tell me any of them. "We met on a case a couple of years ago."

"And she liked you?" That's the part I have trouble with. I mean, I have a hard time liking her, but I think I like Morgan a lot, even if a huge part of me is trying not to.

"It was a . . . difficult case. She had time to get used to me."

The way she said 'difficult' let me know I wasn't going to get any more out of her no matter how I asked my questions, so I tried something else.

"Am I going to have time to get used to you?"

"We can only hope," was her response.

"You're pretty normal, though, right?" I asked. There are exactly zero normal people in my life whom I actually like, and I couldn't see her becoming the first.

"Fortunately and unfortunately," she said calmly.

Interesting and surprising. Most normal people would never consider that there could be an unfortunate side, and I finished the rest of the meal in a thoughtful silence.

After dinner, she took me out to the beach. It was still light out, but beginning to get cool. Charlotte went to the nearest empty bench along the edge of the sand and took out her cell, so I walked a short distance away from her and found my own spot halfway between the ocean and the bench, then sank down to the ground. The sand was very soft, and stretched out for what seemed like miles in either direction. Even though nobody was near our particular patch of sand, happy shouts drifted over on the wind from the volleyball nets stretched out in a line off in the distance, and some squealing from the slacklines a bit nearer, that were tied between trees where the sand ran out into forest.

A lone lifeguard chair speared into the sky about half a kilometer away, near a dock with a huge slide mounted on it. A few kids jostled for a turn on the slide, but most had gone home by this time, and the splashes as they entered the water were drowned out by the regular wash of the waves onto the shore.

I watched the waves for a long, long time, pushing my toes through the sand and picking up handfuls to run through my fingers back on to the beach, over and over. The sand was still a bit warm and the little grains tumbled between my fingers and over my toes as I dug through the sand.

Not until the clouds had all turned dark grey and the sky held every hue of blue until it disappeared into black did Charlotte walk over. I heard the soft grinding of the sand under her feet before I heard her speak. "Let's go."

I felt like snapping at her, but she'd only out stayed out this long for me, and she sure wouldn't let me stay out here by myself, so I grumbled silently to myself and accompanied her back to the apartment. I made a beeline for the deck while she got ready for bed, and I stayed there. She hesitated a bit before going in to her room, trying to decide if she should come and talk to me or not. When she didn't, I felt both relieved and disappointed.

I settled into the braided, cloth hammock that was strung between two beams and pushed off gently with my feet, swinging slowly in tune with the waves that washed over the beach below me.

I'm not sure when the darkness of the sky turned into the black of sleep, but I woke up just before dawn to the sound of birds shrieking. Pale light had just begun to streak across the sky and the whole world looked fresh and new. Off in the distance, a lone person wandered across the sand, taking in the dawn, and I was overcome with the urge to explore the soft, cool, quiet of an unspoiled day. I knew that wasn't an option, and waking Charlotte up to go with me would not be the same. Not that I would.

With a final glance at the silent volleyball nets and the silver slide that was just a dark, clear shape against the lightening sky, I tiptoed back inside to 'my' bedroom, where I locked the door. When I woke again around eight o'clock, Charlotte was up and eating cereal. I had a quick shower, ate a bowl of cereal and drank a glass of juice, glanced wistfully out at the ocean, and grabbed my schoolwork.

For three days, I studied, wrote exams, learned how to make Shepherd's Pie, what veggie ground round was, and why you can use beer to make bread. We rarely left the apartment, except for my supervised beach visits, but I did meet the girl next door, an experience that made me re-evaluate Charlotte once again.

When a knock came at the door, Charlotte swiped her cell phone, which I didn't even know she had on her, handed it to me and then moved to the door, a gun magically appearing in her hand. The Charlotte who'd been teaching me to bake beer bread was completely gone.

"Yes?" she called, in a cool, intimidating voice I barely recognized as hers.

"Um, it's Emily?" a voice called out tentatively from the hallway at the same time the door and walls that led to the hallway shimmered into a sharp transparency. A girl much taller than me stood outside, nervously chewing the end of her ponytail and shifting a towel back and forth from one hand to the other. Obviously, her side of the walls had not changed.

The sight of her, along with the otherwise empty hallway, apparently reassured Charlotte, who managed to wave at me to put the phone away while reaching for the door. Her gun instantly disappeared, and I couldn't even tell where it had gone. As the door opened fully, she looked totally at ease and welcoming. Wow. Charlotte was way cooler, and way scarier, than I'd thought.

"Hi, um, Charlotte?" the girl began nervously, now clutching the towel in both hands. The damp end of her ponytail hung below her shoulder. "My mom says she saw you here with a girl my age?"

"Emily, it's nice to see you again," said Charlotte pleasantly, in a tone of voice she never uses with me. "Caelie, would you like to come meet Emily? I think you're both finishing Grade 8 this year."

Emily nodded, looking up long enough for me to see that she had deep brown eyes that matched her hair. "Hi."

"Hi," I said, walking towards them and trying to close my mouth, which had been open since Charlotte's gun had leaped in her hand.

"My mom said she saw you out by the water, and swimming?"

I wasn't sure if it was a question, but I nodded anyway, even though she was back to looking at the ground, with quick glances directed mostly towards the windows, skittering near Charlotte and me but never quite landing on either of us.

"Well, I'm not allowed to go in by myself, so, um, d'you wanna gowithme?" she finished nervously, her eyes fixing themselves on my sleeve near my elbow.

Once I figured out what she was asking me, and after Charlotte said I could, I quickly changed into the shorts and shirt I'd been swimming in all week and followed Emily numbly down the hall. Charlotte waved us off from the doorway.

It was only the two of us who entered the elevator, but we wouldn't be going alone.

"I'm glad you could come," Emily ventured, after we'd smiled at each other once before turning to study the riveting display of elevator buttons.

"Thanks for asking me," I said, at exactly the same time. She giggled and looked a bit more relaxed.

"How long have you lived here?" I was trying to put all thoughts of Charlotte and her gun out of my mind, even though she'd be out there with us, and presumably so would her weapon.

"Forever," Emily replied, rolling her eyes. "Well, since about kindergarten. Most everyone else just vacations here, so there's never anyone to hang out with."

I nodded at her politely, looking interested.

"Is Charlotte moving back here?" she asked me.

Back? I shrugged, at a total loss. "I don't know." I was very motivated to get Emily off the topic of personal histories since I definitely couldn't answer any questions she had about Charlotte, and I cast around for something to say that would distract her.

"So what do you like to do? Do you have a boyfriend?" I grimaced internally, but it was better than having the conversation veer towards me or Charlotte.

"Ewww," she replied, wrinkling her nose. "No, thanks."

Her obvious nervousness had drawn me to her from the start, and I was liking her more and more as we talked.

"You don't, do you?" she asked me as the elevator settled down and the doors opened smoothly, worried that she might have to backtrack a little.

"No. Gross," I answered. We both grinned and then sprinted for the ocean. She was a lot taller than me and obviously had lots of practice running over the sand, and she won easily. It was strange to play with her as if nothing in my life were wrong, but I liked it, too. The weightlessness of the water and pull of the waves as we floated, dived, chased and leaped through them took everything else out of my mind.

For the first time ever, I felt safe. Free, maybe. Happy? It felt weird, and perfect. Knowing that Charlotte's read my letters, has memorized everything about me, and is kept up to date with whatever's going on back home keeps everything close to the surface, even while we're cooking or I'm writing finals.

Out here, none of that existed, and I only reluctantly followed Emily out of the water when our sanctioned hour was over.

"Is Charlotte strict?" she asked me, as I glanced quickly at a clock on our way back up to the apartment. We'd done our best to dry off on the beach, but were now dripping water and sand everywhere we walked.

I shrugged. "How about your mom?" I turned the question back to her for the thousandth time since meeting her. She wanted to know everything about Charlotte, but she already knew way more than me. I couldn't make things up or ask her anything I, as the one currently living with her, should know.

"Pretty much," she shrugged. "I mean, I've lived here my whole life and taken so many swimming courses that I could be a lifeguard myself if I weren't too young, and she still won't let me go out by myself."

"Want to go again tomorrow?" I found myself asking her.

She nodded and smiled eagerly. "Meet you after school," she offered, walking me down the hall.

"Where do you live, anyway?" I asked.

"Right beside you," she pointed back to the door at the other end of the hall. I smiled at her, said "See you tomorrow," and we both walked in our own doors.

Charlotte was already back at the stove, stirring the chili.

146

"Hey," I said to her, heading to the bathroom to strip off my clothes. I poked my head out the bathroom door and said, "Charlotte . . . thanks." I was sure she was out there the entire time, and neither of us had spotted her. She wasn't lying when she said she was very good at her job.

She had no answer for me then, aside from a slight, acknowledging nod as I disappeared back into the bathroom with the scents of tomato, chili spices, beer and saltwater swirling thickly through the warm air, but she surprised me again the next day, in a totally different way.

I'd barely finished pressing 'Send' to submit my last exam when she grinned at me. "C'mon," she said, "let's take a real break."

I narrowed my eyes at her, but she was in a strange mood, and positively beamed back at me.

"Have you been taken over by a pod person?" I asked warily, pretending to hold back.

"Trust me," she said cheerfully, waiting expectantly for me to follow.

I almost reminded her that she's not the one I trust, but she's the only one I have, plus she was so excited.

It turned out that her idea of a real break was to go to an amusement park and it didn't take me long to notice that for someone who survives on organic multi-grain flax foods, she can sure eat a lot of junk. We stuffed ourselves with clouds of cotton candy, brightly coloured sno-cones, lemonade that managed to be both sweet and tart, the softest, sugar-covered, hot doughnuts in the world, deep-fried strawberry butter and the best barbequed chicken I've ever eaten. When we'd finally crammed as much into our stomachs as possible, we headed for the rides.

The log boat waterslide was definitely the best ride, but Charlotte liked this old wooden rollercoaster that I thought for sure would kill us, and she didn't complain once about how wet we got on my ride as we tried absolutely everything and then rode our favourites over and over. The park got quieter about an hour before closing, and we found that we didn't have to wait in line any more; we just stayed on the ride of our choice and kept going. At the end, we got on the Ferris Wheel, riding up and around, with the whole city spread out beneath us.

"Thanks," I said, not looking at her. "I had a really good time." I can't figure Charlotte out. Sometimes she's all bossy and annoying and treats me like an infant, and sometimes she's really nice. Factor in that whole supercop thing and the cool technology she barely even notices, and I'm really not sure about her. I'm impressed, definitely, but comfortable? No, and I shouldn't be, either. *She's a cop, Cael. Let's not forget that, okay?*

"Well, I'm not all bad," she acknowledged. I glanced over and saw that she was smiling.

I grinned back at her and she seemed really happy about that, which made me nervous. I don't want her to think I trust her now, because I don't. I shrugged and turned back to look at the lights in the city.

It was almost midnight when we got back, and I was tired enough to fall asleep right away. Charlotte waved as I walked into my room and shut the door, and even though I heard her phone ring, I was too tired to even pretend I wanted to listen in. After all, she has a life beyond me. She definitely has a job beyond me. *And she'll go back to it in two more days*, a little voice whispered.

CHAPTER SIXTEEN

When I woke up, my father was there, towering over my bed in imagination the way he had never done in life. His muscles were honed to perfection, face smoothly shaved, skin evenly bronzed, no hair out of place—just as in real life. His stony blue eyes palely reflected the familiar cold disdain that crept into them whenever I was unlucky enough to draw his attention, but it couldn't be real. For a moment, I was back in my own bedroom, where I had so often gone when it hurt too badly to move.

His image faded away slowly, but I lay paralyzed for what seemed like an eternity before I finally got up the nerve to reach out and turn on the overhead light. I could have made the walls light up, too, if I'd been thinking of anything other than him, but I wasn't. The overhead light helped, but I absolutely had to get out of the room that seemed to be clutching me tightly in malicious anticipation of his inexorable return.

The smothering silence of the night and the darkness seeping out from under the door and bed made me too scared to move. I couldn't force myself out of the bed, but I managed to grab the photo of Amy from the bedside table and stared at it, willing the blackness and violence in my thoughts to go away and be replaced by her.

After a long struggle, I remembered that I'd copied her number onto the back of it. I reached for the closest bit of wall and activated the phone function without wondering if level 3 access would allow me to use the phone on my own. Charlotte's words, "When you need help, ask for it," were echoing in my mind, and I hoped it would work.

Amy picked up on the third ring, looking like she was either just finished or just starting a shoot. In other words, the most gorgeous and perfect woman on the planet.

"Allyson," she said coolly, then bit her lip. "Hi, kid," she said, and waved someone away. She was definitely on the set.

"Amy," I almost cried.

"Caelie," she acknowledged briskly, her eyes narrowing as she studied me to figure out why I was calling. "Are you okay?" she asked. She took up an entire panel of my wall, but I would only be as big as the screen on her mobile.

"No. No, no, no, no, no," I whispered.

"Where are you?"

I shrugged. "Apartment."

"Charlotte's?"

I nodded.

Deciding there was no immediate threat, she relaxed. "Well, I'm okay, so maybe we can get you there, too," she stated, now as calm and professional as Amy always was. "How about I tell you what I did today?"

I nodded gratefully, and she spent the next few minutes rattling off a bunch of everyday things she had done, her eyes warm and soft and interested in reliving her day for me. I couldn't hear any resentment at my having called her, even at this hour, and I calmed down as she talked about going to the store, cleaning out her fridge, and working.

She finished up with, "What did you do today?"

"I wrote my last exam," I told her, starting to relax now. "And Charlotte took me to an amusement park. We ate lots of junk food and stayed on the rides until the park closed."

"Good for Charlotte," Amy said. "Avoid the media, hey?" she added in a way that sounded like congratulations instead of warning.

"What?" I managed. Except for publicity shots at Christmas and Easter, and the odd article about skating meets, the media had no interest in me at all. Why would I have to avoid them?

"Oh. Haven't talked to Morgan yet." It sounded like a statement, but I knew it was a question.

"No. What media?" I pressed. What was she talking about, and why would I talk to Morgan? I hadn't talked to Morgan since the car.

"Probably all of it," she said wearily, but with a hint of humour. "Hang on a sec, okay?"

Her image froze in place, deep, sapphire-blue eyes looking out at me through long, dark lashes, with freckles sprinkled across the bridge of her nose, and a faint smile curving her mouth. A few seconds later, I heard the muffled tones of a cell phone ringing, some murmured and one-sided conversation, then someone knocking at my door.

"It's okay, Caelie," Amy's voice returned and her image shifted smoothly to life on the screen. "Go ahead," she urged me, when the knocking continued.

I disengaged the door lock without getting out of bed, even though I was sure Charlotte could over-ride anything I did, which rendered the lock pretty much meaningless. It waited for my command to slide open, revealing Morgan waiting on the other side.

"There's no way to keep her out of it now," Amy said to Morgan as she walked in and sat down comfortably at the foot of my bed. "And I'd only make it worse by coming. She doesn't need the increased media pressure that would bring."

Morgan nodded her agreement, but I nearly missed what she said next because *Amy would come out here?*

"Sorry, kid, but your life is going from bad to worse. It is your mom," Morgan told me, shifting up the bed to sit facing me, with one hand placed on my shoulder bracingly. "But there's not enough evidence to prove that your father was the one who killed her, or even that she was intentionally killed, so you and your letters are going to trial and the story is out. Unfortunately, it's just the kind of—Charlotte!" she shouted.

I was gagging, and Charlotte immediately brought in a bucket for me to throw up in, like she'd been there waiting all along. She'd probably been alerted the second I accessed the phone, and it didn't make me like her any more. When I finally couldn't throw up anything else, Charlotte took the bucket away, and I only then realized that Morgan's arm was draped comfortably and companionably over my shoulder. When I leaned back, she shifted her weight, pulling me in solidly against her before Charlotte returned with ice and a wet cloth.

Amy waited silently until I lifted my face out of the towel, and Morgan relentlessly picked up where she had left off.

"It's just the kind of situation the media love," Morgan continued, in a voice that made it very clear she considers the media one of the world's greatest and most vulgar evils. "Pretty young daughter, popular, handsome father in the public eye, violence," Morgan summed up. "Good looks, domestic abuse, even a possible murder. You're the story of the hour, kiddo," she finished in a mock-congratulatory manner. I tried to stop myself from heaving, not that there could possibly be anything left to throw up.

"I watched you on the late news," Amy added. "Just your school picture," she tried to reassure me, "and some of you in sports. No live footage. They don't know where you are."

"Yet," Morgan added warningly.

"So that's why you came," I accused, as Charlotte glared at her. Amy's exasperated 'God, Morgan' was drowned out by me, but she didn't seem upset with Morgan the way Charlotte was.

"Yes," Morgan said calmly, waiting to make sure I was looking at her. "If you don't know what's going on, how can you deal with it? It's not good, Caelie, but that doesn't mean it's not real." She winced as the last words came out and I turned away from her. *Had she forgotten that my entire life could be described with that sentence?*

I turned on Charlotte. "You knew today! And you didn't tell me!"

She held my gaze without flinching, giving me enough time to imagine what it would have been like if she'd been the one to tell me. What I would have been like.

"Besides," Charlotte added, "I didn't know until we got back." The sound of her cell phone ringing as I was falling into bed last night came back to me clearly.

The rest of it was a lot less articulate, and even I'm not sure what I yelled as my face burned and my insides froze, but none of them went away. I ended up begging them, pleading with them, not to let my letters go to my dad. I didn't even care about how humiliating it was—I would do anything to stop that from happening.

"I'm so sorry, Caelie," Amy said, her eyes firmly on mine after I finally gave up. "It was the only way I could help you. The only real way. I wish it wasn't."

"Hey," Morgan said gently, and her hand was warm and soft and solid on my arm as I sat slumped beside her. "You have to get through this, so you will. However hideously you manage to do so will be fine, because getting through this perfectly, or even well, is a ludicrous and cruel expectation that you will not have of yourself."

"Yeah," Amy agreed. "What she said."

"In the meantime, though, we're going for a walk," Morgan decided.

"Ciao, kids," Amy smiled, adding more seriously, "we'll get you through, Cael. Kicking and screaming if necessary."

I managed a wan smile at that.

"Love you," she said easily, her image disappearing before I even had time to react, so Charlotte got the full force of my frown.

Wisely, she said nothing, and I barely noticed that Morgan had taken my hand until we were already in the elevator.

In my Strawberry Shortcake pyjamas, I followed her as she really did take me outside, right to the edge of the waves, and we sat there in silence as the darkness turned to grey, and the pink and peach hues began to tinge the sky. When the first tendrils of light hit the clouds on the horizon, Morgan quietly said, "I went to a foster home when I was a bit younger than you."

I didn't say anything, but the curiosity inside me swelled a little bigger. She didn't have to tell me anything. Why was she telling me this? As the sun burst above the horizon and began to shed some warmth, I became aware of the heavy cold that had settled inside me, and my body began to shake uncontrollably.

Morgan pulled me in to her side and wrapped both of her arms around me. A few seconds later, there was a dull thud, to which Morgan did not react at all, except to reach out with one of her hands and pull a soft, cylindrical object towards us. Unrolling a blanket, she tucked it around me and settled me back against her as if nothing had happened.

I turned to look at her, and she smiled. "She's not here, she's not listening to us, and she's not stupid."

I knew she was talking about Charlotte and I frowned. "Just ignorant."

"Yes. Lucky her," Morgan reminded me patiently, and without reproach.

"Did your dad go to jail?" I asked her, after a while.

"No," she said calmly, so I knew she had expected me to ask questions. "He went to hell, preceded only slightly by my mother."

'What did they do to you?' seemed like the obvious, if wrong, thing to ask. "Were they nice?" I asked her instead, about the foster home.

"I guess," Morgan decided, and it seemed that she'd never thought that much about it before. Maybe she didn't care whether they were nice or not, but just whether they left her alone. That's all I would care about, too.

"I didn't see them very often, but when I did, they were kind to me. They never hurt me, and they made sure that I was clean and fed and educated."

"Did they have any other kids?" I asked. I wouldn't like to be around other kids all the time.

Morgan shook her head. "Just me."

"Do you still keep in touch?" I wondered. It sounded more like a place to stay than a family, but I could definitely live with that. As long as I knew what the rules were, I could keep a pretty low profile.

"Sometimes," she said. "Not very much. They had their own lives, Caelie, and I wasn't really a part of them. I don't know why they wanted to be foster parents because they didn't do that much parenting, but they routinely took one child, a teenager, and kept her until she went to college or got a job." It didn't sound like she'd met any of the other girls. "They never took boys. I was their third one, and they were getting older when they took me in. I think they only took one more after me."

Her description sounded pretty good to me, and I decided that a foster home might not be so awful, if that's what it came down to.

"It worked out okay for all of us, Cael," she decided. "I was safe and left alone and provided for. That counts for a lot. I don't see them anymore, but I write to them, sometimes send them pictures. They did a good thing, and it's only right for me to let them know."

"It's not about being grateful," Morgan added hastily, suddenly worried about what I was thinking. "It's neither comfortable nor necessary to feel grateful to someone for taking on a job that just happens to be you. It's not your fault you're a minor and don't have anyone else to take care of you."

"That's not what I meant," she clarified, "when I said it was the right thing for me to do. I just understand now how their decision to take me in affected their lives, and the things they had to change in order to do it. It's fair and kind for me to let them know they did a good job, and I hope that I'm fair and kind. That's all."

"Where am I going to go?" I asked her. The way both Amy and Charlotte defer to Morgan makes me think that if anyone is in charge, she is.

"Charlotte's dealing with it," she told me.

"She's not like us," I said. How were they so close to each other that Charlotte knew about Morgan?

There was a long pause before Morgan said simply, "No."

"You like her," I said. It wasn't really a question or an accusation, although there was a bit of both in my tone.

"Mm-hm," Morgan agreed lightly.

"She said you had time to get used to her," I added, hoping she would tell me more. It was an interesting thing for Charlotte to say, because it implied that she was the one who had to impress Morgan, and normal people don't often care what non-normal people think.

Morgan started to laugh, and I looked up at her. "Get used to her, huh?" she asked, grinning broadly. "I guess we got used to each other."

"You said that you trust her," I probed.

"I do," she answered, and it made me relax a very little bit inside about Charlotte. Not a lot, but a little.

"She knows about you," I said. I wanted to be sure about that.

"Yes, she does."

Was I wrong, or was she a bit uncomfortable about that? "She knows about me, too," I said. It makes me feel a lot worse than uncomfortable.

"I know," Morgan said, looking at me again. "You can trust her."

I shook my head slightly. I could maybe—*maybe*—trust Morgan, but she's the one trusting Charlotte.

"You don't have to," she said agreeably, reading my thoughts very easily, and shrugging and smiling slightly. Nobody's ever come remotely close to understanding me in the past, so how can it feel so normal when she does?

As the first real rays of light speared across the sky, Morgan gave me a gentle squeeze. "Want to see what Charlotte made for breakfast?" she asked, and I realized I was starving.

"She's a good cook," I said. Was I defending Charlotte? For what? Geez, I had to get a grip.

Morgan just smiled at me as we stood up and walked across the sand to the building. Emily was in the elevator when the doors opened to take us up and she looked first surprised at the sight of us, then embarrassed, her eyes dropping to the floor. In a flash, I remembered that I was supposed to have met her yesterday after exams, but Charlotte and I had gone out. Thinking about her waiting for me after school yesterday and me never showing up made me feel kind of sick.

"I'm sorry I didn't meet you yesterday," I apologized quickly, my face feeling as red as it probably looked. "I just finished exams, and Charlotte took me out right away afterwards, and . . ." I trailed off. 'I forgot' seemed a bit too cruel to say out loud, and I was sorry it was true.

"Oh, that's okay," she said, looking up for a second before returning her gaze to the carpeted floor. "I saw you on the news."

Great.

I barely had time to think it before Morgan's fingers reached out and skimmed over the normal-looking elevator pad, turning it opaque even as the doors shut much more quickly than any elevator doors I've ever seen before. Was that glass everywhere, for secret society members or Big Brother or whatever?

The glass responds to Charlotte's touch immediately, but it works so quickly for Morgan, it's almost anticipating her requests. Emily had no time to get out, and Morgan glanced at her apologetically as she made the normal elevator buttons appear. "Sorry, Em," she said.

Emily stared at her blankly, and Morgan winked back. "Of course Charlotte talks about you. She likes you."

Can Morgan read everyone's minds? Emily flushed, but didn't look away.

"I can see why," Morgan added. "Now, the smart thing for you to do now is?"

"Stay inside my apartment all day and don't talk to anyone or let anyone in?" Emily guessed, a bit glumly.

"Sounds boring," Morgan commented, looking up at the ceiling panels.

"Or . . . go out on the beach and pretend I have no association with the building at all?"

Morgan flashed a quick grin at Emily as we stepped out of the elevator and walked quickly down the hall. The doors closed on an Emily who was just beginning to smile back, and I waved to her before we got to Charlotte, who was waiting in the doorway with our packed bags. Nothing of us was left in the apartment, and I guess that was why she didn't want Morgan to take me outside, not because it was unsafe, but because she wanted to get us out of there earlier.

"Emily knows who Caelie is," Morgan told her quietly.

"I know. Let's go," Charlotte replied.

"Would she tell someone?" I asked, not believing it, and Charlotte spared me a pitying look.

"Caelie, if Emily saw you on the news, so did a lot of other people, including ones at the fair, the store, the hospital, and on the beach. It's only a matter of time before they find you here, and I think we want to avoid that."

She was already walking away, and only Morgan's presence beside me stopped me from calling out after her. Instead, I pressed my lips together, ran to catch up, grabbed my bag of books from her overloaded arms, and allowed myself to be pulled along in her wake.

We were almost at the car when about three different news crews, all converging on the building at once, came zooming down the street.

"Hey! Caelie!" one shouted, waving his arms frantically through the open window as they veered towards us. "We want to talk to you!"

"I'll race you," Morgan offered, as we leapt towards the car. I automatically went for the backseat, and as soon as Morgan shut her door, she flicked her fingers over the dashboard and entered a command. It didn't seem to do anything, and as Charlotte pulled away from the curb, the vans were right behind us.

"They're going to follow us!" I warned Charlotte and Morgan.

"Yep," Charlotte agreed calmly, her focus on the road.

"They can't see in," Morgan told me, making a slight gesture towards the dashboard that was now filled with words, several sections scrolling through different kinds of reports or possibly articles. I couldn't tell, since I can't read Cyrillic. I'd looked up the strange characters I saw last time.

"Sorry," Morgan apologized, following my gaze. "We know you've never studied Russian, but it's Charlotte's worst language, if that makes you feel any better."

It actually did.

"So," Charlotte asked briskly, "how do you feel about cutting and dyeing your hair, Caelie?"

"No." Like, really no.

"What about braids and hats?" she suggested.

"I feel tolerably well about braids and hats," I replied stiffly.

"Temporary dye," she persisted.

I looked at Morgan, who was clearly not going to help me out on this one. "It'll come out, Cael, I promise," was all she said, her attention on the words scrolling down the dash.

"Not black," I stated, closing my eyes just as Charlotte nodded, then accessed the phone and put on her headset. Obviously, they were used to working together in this car.

"Morgan . . ." I began, once Charlotte was safely talking to someone else.

"Okay, Cael, here's the deal," she said, pausing in her work to look back at me. "There are no foster homes available at the moment, and if there were, the media would make that option impossible for you. Most of the time, kids your age get sent to a hotel, apartment or group home, but there's no way you can be left in any of those right now either. We're really pushing to get everything settled before you start school in the fall, but I can't guarantee anything, and that still leaves the whole summer to deal with, so Charlotte's arranged for you to go to camp."

She turned to Charlotte, who nodded at us, apparently confirming the camp thing without taking her eyes off the road or her attention off her phone call.

"It's not the perfect solution, especially with your nightmares, but it's better than a hotel," Morgan repeated, now frowning at the dash again.

I'd learned more in a few hours with Morgan than 6 days with Charlotte.

"You're sending me to camp?" I asked, a bit stunned.

"Charlotte will drop you off in the morning," Morgan said, tilting her head towards Charlotte, who was still on the phone but managed to smile at me while continuing to threaten whomever she was talking to.

She didn't pause in her diatribe, her eyes were very clear and determined, and I've never heard anyone speak with such certainty and assurance. For a moment, I wished very hard that we could just go back to the condo and I could stay with bossy, normal Charlotte, swimming, studying and cooking.

"With them?" I waved my arm towards the windows, where it was easy to see that we were surrounded by news vans. I didn't have to take Morgan's word for it that they couldn't see in because they weren't even trying to film, just keeping pace with us until we eventually had to get out of the car.

"Nah," she said dismissively, "with guards."

"What?"

"Oh, you'll never see them," she assured me, fingers dancing through the streams of writing on the dash, moving, altering, and adding to them. "Well, probably never." She glanced over her shoulder and smiled. "Trying to leave the camp will definitely enable them to make your acquaintance."

"Great," I said sarcastically. "How do I explain guards to a bunch of other campers?"

"You don't," she said absently. "They're Charlotte's guards."

"What does that mean?"

She stopped scrolling through whatever was on the dash, but didn't turn around. "It means nobody else will know they're there."

I frowned, and she caught a glimpse of it in the rearview mirror. She turned back to look at me. "Hey."

"Hey," I replied grudgingly. Summer camp? With guards?

"You'll be inconspicuous there, Cael, I promise. Just one kid among a whole bunch of other kids," she said, reassuringly. "It would be very surprising if the guards ever had to do any work at all, but Char doesn't like to be surprised."

Char. I looked at Charlotte and considered ever trying to use that name for her.

"You don't have choices now, Cael, you have us," Morgan said. "It'll be okay."

I looked away.

"And every night, when Amy calls to talk to you, you'll remember why it's okay."

"I don't need to be anyone's job," I replied sullenly.

"Yes, you do," she corrected me, turning back to her displays. While we'd been talking, the news vans had slowly peeled away, and Charlotte had gotten off the phone. "But in Amy's case, you're not," she added, almost absently.

And in your case, I am, I decided. It shouldn't have hurt me to think that, but it did.

"So we'd better get busy today," Morgan told me. Reading in Russian while carrying on a conversation with me in English made her phrases halting. "We need to dye your hair, get you some extra boxes of dye to take with you, teach you to French braid-" she looked quizzically over her shoulder at me for a second and I reluctantly shook my head. I don't know how to French braid. "And get you packed for camp. You need a bathing suit and towels, toiletries, hair stuff, and underwear. Oh, and a cell phone," she added.

"We're bathing-suit campers?" I asked dryly.

"Uniforms, baby," she grinned. "Don't you watch camp movies?"

Real life isn't like movies, though.

CHAPTER SEVENTEEN

Our first stop, after losing the media, was at a drugstore to get hair dye. Charlotte went in to pick the dye and came out with six boxes of a chestnut brown. Did she pick the colour of her own hair on purpose, or was it just a good one to cover up red?

"Two to do it today because you have so much hair, and one to use every week and a half after this to make sure your roots don't grow out, and to keep the colour in the rest," she said, answering my questioning glance. "You're lucky to have such a lot of nice, thick hair," she added, sounding envious.

Nobody, especially a powerful and beautiful cop who obviously grew up with decent parents, should be envious about anything that had to do with me, and I decided she was just trying to be kind. She does try to be nice, when she isn't being completely annoying.

"Your hair is pretty," I offered. "And you can actually get a brush through it."

She smiled back, kind of surprised, and looked at Morgan. Morgan smiled, too, and winked at me. "There," she teased me, "that didn't hurt at all, did it?"

I wanted to smile back at her but instead I stared out the window until we pulled into the police station and stepped out of the car.

"How did you get rid of the reporters?" I wondered. A full-on assault to absolutely nothing just seemed strange to me. "We didn't actually lose them, so they were either driven away or decided to leave us alone. Right?"

"I did my job, Caelie," Charlotte reminded me, her face closed.

Fine.

Going into the back areas of the police station felt like going into the staff room of my school, and I was just as acutely conscious of the fact that I was not supposed to be there. The floors were ugly and scuffed like my school, and the cement walls looked like the layers of paint in the hallways were just covering up all kinds of stains I didn't even want to think about.

It was a far cry from the light, airy, clean spaces that Charlotte thrived in, but she didn't get any less confident in the dingy hallways. Almost the opposite, in fact, and it didn't hurt that she was treated with immediate deference by everyone we passed, despite being in a city she didn't work in without her uniform, if she even had one.

There were some murmured acknowledgements of "Lieutenant", but she barely nodded back in response. The weight of the laptop in my backpack reminded me that I could probably find out everything I wanted to know about her by just entering her name into Google, and I was tempted for a minute. Just a minute, though, because being interested in her is almost the same as liking her, and what would be the point in that? I'm her job for a while, that's all, and she's made it clear she doesn't want me to know anything else.

We finally got to the changeroom, which was a bit of a letdown, actually. I was expecting something more . . . military, maybe. Something secret or cool or anything different at all, but it was disappointingly exactly like the change room at the swimming pool. Green lockers, green tile floor, and grey everything else, including the long bench between the lockers, and upon which I was instructed to sit.

Morgan and Charlotte got busy dyeing my hair, then told me I had to stay relatively still for at least half an hour, depending on how my hair took the colour. As they were cleaning up the mess, another policewoman walked in with a Cabbage Patch doll and handed it to me, smiling. I took it to be polite, but I mean, I only *look* seven.

"It's for French braiding," Morgan enlightened me, somewhat amused at my reaction.

Oh.

While the dye was setting in my hair, Morgan showed me how to French braid. You take three clumps of hair from the front of the doll's head and then braid them normally once each. Then you add a bit from the side of whichever section of hair is due to be braided next, and braid it in. It wasn't all that hard on the doll, but yarn must be easier to braid than real hair because no matter what, when Morgan let me try on her, I couldn't do it at all. It ended up all clumpy and I couldn't get it to stay tight at the back.

"Why don't you try your own?" Charlotte suggested after my fifth failed attempt. "I find it easier to do my own hair than someone else's."

After we rinsed and dried my hair, which took forever, I stood up in front of the mirror and gave it a whirl. Charlotte did hers, too. Mine was kind of lumpy the first time, but the back was tight and it looked mostly even. I pulled it out and tried again, but it was still lumpy and my arms were really aching from holding them over my head for so long. Charlotte, of course, had this perfect, even, elegant braid that she could make in about 10 seconds.

"Caelie," Morgan said gently, as my eyes welled up with tears. I swear I'm such a dork sometimes. I know I can't do anything right, but why I should care about a stupid braid . . .

"Charlotte's hair is a lot straighter than yours," Morgan told me, still speaking softly. "It'll always be smoother than yours. Even in the braid, you can tell that you have really curly hair. Let's try it when it's wet," she suggested.

So, we wet my hair down and I tried again. It was a little better, but I had to use a comb each time I picked up a new strand of hair, and it took ages. I thought I might never be able to use my arms again.

"It's not bad," Charlotte commented, looking at my hair critically, "but you'll still be able to tell it's curly from the growing bits around the edges."

I peered at myself in the mirror. All along my neck were tiny, soft little corkscrews, and they looked very foreign now that they were brown. I hadn't realized there was anything I liked about myself, but red hair was it. Brown hair could be anything when it got in your face—a spider, a mosquito, a glimpse of someone standing far away . . . but red hair is always hair, and nothing else.

I frowned at Morgan and she looked back at me, her eyes meeting mine directly. "No, you're not in charge of even your appearance anymore, kiddo. It sucks, but try to remember that this will all be over soon. In geological terms, anyway," she said, trying to get me to smile. When I didn't, she sighed. "Just . . . let us take care of you, okay? Please," she added nicely.

I took a deep breath, looked at myself in the mirror for a second, and then looked down at my feet. When I looked back up at Morgan, pleadingly, she nodded and pulled Charlotte out of the locker room. She understood exactly what I wanted without me saying a word, and I was too grateful for the reprieve to wonder about it. I'm not sure I could have spoken without crying anyway.

I sat down on a bench and looked at my shoes. I wasn't going to be me for a whole summer, which had its good side, but I would have to eat and sleep and exercise and talk with a bunch of other girls all day every day for weeks and weeks. And then at the end of it . . . Well, I couldn't do that, so I wasn't going to think about it.

What if I woke everyone up by screaming in the night? What if I made a mistake and got recognized? What if it was too hard? At least at school and skating I only had to pretend for a while, and then I got to go home to—*oh, yeah, that was much better*, I interrupted myself sarcastically.

I lay down on the bench and cried until I was exhausted, not caring about how hard the plastic was, or how one of the metal rivets pressed into my knee. There was no 'back' to go to, and I wouldn't want to go there even if I could. The last few days, horrible though they'd been at times, were still the nicest ones I could remember. *What do you do when you have no parents, and nobody else wants to look after you?* my inner voice asked treacherously, and I quickly shut down that train of thought.

The summer was all I could manage to get my head around, and even that was a stretch. After a low tap at the door, I picked myself up off the bench, washed my face in cold water and re-tied my already perfect shoelaces. After that, I went to open the door for Charlotte and Morgan.

"Thank you," I said, looking at a space between them. "What's next?"

They didn't try to pretend I hadn't been crying, but they also didn't act all sympathetic.

"You need to learn how to do a bun," Morgan said, "then we can eat and answer any questions you have about camp and the trial. After that, you and Charlotte will go shopping and check into a hotel while I go back to work," Morgan finished. She should probably be back at work already, and I was really grateful that she'd stayed, but I didn't want her to go back.

"I've put my hair in a bun millions of times for skating," I told them.

"Food it is," Charlotte decided. Sandwiches, fruit and pretzels were set out for us in the police break room that looked a lot like the break room at City Hall, and which gave me a nasty flashback to when I was younger and had to stay there when my dad was working late. I could always tell how bad it would be when we finally made it home by how much he smiled when his underlings and colleagues commented on my presence.

This room was pretty much the same, and maybe all break rooms are. Along one side there was everything you need in a kitchen, and the rest of the space was filled with ugly metal and plastic chairs and tables. The walls sported the same kinds of posters and newsletters as City Hall's, but about law enforcement instead of zoning bylaws or something else hideously boring, tacked onto ragged bulletin boards or scratched-up walls.

The chair I sat down in was not completely balanced, and it rocked back and forth if my weight shifted, so I tried to keep still as I picked a chicken salad on whole wheat and dug in. I was starving. Charlotte and Morgan must have been just as hungry, because none of us tried to say anything until the sandwiches were done. While we munched on sweet, ripe blackberries and dry, salty pretzels, Morgan asked, "Well, Caelie? Any other questions?"

"Is there any point in me asking where the camp is?"

"No," Charlotte answered.

It figured.

"What will happen after the summer?"

They exchanged a glance, then Charlotte looked away while Morgan shifted towards me.

"Caelie." She paused. "Well, for one thing, you're never going back to him and we'll always make sure you're safe. Okay?"

I nodded. But?

"We're waiting on a trial date. I hope before school starts. You're going to have to testify."

No.

"How close will I have to be to him at the trial?" I asked, amazed at how calm I sounded. I wasn't going to a trial. I mean, I was NOT going to get up in court and testify against my dad. Not ever.

"You don't," Morgan assured me. They both looked surprised that I wasn't freaking out. "You can be completely screened from the rest of the courtroom, or in a totally different room to participate by video."

"So I don't have to see him?" I asked. I don't like lying to Morgan, but it's definitely Charlotte's job to get me into that courtroom and if she thinks I accept the idea of a trial, it'll be easier for me to get away before it happens.

"No," Morgan answered, and I noticed that even as she began to speak, Charlotte laid a restraining hand on her arm. Morgan ignored her, and Charlotte jerked it away as if she'd been burned, but neither of them said anything else.

"Who gets to decide if I see him or not?" I asked, after thinking that over for a minute.

"You will have some say," Morgan answered cautiously. I assumed that meant someone else would choose, but if I entirely freaked out at whatever option they gave me, another one might conceivably be offered.

"Okay." I went on to camp. "What am I supposed to tell people about myself this summer?"

"Ah, well, there you'll have to be a little selective, but I would stick to the truth as much as possible. Avoid questions if you have to, but lie as little as you can, so you can at least remember what you've said," Morgan told me. "It's a sought-after camp and they don't accept everyone. Maybe focus on books and things?" She shrugged.

Yeah, because teenage girls are super interested in books. There were never more than twenty people in the school library at lunch, out of a school population of over four thousand. I was going to be weird again, but at least I know how to do that well.

"You did very well with Emily," Charlotte praised me. I got the feeling it was taking all of her willpower not to glance reproachfully at Morgan. For what? Knowing that I'm weird?

"Just remember that people like to talk about themselves," Charlotte went on, "so keep directing questions back to them. There are visiting days every second weekend, though, and obviously your parents will not be showing up."

"It's okay," I assured her, wondering how bad it was going to be, but figuring that if they could pretend everything was fine, so could I. All I had to do was keep a low profile, be good but not too good, and never call any attention to myself while trying to find a way to get out of the trial. How hard could it be? I've spent every second of the last several years doing most of that.

I licked the last bit of salt off my blackberry-stained fingers and started to get up, but Morgan reached for my hand and pulled me back down.

"Cael," she said, holding on to my hand under the table, "Your cell phone will have all of our numbers programmed in to it, and those numbers will always be open for you. Call us anytime you want to or need to, okay?"

"When you get to camp," Charlotte continued, "scout out a few places that will be private and safe for you to call from, so you'll know in advance where you can go." Her voice was slow and assuring, but there was an underlying warning tone in it that I knew was for Morgan and not for me. It made me look from Morgan to Charlotte with open speculation. You have to be pretty close to someone to communicate with them like that. Of course, they do sort of work together, but not in the same field.

I filed it away for future consideration and got back to what I didn't want to be thinking about. Me.

I looked at Morgan for a few more seconds, weighing her words. She was still holding my hand, and it felt like the most comforting thing in the world. I didn't want her to leave, but I knew she'd have to, very soon.

They looked back at me as I tried as hard as I could to make time stop. I was safe here. Inside an unpleasant police station with strangers pretending they weren't staring at me, but safe. Camp would be totally different, and my best attempts at normal might not be good enough. *Wait a minute, what was I thinking?* If I'd thought like that when I was living with my dad, I'd have been dead years ago.

"I'll be fine," I said, adding, "and I'll phone," for what it was worth. Morgan nodded acknowledgment and started to gather her things together. She squeezed my hand once before she prepared to stand up, and looked right at me. "See you, Cael."

She barely glanced at Charlotte, who was similarly ignoring her. Hmm. No wonder they're worried about me, if that's their idea of concealing something.

Morgan smiled at me as she stood up, and I gave her my best normal smile back, which caused her to immediately pause, then sit back down.

"I need a minute by myself," she said pleasantly, and even though she was looking at me, it was Charlotte who got up and walked away. When she was far enough away not to overhear us, Morgan took a deep breath and then looked into my eyes.

"You can do this, you know, even if you can't imagine anything worse in the world than standing in front of your father and talking about what he did to you."

I looked away, and she just sat there calmly, waiting for me to meet her eyes again. I tried not to, but she wasn't going to do or say anything else until I did, so I finally looked back up. I didn't *want* to imagine it, but I couldn't help it.

"If you find that you can't go through with it at the last moment, I will deal with that," she said. "Do you understand me?"

I wasn't sure, and I said nothing.

"It will be my problem, Caelie, not yours," she elaborated unhelpfully. "You need to go to camp, and you need to put all of this out of your mind. And no matter what happens, I want you to trust Amy, okay? She's not going to lie to you."

I do trust Amy. I even trust Morgan.

"We are not leaving you," she said, and it was a promise. "Believe that now, and believe whatever Amy tells you later."

"It's going to get worse, isn't it?" I asked her.

"Yes," she said.

It made me smile, and she grinned back at me. "Remember what I said," she told me, standing up again. Charlotte was still across the room, but watching us. "And don't do anything—stupid."

I couldn't promise that, but she did have a good Captain Jack Sparrow voice.

"If you think Charlotte is going to send you to that camp without both surveillance and security, then you definitely need to think again," she said when I hesitated, bending down again and speaking quietly but intently. "She's going to keep you safe, Amy's going to give you hope, and I'm going to get you free." She lifted one eyebrow at me and was then across the room almost before I could blink.

"Good luck," Morgan called back from the door, and I crossed escape from camp off my mental list of possible options. It was my normal, unconcerned smile when she was about to leave that had tipped her off, and if she'd just said, "Don't run away," I wouldn't have listened. Morgan is just as cool as Amy, and just as scary smart. That was a problem.

Her ride was waiting for her at the door, and in a flash of soft, strawberry-blonde curls, she was gone. I looked ruefully at my new brown braid, then tossed it back over my shoulder, cleared our garbage off the table, and turned to Charlotte. I was just a part of their job, I reminded myself, trying not to be stupidly disappointed that Morgan seemed quite content to leave me. I'd feel the same, if I were her.

"Where are we shopping?" I asked. Charlotte smiled at me, probably glad I wasn't freaking out already, then collected her own things and motioned for me to follow her. Once we were back in the car, she slipped her headset on to continue making arrangements, bullying people, and whatever else she had to do. Between phone calls, I heard her whisper, "She'll miss you, too." I looked over at her sharply, but she was already busy threatening some other poor phone-answerer.

CHAPTER EIGHTEEN

We spent the rest of the afternoon shopping, and I ended up getting two pairs of jeans, five pairs of shorts, only one sweatshirt because she didn't expect it to be cold too often, five t-shirts, two nice outfits for special dinners or whatever, underwear, socks, and five different hats. I couldn't possibly need that many hats, but it was fun to try them on and Charlotte said they would be good for covering up my hair and protecting my skin from the sun.

I also got a cell phone, which made me start to worry about money, but all I could get out of Charlotte on the subject was: "Responsible adults are looking after you now, and there are a lot of policies in place to deal with this exact situation. There have to be some things you don't need to worry about, and the money and mechanics of keeping you safe are going to be two of them. Okay?"

Whether it was okay with me or not, her tone of voice indicated that it, along with so many other things right now, was not open for discussion. I nodded, but reluctantly, and she sighed and bent down so she would be level with me.

"No one else is worrying about it. I don't want you to think that it's a problem for anyone. It's not. At all," she said firmly.

Was this part of her job, too? "Okay," I said, giving up. "Do you like it?" I asked her, holding out the electric blue cell phone that I'd chosen, and she grinned back at me.

"No."

I smiled back. "Can I have it?"

"Yes." She grinned at me and we registered the phone under her plan and my new name: Kaylee McLeod. I was Charlotte's niece for camp, which I wondered about. Obviously, the media would be smart enough to track me down under her name, since they already know I'm with her, but equally obviously, she has the authority to somehow get rid of reporters pretty easily. *And maybe the guards weren't just to keep me in the camp, but to keep other people out.* I didn't want to think about that.

It was a pretty good afternoon, even if I couldn't get used to my new brown hair, but then we drove for hours and hours. I was really glad when we finally got to the hotel, and Charlotte was in a good mood too, as I followed her up to a huge room with a central sitting area and kitchen, and two separate bedrooms with doors. There were parcels there waiting for her, several small ones and one large one.

"Wow," I said to her, looking out of the giant, wall-length windows that provided a gorgeous view of the horizon.

She looked out, too, and smiled.

I spent the next half an hour unpacking my cell and plugging it in, setting up my room, staring out at the thousands and thousands of lights that meant people were living their lives, and having a shower. When I walked out of my room again, a compact rolling suitcase that somehow managed to look both ultra modern and incredibly old-fashioned was sitting in the middle of the living room. I looked at Charlotte.

"You have terrible taste in colours," she told me, indicating that it was mine, and beckoning me over. I grinned. The blue phone was a bit over the top, but I liked it.

Wow. The suitcase she was giving me for camp was made of soft, creamy, light leather. A strip of darker leather that had been carved into a long row of sunflowers ran around the top and down both sides, and the sunflower padlock at the front looked like it took a key, but actually required a code.

When I looked at it closer, I could see that the petals around the lock were all slightly different sizes, buttons you pushed to lock and unlock the suitcase. It was absolutely beautiful, and very cool. Like Charlotte when she's working. I looked up to thank her, but she waved me away.

"By the way," she said from the doorway, "please take those off."

I was wearing the only pyjamas I had, the Strawberry Shortcake ones she'd hated at first sight. She tossed me the smaller parcels that were still wrapped in brown paper and tied with string. "You can't go to camp in those."

Inside, I found the softest pairs of pyjamas ever—one short set for cool nights, a longer one for warm nights, and both of them in plain cream. I looked up to thank her but she was already gone, so I yelled out my thanks instead.

I heard her mutter, "Strawberry Shortcake" derisively, and decided that was the only response I was going to get. She left me alone while I packed all of my stuff into the new suitcase and played around with the lock until I figured out how to arm it and had chosen the perfect sequence of petals for my code.

While I was doing that, Charlotte ordered food for us from room service. Crisp, green salads, noodles in a cream sauce, and fish baked in spices. It was really good, but after we ate, I realized how tired I was. Charlotte said the phone would be charged enough by now and that I had to learn how to use it before going to bed, so I stifled my yawn and followed her back to my room.

It was my first phone ever, and the manual was bigger than the actual phone even though phoning and texting were all it could do, so she showed me how to program numbers into it, and then let me put in hers, Morgan's and Amy's. I called Amy just to practice phoning, but she didn't answer, and Charlotte made me leave a voicemail, telling me to never, ever call one of them without leaving a message. If I did, she'd send security in for me immediately.

She went on to assure me that kind of situation would not arise in camp, but I couldn't help thinking that if there was a policy to deal with the possibility, it had to mean that it could happen, right? Charlotte seemed happier not knowing I could make that connection, and went on to use the hotel phone to call my cell so that I could practice answering.

When she stood up to leave my room and get ready for bed, I stood up, too. I've never had a phone before, or clothes I chose for myself, or my own suitcase. Especially a suitcase as beautiful and unique as the one she managed to have magically appear in our hotel room. I've never seen one even remotely like it.

"Charlotte?"

She paused on her way to the door.

"I normally don't like shopping. But I had a good time today. Thanks."

Charlotte smiled a little. "I don't, either," she confessed. "Normally. And you're welcome."

I smiled back at her before she walked out, and then realized I wasn't tired at all anymore. I didn't want tomorrow to come.

CHAPTER NINETEEN

Mornings always come, whether you want them to or not, and I was at the camp saying a subdued good-bye to Charlotte before I knew it. The campus was a super-modern one with huge wood and glass buildings all over the place, a beautifully kept lawn, nice cedar walkways throughout the entire place, and it was completely surrounded by forest.

It was also surrounded by the cars of over a hundred families who had come to see their kids off to camp, and I felt very tiny compared to all of them.

The other girls looked ridiculously happy and excited, and their families seemed sad and proud at the same time. Lots of the moms were crying and beaming at the same time, especially the moms of the oldest girls, which was kind of weird. The moms of the youngest girls were the ones who seemed the proudest.

I glanced up at Charlotte, who'd walked me to the edge of the parking lot, and she looked back at me soberly. Was she having second thoughts now that she could see what it was like? I hadn't spoken to her after she told me, on the drive here, that it was a cheerleading camp.

Cheerleading! I couldn't believe it. That has to be the most typical, normal-girl activity ever invented, and my letters make it perfectly clear how much I do *not* get along with normal teenage girls. What is the point of her knowing everything about me if it never helps me?

"Do you want me to take you in?" Charlotte asked me, and I turned away silently, giving up all hope that I might get to go back with her instead of staying here. I could see a whole bunch of colourful signs telling us all where to go next, and girls were already bumping along the path with their suitcases and families in tow. I would find my own way.

"It doesn't feel right to tell you to have a good time," she said, undaunted by my silence, "but I hope that it all goes well for you. Don't forget to call us whenever you need to."

I began to walk towards the path, but just before I got to the gate, I turned around and she was still standing there, watching me. It made me feel a tiny bit better, that she hadn't taken off immediately to get back to her regular work. She waved and smiled at me, and I nodded back before joining the swarm of girls heading for the main buildings.

The signs led us right into the gym, directing us to whichever table had the initial of our last name on it. I was heading for A-F before I remembered that I was registered under Charlotte's last name and detoured to M-Q, where I received a huge package with instructions for absolutely everything: where my dorm was, the names of the other girls in it, the name of my team (there were a hundred and sixty of us split into eight teams of twenty), a map of the campus (which was an IB World School for Grades 11 and 12 during the school year), and my practice schedule.

It also held my uniforms: two white skirts, two pairs of white shorts, and four emerald green tops—oh, and one pair of white runners and twelve pairs of white ankle socks. Every single piece of clothing had my name stitched into it in white or emerald thread, including the individual socks.

Following my map, I lugged my package and my own bags over to my assigned dorm and chucked it all on a top bunk against the rear wall. I was assigned to bunk with five other girls in a relatively small room that had nothing but beds and dressers in it and I put my stuff away quickly, liking that my bunk was near the only window. Two of the bunk beds were together right at the entrance to the room and four girls had already claimed those. They were talking a mile a minute and didn't say anything to me, although they did smile at me whenever I looked at them.

I wasn't sure what to do next, and felt awkward standing there until a really tall, strong-looking girl came in and went straight to the bunk under mine. She introduced herself as Lora and tossed her stuff onto her bed, too. We reviewed our schedules together, and she told me there were twenty other first-timers this year. I was more than a bit relieved I wasn't the only one, because the girls by the door looked like a professional cheerleading squad even without their uniforms. Very perky and bouncy, with perfect makeup and their hair pulled up into tidy, cute ponytails. Lora was friendly enough that I felt a lot more settled by the time she went off to check on her sister who was on a different team and in a different dorm.

I looked over the schedule after she left and saw that today was just an introductory day but it got very busy after that. In the mornings, we'd get up and have thirty minutes to eat breakfast before doing three hours of cheerleading practice. Then lunch, an hour of free time, two hours of something called skills training, and we'd alternate each day between an hour of weight training and an hour of running before dinner. After dinner would be free time, and there were all sorts of things like movies and games and sports, but they weren't compulsory.

I checked the map more carefully and found that there was a library, thank goodness, that was open in our free time and on weekends. Charlotte had only let me pack two of my books, and I can easily read two books in a single day. I planned to hit the library as soon as I figured everything else out.

The schedule indicated that we wouldn't train on Wednesdays or Sundays, but there were a bunch of expeditions planned for every single one of those days, including nature walks, reviewing past cheerleading competitions, lake activities, field trips to museums and science centres, and a trip to the waterslide park. Plus, every other Sunday was visiting day, to show parents whatever we'd learned in the preceding two weeks.

Still using the map, I walked around the campus to scout out other spots. I smiled briefly at all the girls I passed, and everyone smiled back and pretty much left me alone. They seemed to all know each other and I was as invisible as possible, which came in handy for exploring the campus.

It didn't take me long to find a little alcove along the shore of the lake that was quite sheltered and far enough away from camp that probably nobody would bother with it. I also found a good tree to climb. People hardly ever look up, and the old, very thick branches would be easy to climb, plus the vines growing over them would hide me from view entirely once I got high enough.

After that, a tightness inside my chest melted a bit, and it felt easier to breathe. Maybe Morgan was right and I would get through this, although she hadn't been encouraging me at the time. More sort of ordering me, in a way that let me know there was definitely an 'or else' that I didn't want to know about.

Finally, I found not only a quiet bathroom in the library (all the bathrooms in the dorms were already occupied by groups of chattering girls messing with their hair, checking their perfect makeup, and complaining about imaginary blemishes) but a whole room full of computers with internet access. I asked the librarian, and he said that during free time we could use the internet. I was determined to learn Russian before I got back in Charlotte's car.

Lora was waiting for me when I got back to the dorm. "C'mon," she urged, "it's a huge deal if we're late for the welcoming speech."

I followed her out the door and across the campus to the mess hall, where we found two spots together at the emerald table. Lora must have been right, because the place was packed with girls that were, in my opinion, way too thrilled to be there. I felt like Alice, gone down the rabbit hole, but probably less scared than her, because my real life is the nightmare. This was just bizarre.

Almost immediately after Lora and I sat down, the headmistress showed up. She was short, thin, and muscular. She also had perfect hair and makeup. Everyone went completely silent when she showed up, and girls exchanged excited glances. I was puzzled, but tried not to show it. Was she famous or something? For cheerleading? I didn't get it.

"Welcome to the most difficult and most rewarding cheer camp experience of your life!" she boomed. Raucous cheering (ha-ha) broke out and lasted for a good five minutes. When everyone had settled down again, she went on about how much we would learn, how hard we would work, and what great rewards there would be when we went back to our schools and our cheer squads to share this experience.

She kept talking for a while like that, and I pretty much tuned out after learning that her name was Ms. Medley. I would not be going to a cheer squad after this; in fact, I was hoping to forget all about cheerleading the second the summer was over. I can't get excited about an activity that's designed to make girls into pretty, useless ego props for boys, no matter how sincere or enthusiastic Ms. Medley seemed. I'd rather do an actual sport on my own than cheer on complete strangers in theirs, an opinion I'd have to conceal here if I wanted to avoid being lynched.

As she began to wind down, she told us about how we could approach her at any time if we had a problem or needed something, and then looked straight at me to add, "My office is always open for you, even if you just need a quiet place for a bit."

I looked away. I don't want complete strangers knowing stuff about me when I know absolutely nothing about them. Luckily, we were allowed to start the meal after that, but that just meant listening to girls chattering on about how great Ms. Medley is and how amazing she was at cheering, and how nice it was of her to let us come and talk to her if we want to, blah, blah, blah.

I tried to concentrate on my salad, roasted vegetables, and mushroom burger without bun instead. We helped ourselves to no-fat frozen yogurt with fresh strawberries for dessert, and it was all delicious, but I decided nobody could gain any weight here.

After dinner, I stopped by the library again, where I signed out two books.

When I got back to my room, I pulled on my pyjamas and suddenly became the center of attention. It took me a few moments to realize it was because of the pyjamas, but I still had no idea why. They're really comfortable, but simple and plain. The thick, old-fashioned, brown paper wrapping popped into my mind for a second, as did their luxurious softness, but I couldn't guess what either of those things meant.

"I'm Jean," said the smallest of the four. Lora was nowhere to be seen. "Where did you get those?"

"Hi," I said. "I'm Caelie." Or Kaylee, now. "I don't know," I said honestly. "I got them from my aunt. Charlotte," I added stupidly.

"Around here?" she persisted. "I thought you could only get them in England."

I shrugged. As far as I knew, all Charlotte cared about was not sending me to camp with Strawberry Shortcake plastered all over me.

"What's your last name?" she asked me, and I was happy to give her Charlotte's. I could almost pretend I really was Kaylee McLeod, which sounded like a girl with a blonde ponytail, blue eyes, a cheerful smile, and an empty head.

"Is that your aunt's name, too?" she asked, and I nodded.

They all looked at me in awe again. What was wrong? They were just pyjamas. Nice, simple, comfortable pyjamas that fit me and had no cartoon figures on them, but still pyjamas.

"I'm Gurpreet," the girl beside her said, smiling at me.

"Hi." I smiled back, knowing the rules of Girl World.

The others introduced themselves, too, as Neveah and Julissa. "What team are you on?" they asked.

"Emerald," I told them, and they seemed disappointed.

"We're Yellow," they said.

I didn't know what to say after that, but they all seemed to be waiting for something and I'd much rather have them think I was nice and leave me alone than think I was weird and talk about me behind my back. "Where are you from?" I finally managed.

Jean seemed to be the leader, and she immediately smiled at me and took charge of the conversation. Thank goodness. For some reason, though, she seemed to assume I was from New York, and asked me all kinds of questions I couldn't answer. Thankfully, she was asking them so quickly that she didn't really expect an answer.

I found out that they were all from the same school, and felt incredibly lucky to have gotten in together. Last year, only Jean and Gurpreet had been accepted.

After that, the conversation devolved towards clothes, and they wanted to know what else I had. I shrugged and pulled my suitcase down off the bed. They all exclaimed over it, reaching out to run their fingers over the leather, especially over the sunflowers, and when I opened it, they lifted my clothes out excitedly, holding different things up in front of them like they were trying them on. Jean was almost as small as me, and when she couldn't stop talking about one of my pairs of jeans, I smiled at her.

"You can borrow them whenever you want," I offered.

"Really?" she said, and I shrugged.

"Sure."

"Thanks! You're so nice!"

"No problem," I said. Did Allie and Jill feel like this all the time?

"Do you cheer at school or at a private club?" Jean asked me, tilting her head in the mirror as she tried on one of my hats. "Or both?"

This was going to be the weirdest thing about me, but I couldn't see any way of getting out of it. Listening to people talk at dinner had made me quickly realize that as soon as I got into training tomorrow morning, everybody would be able to see that I've never cheered before. Even the other 'new' kids have competed for years.

"This is my first time," I told her, trying very hard not to look embarrassed about it. When she didn't look sorry for me, I figured I had succeeded.

Their eyes all widened as they fell silent, though, and then Jean stepped back to look at me critically. "Were you a gymnast?" she asked, and I nodded. It was true, just not all that recently true, since I switched to ice skating two years ago.

"Yeah, you look good," she decided, after looking me up and down.

"Thanks," I said, not knowing what else to say.

"How old are you?"

"Thirteen."

"Yeah, I thought so. Ms. Medley likes to keep all the ages together in the dorms. You're lucky," she said. "You look like you're six."

"Thanks," I said again. "You look perfect," I told her, and she smiled before turning back to the other girls.

"Come on," she said. "We need to start getting ready."

They reluctantly handed my stuff back to me, and I decided to put it all away properly in the drawers. "You're welcome to wear anything I don't already have on," I told them, even though only Jean was small enough to fit into the bottoms. They loved my hats and tops, as well, for some reason.

"Thanks, Caelie! You're awesome."

We decided to pool all our resources before they went away, each girl offering access to her clothes whether she was around or not.

"Stuff in suitcases is off-limits, though," Jean declared from the doorway, then smiled at all of us with a gleam in her eye. "We might need to save something for later," she grinned, and we all agreed. Was I the only one who didn't know what she meant by that?

They grabbed all their bathroom stuff, which looked like it could easily supply an entire country's toiletry needs for about a week, and headed out, waving and smiling at me as they left. I smiled back, having successfully negotiated girl world for one night, then grabbed my book and climbed back on the top bunk. I had plenty of time to read one of my two book selections, Mary Shelley's *Frankenstein*, which was kind of good, until my hair was semi-dry. In a French braid, it would never be completely dry.

The other girls didn't return for over an hour, and they looked pretty much the same as when they'd left, except their hair was now down and they were wearing T-shirts and underwear, pyjamas or tiny nightgowns.

I was surprised to see that they all got into bed early; without an adult in the room or apparently in the entire dorm, our lights were out by 9:30, although the four girls at the front were still talking quietly. Lora came in just before lights out, apparently having gotten ready with her sister because she climbed in to bed right away. She said goodnight to me and I peered over the edge of my mattress to smile at her before turning my light off and settling down on my pillow.

"Good night, Caelie," Jean said, and I called out good night to them as well, then lay looking up at the ceiling. The moon was out and our curtains were light, so it wasn't completely dark, especially since the sun's rays had not totally faded from the sky yet.

I'd expected to be annoyed and afraid, but instead I felt totally calm. As I drifted gently towards sleep, the thought crossed my mind that nothing bad could happen because I wasn't Caelie Aimes here, I was Kaylee McLeod. It was a very strange feeling.

CHAPTER TWENTY

By six o'clock the next morning, the place was in chaos, and I was the only girl within a 20 kilometre radius who was not up and standing in front of a mirror. After more than a few curious looks, I slid out of bed, pulled on my uniform for the morning's session, and grabbed my book.

Some girls wore a solid coloured top and white skirts like me, but others had the opposite—plain white tops and coloured skirts. The bathrooms were crammed so I could barely find a stall to pee, and the hallways were swarming with girls running up at down, switching skirts or tops, asking their friends if they looked fat, and fetching hairspray, brushes or clips for their friends who'd left them in the rooms. I couldn't blame them, really, because nobody could possibly carry all the makeup, lotions, soaps, creams, perfumes, clothes, gels and hair accessories that each of them seemed to need at all times.

Lora was one of the girls in coloured skirts, and so were the two taller front door girls, Neveah and Julissa, who looked out from the bathroom as I passed.

"You're so lucky to have perfect hair!" Julissa called out enviously. I shook my head, smiling.

"No way," I answered, having heard a million conversations like this in the halls at school last year. "Mine's way too curly. I love your hair! It's totally sleek and bouncy." She seemed satisfied and turned back to the mirror.

I felt a bit self-conscious walking past everyone, like I didn't know all the rules of getting ready and was going to look stupid later on, but I didn't look that different from anyone else. There were girls in yellow, navy, orange, red, purple, pink, and blue uniforms to go along with my green, and we all had our hair pulled back neatly. Mine was still in the French braid, looking better than last night now that it was dry. I had on my requisite white socks and white runners, and couldn't see what else I could possibly do to be ready or look normal.

After I quietly slipped out the door, I headed for the tree so nobody would find me and drag me back to the bathrooms, or just look at me like I was doing something wrong. The tree was super easy to climb, just like I thought it would be, and it was cool and quiet in the early summer morning.

I wanted to climb all the way up and then find the best spot, but about three quarters of the way up, I almost ran into a spider web and decided to stop. It was one of those dome ones where the spider sits upside down at the top, and besides not wanting a spider in my hair, the web looked like it had been a lot of work. Going back down a few branches, I peered around through the leaves to make sure I hadn't been noticed, then immersed myself in my book for an hour.

When my time was up, I tucked the book under my uniform and climbed back down the tree, waiting for three groups of girls to pass beneath me before taking advantage of a lull to emerge from the vines. I joined the tail end of the next group to pass, which included Jean and her posse.

"Caelie! Hi. Are you totally excited?" Jean asked when I caught up to her, and didn't wait for me to answer. I love how she does that, and that she makes me feel included every time she sees me.

"Now, definitely eat breakfast, but try not to eat too much because we get a snack later, and it's hard to work out when you're full. But you'll totally need the energy. Think carbs, but not too many. You know what? Just limit what you drink. That'll help. Good luck!" she said, squeezing my shoulder quickly before we headed off for our team tables.

"Thanks!" I called back, slightly bemused, as Lora ran over to me. I wondered if I would ever see her outside of meals and group training.

Yellow table was nowhere near Green, or Emerald as we were officially called, so I didn't see Jean at all during breakfast. We had granola, yogurt, and all kinds of fresh fruit, plus one boiled egg each. One of the older girls tried to give her boiled egg away, but a counselor (coach?) swooped down on her right away and she had to go eat with Ms. Medley. I like eggs, but I don't think you should have to eat them if you don't like them, an opinion I was not planning to give.

Standing up for this girl would not have been the best way for me to remain inconspicuous. Instead, I concentrated on re-filling my drink. We could choose between herbal tea, skim milk, green juice or orange juice. The green juice had banana and apple in it to go along with all the spinach and stuff, and it was pretty good, but I took Jean's advice and only had another half glass of it.

After breakfast, they handed each of us a cloth bag with a round, white goat cheese, a bran muffin, a handful of almonds, two dried apricots and a box of raisins. They weren't those tiny boxes that you get in kindergarten, either. I estimated that there was at least half a cup of raisins in my box, and they were organic. My bag was green to match my uniform, with my name on it in white puffy letters. I stuffed all the food back inside it and then pulled out my map. Lora probably knew where to go, but she'd already run off to talk to her sister.

I was kind of sorry they weren't on the same team, because they seemed to like each other a lot, and they spent so much time arranging meetings that neither of them was totally focused on their own teams. Maybe Ms. Medley would notice that and put them together, although all the effort that had gone into correctly sizing the coloured uniforms and writing our names on matching bags made me doubt it. I shouldn't spend a lot of time with any one person, anyway, in case I let something slip or did something weird.

Following the rest of my team to our first activity was easy, and we ended up in a small gym with four coaches. A gymnastics floor filled all the space from wall to wall, and a row of green bottles of water had been set down in a line. Two of them had my name on them and we were told to drink whenever we wanted, but it turned out not to be that easy because we were never free. I was the only girl who'd never cheered before, and immediately the subject of muttered speculation and pointed stares.

Way to stay inconspicuous, Cael, I thought, as they spent the first hour picking me up about ten different ways and making me practice falling without moving. That doesn't sound too bad, but it turned out to be terrifying. If some girl was holding me over her head and I started to fall, I wasn't allowed to move. I had to pretend to be a board of wood and not move any part of my body at all while I was hurtling toward the ground, almost always head first.

The first few tries were epic fails on my part, but after I got chewed out a lot by the coaches and had all the girls glare at me, I shut my eyes and forced myself to hold still while I was falling. The girls on the bottom did catch me, but I completely hated it. I'd land perfectly well if they'd just let me go! At the end, they still weren't very pleased with me and I'd learned to hate falling in a way I'd never imagined possible before. What if my bases got distracted or something and forgot to catch me properly? Or just screwed up?

I learned a lot, though, including that girls wearing coloured tops and white skirts like me are the "flyers" or "tops" and our job is to get thrown up in the air and then caught again by the girls with coloured skirts and white tops who stay on the ground and are called "bases", but I was having serious issues with the whole trust thing and it was not making me like cheerleading any more than I had when I woke up, which was not at all.

After an hour and a half more of trying to hold still while someone held me up in the air, we got a ten-minute break. The coaches stood over us and watched us eat our snacks, then made sure we drank from, and re-filled, at least one of our water bottles before we started all over.

"From now on," the tallest coach said sternly, "you carry those water bottles and food bags with you to every meal and training session."

We practiced for almost another two hours, past our scheduled time, and then drank some more water and ran to lunch, which was tuna sandwiches and veggies with dip, plus juice, milk, or unsweetened iced tea. The egg girl was eating with Ms. Medley, and after lunch, instead of getting free time, she had to go to the head's office. Geez. I was hoping I never disliked anything they served us when I walked into Jean. Literally. She grabbed onto a railing to steady herself, and grinned at me.

"Caelie! How'd it go?"

"I hate falling," I told her sourly, and she laughed.

"Silly! Hey, did you see Preedi this morning?"

I shook my head. Who, or what, was Preedi?

"She tried to give up her egg, and got caught! She's got to spend two weeks in food counseling during free time, and be observed by Ms. Medley during and after every meal. They even went through all of her stuff and moved her to the san so she can be watched at night," she told me, looking both sorry and excited. "I thought she looked thinner than last year," she added.

I frowned. "What?"

"Hello!" Jean said, impatient with my slowness, but happy to get to tell me stuff. "Eating disorder! Now, aren't you glad I told you to eat breakfast?"

She didn't wait for me to answer, but dragged me back to the room. "We have to get changed for special training," she told me. "You're like having my own cheer doll," she decided, pulling the right shorts out of my dresser and handing them to me.

I smiled at her instead of being rude. Morgan would be proud. Maybe. "I don't know what I would do without you," I told her. "This is so different from gymnastics, and everyone's so good."

"I know!" she said. "Well, I can't have my roomie looking dumb, right?" she grinned, adding, "You can change your top if you want—I'm not," she said. "About five minutes into special training, it won't matter anyway."

I decided not to change my shirt. If special training was anything like the workout this morning, Jean was right and I'd just get it sweaty right away, and I don't want to go through three shirts a day. Lora came in to change too, then ran off to her sister to compare notes on their morning, and Jean headed back to the bathroom with the other three. She invited me, but I told her I was going to check out the campus. "It's gorgeous," she told me, before running off.

It was just like high school, only nobody hated me yet, and I was kind of glad for Jean's help. I don't want to be the world's best cheerleader, but it's easier to fit in if you don't make a bunch of newbie mistakes. Also, cheerleading is a lot more work than I thought. It's hard and it hurts.

The first thing I did after leaving Jean was exactly what I said, because I didn't want to be late for my next session. It took me a little while to find the gym, even using the map, and it was a much bigger gym down the by lake. All the windows were open, like garage door windows at a public swimming pool, and there was a breeze coming from the lake to combat the heat of the midday sun.

Confident I could find it again a lot easier, I reported back to the dining hall to collect my afternoon snack, which was bean salad, trail mix and fresh fruit, and still had more than half an hour left over to read. I ended up heading back to the afternoon gym and finding a rock down near the lake. When I sat behind it, nobody could see me, and I finished *Frankenstein* in time to not be the last one back.

After the horrible morning of falling, I was a bit nervous about special training, but it turned out to be gymnastics.

We started on back tumbling first, after an intense warm up pattern which I did as well as even the veterans on our team, and when the coaches saw that I could still do a full easily, I got sent off with my base partner Heidi to work doubles into the pit.

She watched me do a few, then smiled a bit. "Well, if you're going to be my top, I'm glad you can tumble, but you suck at lifts."

I smiled back at her weakly.

"Get better," she suggested, looming over me.

"Okay," I agreed. *How?*

"You know we'll for sure be assigned extra workouts in our free time on Wednesdays and Sundays because you're so far behind."

"I'm sorry," I apologized.

"Nah," she answered, grinning suddenly. "I'll learn a lot by getting one on one training. Last year I didn't get singled out at all."

After that, an assistant coach came over to watch us, and we didn't talk any more except to compliment one another on a good job, or give encouragement when we messed up. The assistant threw a mat in after we'd warmed up in the pit, and after four easy ones, he had us do them on the floor. We were both fine, so after we stuck five each, he sent us back to the pit for triples.

We also had to get stretched by the coaches, do a million straddle jumps and split jumps on the floor and on mini tramps, climb ropes, practice standing back and front saltos, and do tuck jumps on crash pads, which are really big mats full of foam that are *very* hard to jump on. They didn't let up for a second and my muscles began to shake at the unaccustomed demand, but at least I didn't feel hopelessly outclassed. Just like this morning, though, our practice went overtime, and this time it made us late for a scheduled activity.

"Let's go! Let's go!" The running coach shouted at us. We'd been fitted with Camelbaks for running, but were late starting and she wanted us to catch up to the others. Running took place with four of the eight teams, and we had five miles to do, an entire circuit of the paths outside the campus. I didn't ask how many kilometers that would be, figuring I'd feel better if I didn't know.

I thought I was going to die at about the half-mile mark, but the coach physically put my bite piece in my mouth and ran beside me until she was satisfied that I was drinking. Our drink bladders were filled with orange Gatorade, which normally I hate, but now couldn't suck down fast enough. We ran hard for three miles to catch up to the others, who were being pushed and shouted along as well, and we didn't get to go any slower once we had caught up. I found myself by Jean, who was struggling, too.

"I hate the running," she gasped, "but it does feel good when you're finished." That was all she could manage and I didn't even bother to reply. My legs felt like spaghetti after the six hours we'd already worked out, although the longer I ran, the better I felt. Especially with the Gatorade. At the end, I was pretty proud of myself, and even with my lungs totally on fire, I finished near the front of the pack, earning one approving nod from a head coach before being sent to rinse out my Camelback and get it back to the refill station for tomorrow.

For about forty minutes I felt great, but by supper, my muscles were ready to collapse and my brain was full of cotton. The food was pretty good, but I was so tired from running, on top of all the other training, that I could barely eat my spaghetti and salad.

Thanks to Charlotte, I noticed that the "meat" in the spaghetti was veggie meat, but I don't think anyone else did. I was not the only person to have two helpings of blueberry shortcake for dessert, where we were told to drink as much as we could tonight because it would help us be less sore in the morning.

I had to get up twice in the middle of the night to pee, and was so sore I could barely move the next morning.

CHAPTER TWENTY ONE

Every day at camp was like that. I got to know the other girls a bit, but because we were all working so hard and so continuously, it was more of a professional than a personal atmosphere, which suited me just fine. I spent most of my very limited free time reading in the library or the trees, but I also studied Russian on the internet, got better at all the cheering stuff that I was terrified of, and discovered trampoline as a sport in itself. It became the only thing I loved about camp, except for getting to talk to Amy every day.

Morgan was serious about that; Amy did call me every night. Sometimes she only had a minute to talk, sometimes she spent half an hour talking to me, and every once in a while she'd make a call when she was with other cast members, and they'd all say hi. It began to feel like I knew them.

I survived being surrounded by cheerleaders every day, and even learned to like some of them. The ones in my room were nice, and we got to know each other a little at a time in the few minutes we had together before falling into an exhausted sleep at night.

The only real surprises at camp came from Charlotte, and the first one came during mail call the very first Sunday. The other girls got letters and packages from home practically every day, but I wasn't expecting Jean to slide a parcel to me as she headed to her own lunch table.

"Hey," she said, smiling, "I bet it's from your aunt."

I smiled back, worried she'd stay to see what it was, but she had other mail to deliver and her eyes lingered on the heavy, compact parcel I was holding only a few more seconds before she turned to Lora. Curiosity was only a small part of what I felt, and it was overshadowed by worry over what Charlotte could possibly have sent. I wasn't sure I wanted to know, and definitely wasn't sure

I should be opening it at the table with everyone else, but how strange would it look to ignore it?

I opened it, and was shocked to find Terry Pratchett's *Carpe Jugulum*, a gorgeous hardcover edition I'd never hoped to own, and I ran my fingers slowly over its glossy surface, looking into Granny's ice blue eyes and softly touching her fierce wrinkles.

When I opened it, careful to keep it out of the juice Elena had spilled across the table and only partially wiped up, I found Sir Terry Pratchett's signature on the title page. My breath caught in my throat, and the other words on the page swam blurrily behind the signature that seemed both bold and simple.

"You okay, Kaylee?" Jenni, a girl who was already passing around the Swiss chocolates she'd gotten from her grandma in France, nudged me.

"Oh. Yeah. Thanks," I said, taking the blackcurrant chocolate she was offering. She looked at my book with disinterest.

"New book?" she asked politely. Everyone was used to seeing me with a book in my hands whenever it was remotely possible.

I nodded.

"Nice," she smiled, before turning to the girl on my other side.

It took me another week, and another parcel, before I decided I'd have to write back to Charlotte. Partly it was because I couldn't figure out why she'd send me something like that, but mostly I was still mad at her for sending me to cheer camp. Falling headfirst towards the ground fifty times a day didn't help.

July 9

Dear Charlotte,

I've been here for two weeks now and this is not a summer camp, it is a military camp. We exercise every morning for almost four hours, stopping just in time to get to lunch. I have to trust virtual strangers with my life in these practices. After lunch, our food gets to digest briefly before we work out for another four hours. Then we drag ourselves to dinner, and I have time to shower and do my hair, and maybe read for half an hour before I fall asleep. Where are you planning to send me after this? The Ironman Competition? The SAS?

Caelie.

P.S. Thanks for sending me the Terry Pratchett. It's absolutely perfect and I've been waiting for it a long time.

While I was at it, I decided to write to Morgan and Jane as well. That proved to be a bit of a mistake, and led to my second surprise from Charlotte, although it really shouldn't have come as a surprise at all.

I got through the letter to Morgan okay, but because I'd written so many other letters to Amy, the simple typing of 'Dear Amy' made them all come flooding back, bringing my father with them. I was so busy and tired that he'd faded from my mind exactly like he was supposed to while I was here, but at those familiar words and the memories they sent flooding through me, he slipped past my defences.

Bile rose in my throat and I tried hard to push him away, concentrating firmly on the picture of Granny Weatherwax on the cover of my new Pratchett book. The piercingly blue eyes, light ones like mine, almost got through, but in the end I had to run to the bathroom where I threw up everything from lunch.

I hate throwing up, and I leaned weakly on the stall door before moving out to rinse my mouth with water about a million times.

The revulsion I felt and the repetitive action helped me block all thoughts of my dad, and I reached the following conclusion: if I lack courage at the end, thinking of him with my letters will make it possible for me to use the razor I was planning to take from the showers, and not just to draw blood and cause pain like I did before, but to finish what he started before he got the chance to do it himself. It would be faster than the death he'd give me, and a lot less scary than walking into a courtroom.

Afterwards, I walked back into the library and forced myself to get back to the letter. There was no way I'd let him take Amy away from me, and maybe I could slip her a few hints that I'd never get away with in a phone call, so she'd kind of be prepared at the end. Just in case. She does most of the talking on the phone but when I write, I'm a lot braver.

July 9

Dear Amy,

    I can't believe this camp! Charlotte is a sadist.

    I'm doing okay here. Sport-wise and head-wise. Thanks for sending me your new headshot, but I can't put it up because the girls here are insane over half the guys on the show and I would be the most conspicuous person here if they found out I know you. They're SO normal, it's depressing. They went crazy over my pyjamas! I keep your photo in the side pocket of my suitcase so it doesn't get damaged. Also, thanks for sending me your shooting schedule.

    We stay super busy and tired, but whenever I have a break, I get really scared about the trial. We don't get a lot of time off, so I don't think about it all the time, but whenever I do it makes me feel sick.

    I'm trying to take your advice and just live in the present. Charlotte's sent me two parcels with books now, which is really nice of her. She sent a signed hardcover of one of my favourite Granny Weatherwax books! I love it, and keep it safely in my suitcase or on my bed when I'm not reading it.

    Tomorrow is parents' day, but lots of kids' parents aren't coming, so nobody will notice about mine. From the sounds of it, though, everyone's will be coming out for the show on the last day of camp. Girls are already talking about it.

    I'm doing what you told me to do—being polite and evasive and a bit friendly. It's pretty easy because everyone is rushing around all the time, or

concentrating on getting a trick right, or doing extra
practice to make up for not learning something fast
enough. I am, too. Who knows if I'm getting any better
at falling (I guess I am) but I hate it just as much as
ever.

Love, Caelie.

The next surprise from Charlotte didn't come until after dinner,
which was spinach salad, grilled lemon chicken and new potatoes,
with fresh raspberries for dessert. I was starving, and ate all of it
up, so when one of Ms. Medley's older 'guard' girls came up to me
proprietorially, I had no idea why. Their only job is to take care of
the eating disorder kids, and I don't have trouble with food. Except
for today in the library . . .

"Hi," she said.

"Hi," I answered back guardedly. What did she want?

"I got assigned to you because you threw up after lunch today,"
she explained, confirming my suspicions. "My name's Ginn, and
you're all mine for the next hour."

"I'm Caelie," I told her. *Great.* But how did they know? I was
alone in the library after lunch and it had nothing to do with an
eating disorder, anyway.

"Everyone knows who you are."

When I looked at her in alarm, she ticked the reasons off on her
fingers, talking in the voice you use when you think someone's very
stupid and a total waste of your time. Index finger: "New kid." *Duh.*
Middle finger: "Teacher's pet." There was some resentment there.
Ring finger: "Über-talented." How did this girl, who looked like
painting her nails perfectly was her highest ambition in life, learn
German? Pinkie: "Tiniest, lightest, strongest flyer in camp."

As she worked her way through the list, my initial alarm faded
and I ended up frowning at her in puzzlement.

"Uh, hello?" she said. "You're already completing tricks that
nobody else is even working on yet."

No way. All the teams train separately, except for trampoline
and running, so it's not like I ever see any of the other teams

cheering, but I'm always having to go in for extra sessions because I'm so bad at it.

"Why'd you do it?" she asked, pulling me outside with her, but I was hardly listening. I couldn't tell her even if I wanted to, but if Ginn knew about me throwing up, Charlotte certainly did. In fact, Charlotte had to be the reason Ginn knew in the first place.

"Can we go to Ms. Medley's?" I asked, as resignation, admiration and resentment for Charlotte's omniscience fought a brief battle for supremacy in my mind. My timing—or Charlotte's—was excellent; an assistant coach flagged us down before I even finished my question.

"Caelie, phone call. Ginn, I'll take her from here."

"Thanks, Jason," Ginn said happily, looking up at him through her eyelashes and acting like he'd just pulled her from a burning building.

He grinned. "I told you, after the summer. I'm not looking to get fired."

"I'll be waiting," she said, in a tone that made colour flood his cheeks.

I pretended not to be there, wrote Ginn off my list of salvageable human beings, and waited for Ms. Medley to thank Jason before waving me into her office. She showed me how to take the call off hold and then surprised me by leaving her office and closing the door behind her.

It was impossible to spend more than five minutes at this camp without learning that cheerleading is a seriously competitive sport, but Ms. Medley's office was like a shrine. Behind her desk, trophies and medals by the dozen stood or hung proudly in a huge glass case with its own lighting. As I watched it, I realized that the lights faded in and out, illuminating different awards. The other walls were covered with gleaming plaques and glossily framed photographs of teams in mid-routine or all lined up formally. Even the windows were covered in a light film of cheerleader images.

The overall effect was a bit scary, even though I could tell it was designed to be both inspirational and beautiful. Maybe it was just the silence, the too-soft carpeting and the orange light on the phone blinking on and off, on and off. I reached out to stop it.

"Hi, Charlotte," I answered in resignation, knowing it was her.

"What's up, Cael?"

"I got your letter," I told her accusingly. Two letters, actually, one with each book.

"And? My letter made you ill?"

I hate having to spell everything out for her. "Your letter made me think of other letters. Oh, God," I said, as my dinner rushed up. I had to use Ms. Medley's garbage can.

"Oh, Caelie," Charlotte said, when I'd finished. "Hang on a second, okay?"

I waited, spitting the disgusting taste in my mouth into Kleenexes from the box on top of Ms. Medley's desk until Ms. Medley walked in, carrying a glass of water. She didn't say anything as she handed it to me and then collected her garbage can.

"Okay," Charlotte said a moment later, having clearly demonstrated that she had some other way of communicating with Ms. Medley. "Feel better?" she asked me.

"No!"

"Yeah," she agreed. "Well, at least I can assure Ms. Medley you're not becoming bulimic."

I remained silent. Throwing up is disgusting, but I'd rather live with that than my dad.

"I heard you met the guards," she commented, for what purpose I could not imagine. To remind me I was constantly under surveillance? I hadn't been trying to escape, anyway, just sort of checking to see where the boundaries of the camp were. Walking around the camp in my free time. It's not a crime.

"I'm not going anywhere, Charlotte," I told her.

"I'm well aware of that, Caelie, because it is my job to ensure it. However, we both know that your word doesn't mean a lot to me. There are two women it does mean a lot to, though, so which of them would you prefer to give it to?"

"Charlotte, you have me watched in the bathroom! How do you think I'm going to escape?" *And when have I ever lied to you?* The unjust accusation was enough to destroy any guilt I might have felt about lying to her in the future.

"I'm not watching you at all, let alone in the bathroom. At least, not you specifically," she told me. "Ms. Medley's washroom security cams are activated only when someone enters a stall and doesn't sit down. All the parents and campers sign a release form to that effect."

"I didn't!"

"I know. I'm sorry about that," she said, actually sounding as if she were. "I had your paperwork completed, and you didn't get to see it."

"I don't imagine my dad did, either," I said sarcastically.

"Would you want him to?" Charlotte asked.

"Sometimes," I answered defiantly, even though I don't really. Still, no more surveillance, no more cheerleading, no more death runs, no more pretending that what normal kids think about is actually important. Just, no more. It was tempting sometimes.

Had I actually felt better after sending those letters this afternoon? That seemed like another lifetime ago, as everything came flooding over me. How could I keep on doing this? It was too hard. How can older girls I don't even know be jealous of me for being good at something I'm not actually good at? How can Charlotte watch me everywhere? How many more times can I just hold my body still, waiting for my bases to catch me as I plummet towards the ground? *How can I get out of the trial?*

Morgan said it would be her problem, but Morgan wasn't here. She hadn't spoken or written to me once in the past two weeks, and whatever else is true about her or her past, her job is upholding the law, and trials are famous for *being* the law. There was only one way out, and I'd have to be extremely careful to keep it from Charlotte. From all of them.

"Are you thinking of starting to shave your legs? Because I wouldn't recommend it," Charlotte said flatly. She definitely can't read my mind, but it sure felt like it. She knows I don't shave my legs, and could have only one reason for bringing up razors.

"What? Are you watching me in the shower?" I demanded. Anger at Charlotte helped swamp the terrible hatred and pity I felt towards myself, even if it stemmed from terror that she'd prevent me from following through on my plan. There was no way I could walk into that courtroom.

"No. It would be very wrong for us to have surveillance in the showers, or in any room you are routinely naked."

"Wrong but not illegal?" I probed. Her voice sounded like she was reciting something she didn't find interesting or important.

"Wrong and illegal. Just stay away from the razors, Caelie," she warned me. "And the ketchup bottles."

The ketchup bottles are the only glass items in the entire camp, and Ms. Medley found me looking at them once, forcing me to improvise and put ketchup on my scrambled eggs. Disgusting.

I hung up on her and stayed, trembling, in the office. I might not have been able to calm down at all if Ms. Medley hadn't come in, but as soon as she did, I resumed the Kaylee shell to avoid being forced into a conversation. After I politely deflecting her questions about how I was doing, she took Ginn off surveillance duty, and had an extra dinner made for me an hour later.

I was really starving by then, and re-reading my book in the library to forget everything else for as long as I could. Mr. Grere, the librarian, brought me a plate of salmon with lemon wedges, and a creamy curried rice with mushrooms and broccoli. There was a chocolate milkshake to go with it, and I hadn't seen chocolate in any form but mailed parcels since arriving at camp. I looked up at him.

"Now you know why the staff doesn't eat with the rest of you," he grinned, and wrote something down on the top piece of a stack of paper. When he slid it over to me, I saw it was the library keycode. "Stay as long as you like."

I smiled a bit as he left, locking the doors behind him. Once he was gone, I squeezed every last drop of lemon out of all the wedges onto my salmon, and stirred the rice around. It smelled good, and I began to eat, absently pulling the keycode over so I wouldn't forget it. There was something written on the piece of paper underneath it, too, and that was attached to an envelope. I read the note.

I said it would get worse, and it's not over yet. Keep going, Caelie. I will be there for you when you need me.

Love, Amy.

PS—Tell your bunkies that these are from your Aunt Charlotte.

I opened the envelope to find headshots of all the male cast members of *Last Line of Defence*, with personal messages for each of my roommates. Or bunkies, I guess. Since tampering with the mail is a federal offense, I decided it was a coincidence, and not a result of the letter that couldn't possibly have gotten to her yet, but after I finished eating, I locked up the library, carried my plate and cup back to the dining hall and then went back to my dorm. These would give me a way to explain my absence without talking about food or throwing up. I hoped. If not, they'd definitely provide a distraction.

"Jean, look!" I said, knowing that with her attention, I'd have everyone's. With half an hour to go until lights out, they were all still in the bathroom, covered in creams and . . . stuff. I held hers out to her and she squealed before wiping her hands carefully and reaching out to take the stack.

It was a good ten minutes before they stopped talking and squealing about the photos and messages, and then Jean turned to me with mock severity.

"You were holding out on me today," she said accusingly, having designated herself the official mail-call person in our room.

"No," I protested. "Ms. Medley called me in to her office after dinner. My aunt sent them to her this afternoon!"

"You are so lucky!" Gurpreet exclaimed, for about the eighth time.

"Don't forget yours, Cael," Julissa said, waving one that had been at the bottom.

I tried not to look confused, but I really only care about Amy's, which I already have.

"Take them back for us, so we don't wreck them, okay?" Jean asked, already passing them over, so the one Julissa had waved was mixed in with the others.

"Sure," I agreed, realizing that I'd lost most of my own bathroom time already. Could I shower and do my hair in fifteen minutes? I'd have to try. I dashed back and tossed the photos on the correct beds, including Lora's even though she wasn't back yet, and ran for the shower.

Hair dripping down my back, I leaped into my bed with one minute to spare before lights out and almost flopped down right on the photo I'd tossed up so carelessly a few minutes earlier. It was from Jock, one of the few members of Amy's team who treats her like an equal and a friend, and who has enormous, sprawling handwriting.

> *I'm looking forward to meeting you in person. Make sure that I do. Love, Jock.*

I have no secrets from anyone. But I like Jock, and it was nice of Amy to send me a guy picture, too, since I'm pretending to be all normal and everything. I put his photo and hers up together at the head of the bunk, which made the rest of the girls talk half an hour into lights-out time about the possibility of them becoming a couple.

Nobody even asked me how my aunt got cast headshots.

CHAPTER TWENTY TWO

After several weeks of cheer camp, I fit in pretty well and no longer needed Jean's help to figure anything out. Laundry was after dinner, and we had to leave our clothes in a bag with our room number on it outside the huge laundry room before going to bed. By lunchtime the next day, it would be clean and folded and on our beds. Field trips were optional, food was mandatory, and free time, if you managed to actually get any, really was free. No supervision or anything.

Every Saturday after dinner the coaches would post a list of what each person had to work on and the times the specific coaches were available. Not everyone had her name on the Extra Practice list, but mine was always there. Heidi, my base, said it was because I was really good now, and not because I wasn't good enough, but I still don't trust my bases, which put me on the list for practicing basic lifts, falls, throws and catches for at least two hours every Sunday.

The extra practice coach told me that if my basics weren't good, I would never reach my true potential. I didn't tell her that I do not want to reach my potential, or anyone else's, in cheerleading. It's a hard sport, I agree. I respect the heck out of it, and will never let anyone say anything bad about it ever again, but I still don't *like* it.

Practice was hard, and it was all the time.

"One, two, three, GO!" my bases would chant, then toss me up as hard as they could. I'd long ago stopped screaming out loud when that happened, but I was still screaming inside, believe me. I was doing two and a quarter backs with my group of four bases, and the hardest part wasn't my job, but theirs. They had to throw me straight up, all at the same time, and with equal force.

Part of the reason I stopped screaming out loud is that they got better at it. The first several times I went more sideways than up, and the other base groups were deployed around us specifically for the purpose of catching me. We did the same thing for their flyers, although none of them were doing back two and a quarters yet. I was also the only one on our team with a front two and three quarters, and I wondered briefly if Ginn was right about me. The other groups in my team did swan dives at the same time, in a semi-circle behind me, and it looked really cool.

My bases loved how small and light I was, but now that I truly understood what that led to, I was completely freaked. It was only the fourth week, but we were already starting to assemble our routines, and I was not only always in the middle, I was also the one who got thrown up on top of the other flyers at the end of the routine, four people high. I still scream when we do that one.

"Great job, Caelie!" the coach complimented me, when my bases caught me perfectly. I winced slightly, but smiled as she congratulated the bases, too. Bones and muscles are way less comfortable to land on than a trampoline bed, which we practice on three days a week, and my back and arms were thoroughly bruised.

"Okay, let's get all four groups in together," the coach said. "On your marks, please."

We got into formation, counting together so it would all happen in unison. I bounced along with the other flyers, two of them a bit in front of me to my sides, and two behind me to each side. *One*, we bobbed down. *Two*, the same dip, and I breathed in, readying for the third. *Three* was twice as deep, and I tightened my legs for the throw. It felt good, I opened up in time to see my bases, just like I was supposed to, and they caught me securely. *Ow.*

"Great job, girls!" the coach cheered. "Now let's watch it."

Watch it? I seemed to be the only one confused, because all the others ran eagerly, first for their water bottles since we had a few seconds off, and then back to the floor, facing the widest wall. It was entirely white, and we didn't wait long before a projection of us showed up, very brightly considering that the sun was streaming in through the windows.

"Watch," our coach instructed us, and the chattering stopped.

I saw myself get bobbed up and down, then tossed up to do my trick. It was ridiculously high, much higher than it felt when I did it, and my stomach turned over at the sight. The catch looked every bit as painful as it felt, but that could have been because my face clearly showed it.

"Again," we were ordered, as the clip returned to the beginning. "Watch your whole group."

This time, I focused on the bases, who made the toss and catch look effortless, even though I heard them grunting on the toss and caught their low moans on the catch. My back may have been bruised, but they left every practice with bruises on their arms, and their entire bodies trembling from the fierce workout.

I looked scared and in pain up there, and they looked like they were having fun. The coach turned to me and I nodded, knowing what was coming.

"Smile, Caelie," she ordered, and I mouthed the words along with her. They remind me to smile a hundred times a day or more, but now I could see why.

"One more time. Watch the team."

I did. Everyone looked like they were having fun except me. Maybe they were, and maybe they weren't, but smiling was part of the sport and I'd have to do it. Despite their easier tricks, the other flyers looked fabulous surrounding me, and I just looked okay. The video played through one more time, and my stomach flipped over again as I saw exactly how high they tossed me. I'd have to stop thinking about that before I completely lost my nerve and refused to do it at all. Losing my nerve was not an option with four weeks left to go. Four more weeks. I could do it, right?

When she shut the video stream down, we all got back on our marks without being told. This time, I tried hard to smile, imagining that I was back on the tramp.

"One, two, three, GO!"

CHAPTER TWENTY THREE

"Caelie! Letters!" Jean announced, holding them out from the doorway. As the self-appointed leader of our group, she took it upon herself to know all of our business. I was not foolish enough to fight it, especially since she was fiercely loyal. That was lucky for me, since I was careless on a phone call with Amy in only the second week, hanging up to find the other girls from my dorm gathered behind me, mouths agape. I froze, but Jean took it in stride, of course.

"Are you crazy, or are you helping Jane Allyson rehearse?" Jean had demanded. Put that way, I honestly wasn't sure, but Jean never waits for answers when she can think up her own. "It's a secret?" she guessed, and I'd forced myself to nod, hopefully somewhat naturally. "This doesn't leave our room," she told the other girls, and it hadn't. It got a lot of play *in* our room, though, once the door was shut for lights-out. Fortunately, Jean handles both the questions and answers then, too.

There was another book in the mail for me, and I hopped down off my bunk to grab it. "Thanks, Jean."

"No problem," she smiled. "Hey, I hear your group is looking pretty good. Only a couple weeks left, huh?"

"Yeah," I said, grinning when I saw that one of the letters was from Amy and ignoring the reminder that my life was going to change again in two weeks. "Hey, what's the competition like?"

I tried to ask it casually, but the final show was rapidly becoming the only topic of conversation at camp, and I was really nervous because I had no idea what to expect.

"Like the most important day of your life, times a million!" Gurpreet chirped excitedly over Jean's shoulder.

Very helpful.

Jean, who thinks that a girl Jane Allyson speaks to on a regular basis has more important things in her life than cheerleading, rolled her eyes at Gurpreet and answered my question seriously.

"We get to warm up, of course, but everyone's there to watch, so it's both exciting and scary. All the coaches, everyone's parents, grandparents, aunts, uncles, annoying little brothers and, of course, Ms. Medley right up at the front. Some people's parents really sacrifice to get their kids here because it's so expensive, you know?"

When she seemed to be waiting for a response, I nodded. The mere threat of being sent home for underperforming or behaving badly is the reason we don't need adults in our dorms.

"Nobody wants to screw up. We do a full dress rehearsal on the day before, so we'll have a good idea of the other routines before we go out and do our own. Don't worry," she assured me, reaching out to touch my arm. Did I look as nervous as I actually was?

"Oh, and everything except the competition floor will be dark," she remembered, "so don't look into the lights or you'll be blinded. It's televised, so the lighting has to be perfect for them, which makes it harder for us. But we'll get to practice that way first. Awesome, right!?" she asked, carried away with excitement by then.

Oh, yeah, it was awesome all right. Televised? Did Charlotte know? Probably, I thought grimly. Oh, yeah, lie low, Caelie. Don't call attention to yourself. Apparently being filmed under glaring spotlights on a huge stage in front of two thousand people qualifies as maintaining a low profile in her mind, but before I could even begin to understand her rationale or start to plan an elaborate revenge/escape, Lora poked her head in. She's never around except between lights out and reveille, so we all looked up.

"Do you have any extra Tiger Balm?" she asked.

"Red?" Julissa asked, already reaching for it. She'd received three letters and a tin of homemade fudge in mail call today, and passed some fudge to Lora along with the Tiger Balm.

"Thanks!" Lora called, disappearing.

The rest of us exchanged a look, then Jean shrugged. "She'll spend the last night crying and saying she wished she'd spent more time with us. She did it to her group last year, too."

"Why doesn't Ms. Medley just put her with Shyan?" I asked. It was her twin she was spending all that time with, and I thought twins only got split up if they wanted to be.

Jean shrugged. "The parents. They split them up for everything. They went to different daycares, they go to different schools, the parents even switch custody so they never get to live together, but both twins insisted on Cheer Camp. The most the parents could do was request different teams and dorms because they couldn't say no. Do you know how many university scholarships there are for cheerleaders? And most of the winners come from here, no matter what school or team they belong to during the year."

I thought about that. "Their parents like them, right?" I asked.

Jean shrugged. "Who knows why parents do what they do?"

No kidding.

I used my library time the next afternoon to read my own letters and write back.

Aug 12

Dear Charlotte,

Thanks for *Bummer Summer*. It was a good camp book. I told you, though, that this is NOT a summer camp. Can't you find any marine corps books?

Caelie.

I didn't bother asking if she knew I'd be on television in two weeks. Charlotte knows everything.

It was harder to write to Morgan. I don't want to make her feel guilty, or like she has to be nice to me, but I haven't heard from her all summer, even though I've written to her four times. I thought about it for a while before I began writing.

Aug. 12

Dear Morgan,

Hi. I hope you're doing okay. Charlotte and Amy say you're really busy right now. Cheering isn't that bad. I'm getting better at it, but it kind of hurts when the bases catch you, especially now that I'm doing really big stunts. I still don't like trusting other people to catch me, but the coaches think I'm doing all right. I'm keeping my head down for the most part, and I don't have much time to myself. No nightmares yet.

Love, Caelie.

Amy was way easier to write to, and she's been amazing all summer, sending me really fancy candy to share with my bunkmates, and writing to me every week. I wouldn't have gotten this far without her.

Aug 12

Dear Amy,

How come Morgan isn't writing to me or anything? I kind of feel like a baby asking you that, because I know she's busy, but . . . did I do something to make her mad at me?

Cheering is going pretty well. It's still scary trusting other people to catch you, and they show our work to us on videos so I can see how high up I am. Well, that's not why they show us, it's really so we can see what we're doing wrong and how to fix it, but what I mostly notice is how high I am. It's very, very scary and my stomach feels sick every time I think about it, so I try not to.

The trampolines are open in our free time now and I always go. I really, really love it! It's easy and exciting and fun, and there's always something new to learn. I'm surviving cheering and I like the hard work, but tramp is awesome, and being small is good for tramp.

I can't believe camp is over in two weeks. I'm trying not to think about it, but I just wondered . . . do you know what's going to happen then?

Thanks, love, Caelie.

CHAPTER TWENTY FOUR

There were two days of camp left, and I was finally ready for the competition and for what would happen afterwards, which would definitely not include testifying at my dad's trial if my plans worked out. What I wasn't ready for was the aftermath of Amy sending me a terrible teen magazine.

"What turns you on the most about a guy?" Jean read from her low bunk by the door. Lights would be out in twenty more minutes, and this was seriously taking away from my real reading time.

"A) The way he looks, all hot and cute at the same time, B) The way he walks, like he owns everyplace he goes, or C) The way he pretends he's not watching you when he's talking to a group of his friends."

I sighed while they all shouted out their answers.

"Come on, Caelie. Everyone has to answer," Gurpreet reminded me, once Jean had recorded all their answers.

"Isn't there a D?" I asked hopelessly.

"Caelie!" Julissa wailed. It was the fourth question, and none of the answers had been right for me.

"Okay, okay," I said. I was going to get Amy for this. She sent the magazine because it had an interview with her in it, and she'd included a handwritten page with all the answers she secretly wanted to give. They made me laugh out loud, but I tucked them into my suitcase before anyone else could see them. Jean, who always hands my mail to me, asked to borrow the magazine when I was finished with it, and I'd said sure. Now it was almost lights out, and this was her idea of borrowing it.

"I'm gay," I decided.

"Oh, you are not," said Neveah. "You can make up a D if you want."

I would, if *anything* turned me on about any of the guys I know. At least Amy gets to deal with adult guys, who are smart as well as . . . heyyy. I could make up a D if I just described Laertes, my favourite character from Amy's spin-off show, or even Amy's secret love interest, Geller. I decided to go with Laertes.

"D," I announced, "The way he gives up everything to help you when you need it."

They all sighed happily. "Yeah," Jean agreed wistfully. "Good one, Cael."

"You know you're messing up the quiz, Caelie," Gurpreet complained. "I still pick A."

I rolled my eyes in the darkness as Jean read out the next question. "Your favourite look is: A) blond and blue eyed, Cali surfer, B) dark and mysterious, or C) the boy next door."

"Redhead," I said, before they had the chance to ask me. I was describing Laertes. "Tall, lean, with eyes that speak just to you."

"You are so good at this!" Lora said, "I'm with Caelie, except dark hair."

"B," Jean decided for her, penciling it in.

"B," Gurpreet chose.

"A," Julissa said. "I can't help it, I totally melt for blue eyed blonds."

I let my mind wander a bit while they discussed their ideal guys.

I finally had my razor blade, and was still worrying that someone would find out about it, even though I couldn't see how. I'd pretended to shave my armpits, even though I have no hair at all yet, then tucked the razor, cap on, as far into my armpit as I could, holding it there with my arm. Afterwards, I took it down to the lake and went for a swim, concealing it under my arm until I was in the water and could tuck it into my suit.

I waded into the water for a bit, then lay casually in the shallow water, and pressed the razor head between two rocks until the plastic snapped. Pulling the blades out was simple and I carefully tucked one in flat along my stomach, and put the broken plastic back and spare blades under my arm, getting out of the water right away to dispose of the plastic in one of the big garbage cans along the paths through campus, wrapped in balled up Kleenex that I grabbed from the washroom nearest the lake.

There'd been no phone call from Charlotte, and no visit to Ms. Medley's. The blade was now deep inside the tongue of my shoe, where it would stay flat and not cut me, and not be anywhere near where the bases grab my feet all the time. Finally, I felt calm in a way I hadn't since touching the glass from the highway. It was my choice now.

"Last one," Jean told me, and I reluctantly brought myself back to the present.

"You would be most likely to go out with a guy you just met if he: A) invited you to a huge party, B) invited you for a day at the beach with his family, or C) invited you to a concert."

"A rock concert?" Gurpreet asked.

"I don't know," Jean said. "It doesn't say."

"D," I said, making all of them groan. "If he invited me to the morgue, to view my remains after I was stupid enough to go off with someone I didn't know."

"Caelie!" they protested together. "Be serious."

That wasn't? "Fine, E. If he was Davy Jaye, inviting me to do pretty much anything." Davy Jaye is the name of the actor who plays Laertes.

"Yeah, no kidding," they agreed.

"It still doesn't count, though," Julissa added. "It has to be a boy from school, or someone you meet at the mall, or a friend of a friend of a friend. Something real."

"C," I decided, sighing.

"Me, too!" Gurpreet agreed.

Lora and Julissa both picked A, but Jean wouldn't tell us hers. She was too busy tallying scores.

"Okay," she finally announced, "I'm the outgoing girl who knows herself really well, who will not end up in the morgue," she added to me, "and whom guys like to hang out with. I will always be able to get the special guys to ask me out."

I've seen her around guys on our field trips, and was inclined to agree.

"Slow down," she said to Gurpreet, quoting from the magazine. "You've got plenty of time to meet all the handsome guys in the world. If you go through them too fast, you might just race past that one special someone." All of them giggled before Jean turned to address Lora and Julissa.

"The right guy is out there waiting for you, and you're too smart to hang around waiting for him. He's more likely to find you if you're out having fun with his friends anyway. You're party girls, so keep up the great work!"

Ew, I thought.

"Caelie," Jean said, reading pointedly from the magazine. "You're not a kid anymore. Get out and enjoy yourself already!"

"Thanks," I said dryly.

"Well, you had some great answers, but they didn't count. Say thanks to Jane when you write back to her," Jean told me, rolling the magazine up and tossing it onto my bunk. That started a whispering war at the front door about me knowing Jane, and how maybe Davy actually would invite me on to the set.

I lay back in the dark, lights-out enforced by Jean, who I'm sure chose that bunk specifically so she would have the light switches in her own space, but I didn't mind because I was tired. Going through our routine ten times a day in practice with absolutely no fooling around was exhausting. If anybody made a mistake, we had to re-do that part perfectly ten more times, and the routine with the mistake in it didn't count.

I thought it was serious before, but girls were now walking around muttering to themselves, and everyone was spending all their free time visualizing their routines. It was even cutting into their bathroom primping time, although nothing smells like perfume or hairspray or baby powder anymore because of all the Tiger Balm. You can't wear it to practice because it's too slippery, and therefore dangerous, but everyone practically soaks in it overnight.

Nobody'd told me what was going to happen after camp ended, and all I could see beyond cheering was a void of darkness. The one time I tried to call Morgan, it was a generic message re-directing all calls to a number I recognized as Charlotte's. There was no option to leave a message.

CHAPTER TWENTY FIVE

The next morning, I woke up from a dream about Morgan, and could hear her voice as clearly as I had just before she left me in the break room. It left me with a totally overwhelming urge to write to her, and it was light enough to see, but not light enough for anyone else to be up yet, so I got up very quietly, got ready for the day, then went out to sit by the lake with my papers and pencil.

The sun was on its way up, and the coolness from the night lingered everywhere except inside those pale yellow rays. Pink and purple clouds still ringed the horizon, and the trees were still black shapes against the sky. I closed my eyes, trying to pull Morgan closer, but she was gone.

In my dream, she knew that death could be freedom, and she wasn't mad at me because of it. I wanted to make sure she would know that in real life, too, although I'm pretty sure she does, anyway. Charlotte wouldn't understand, and nothing I could say to her would change that.

Dear Morgan,

It's the last day of camp tomorrow and it's weird to think that it will all be over in just two more days. Not even. On the plus side, I haven't had any nightmares at all out here. I've tried to put everything out of my mind completely, and it didn't always work, but we're so physically exhausted that you sleep no matter what else is going on. I'm sorry you couldn't write to me or talk to me at all this summer, but Charlotte and Amy told me that you can't bear to do anything that will make the trial harder for me, and since your evidence and my evidence are the most important, you have to not communicate with me.

Sorry my other letters were so short, but I guess you understand. Did you know Charlotte sent me a book every week, and every one of them was about summer camp? Except the Terry Pratchett. They were all pretty good.

Tomorrow is our big exhibition for parents. It's on TV, so you can watch it sometime if you want to. I'm doing some scary stuff. I have to admit that I've really learned a lot here, even though I only like the stuff on tramp.

Our team has done our routine so many millions of times that I probably shouldn't worry too much about it, but I still do. Everyone here is so hyped! I have this horrible feeling that I'm going to forget the whole thing once we get up there in front of everyone. I also have the horrible feeling that one of the bases is going to drop me, but I always have that feeling.

So . . . it's almost over and I did okay here. I didn't make any friends, but I'm friendly with everyone.

I was pretty happy here, so don't worry about anything. It was much better than a summer of political touring with my dad would have been. Let Charlotte know it worked out, okay? Thank you.

Love, Caelie.

I felt a lot calmer once I wrote it and dropped it in the camp mailbox, and still had almost two hours to fill before breakfast and the mass confusion of dress rehearsals that would follow. I wanted to finish *The Return of the King* one last time.

CHAPTER TWENTY SIX

The last day was a total zoo. Girls ran shrieking all over the place at five minutes to five in the morning, which is not a civilized time to get up, especially not two days in a row.

"C'mon, Caelie!" Jean called, and I tossed back my covers, thinking about the night before as my eyes fell on Lora. Jean was right, and Lora had spent most of the previous night telling us how much she liked all of us and how she wished she'd spent more time with us. She was almost crying when she said she hoped we would understand that she never got to spend time with her twin, and the summers were their only chance.

After Lora fell asleep, Jean announced to the room, "I'm asking Ms. Medley to put them together next year. This is ridiculous."

Jean is super nice and very sensible, but also bossy. She now stood at the bottom of my bunk, glaring up.

"I'm coming!" I called back, jumping out of my bunk before she made good on her threat to douse me with water.

Weeks of begging by my roommates, a bit of curiousity on my part, and the realization that this was really the end made me agree to let them go all out on my hair and makeup for the competition. I couldn't see any reason not to let them, especially since it would make me look nothing like myself for the TV cameras.

"Sit," Jean ordered firmly, once I got myself into the bathroom. She was already dragging a chair in front of the mirror she'd claimed for herself back in the beginning of camp, which seemed like years ago now.

Obediently, I sat.

"Wait!" Julissa called, alarm in her voice. "It'll wreck it if she puts her clothes on after!"

"Nothing's going to move this hairstyle once I get it in," Jean told her. "It'll be like concrete," she added with satisfaction, but in the end, she did let me get dressed first after Neveah pointed out that our uniform tops are so hard to get on we usually have to help each other muscle them down.

"It'll be better for makeup, too," Lora said. It was a whole bunk affair because she'd smuggled Shyan into our dorm's bathrooms this morning. Jean got busy on my hair, yanking so hard every couple of seconds that my eyes began to water, and then Lora scolded me for ruining her makeup job.

"Sit *still*, Caelie," she admonished me. "And no tears until after the makeup's dry."

I blinked and tried to sit still. Ow. I can't believe people do this to themselves every day.

"What are you doing to my hair?" I yelled. "Is that backcombing? It's not 1985!"

"Shh," Jean said sternly. "You need big hair."

"I *have* big hair," I told her. They've only seen it in a French braid or a bun, and have no idea how massively out of control it is when I leave it down. "I won't be able to see *anything*!"

"Shh," she said again, and I could see Julissa roll her eyes in the mirror as she carefully applied what had to be her thirteenth layer of mascara.

Jean started pulling hard and continuously on the front of my hair and Lora gave up admonishing me, ordering Shyan to hold the point of a Kleenex at the corner of my eyes while she kept working.

"This is not helping me think that makeup and hair are good things," I told them, and Lora reacted immediately.

"Caelie! I said don't move!"

Fine. I sat there as they tortured me for almost an hour, and when they were finished, I looked at myself in the mirror. The front of my hair was pulled back tightly into tiny Caribbean braids tied with emerald and white ribbons to match the colours of my uniform. The loose hair at the end of the braids tumbled into the rest of my hair, which fountained up and around, curls springing and cascading everywhere. I had so much makeup on that I could barely feel my face, let alone move it.

"Whoa," I said.

"You look gorgeous!" they shrieked.

I looked like a freak, except for my hair, which I kind of liked.

"Thanks, guys, I love it," I told them, hoping I sounded sincere.

"Augh!" Jean yelled, glancing at the clock. "We only have an hour left!"

"Do you want some help?" I asked, but she only looked at me pityingly.

"You're a hair and makeup virgin, Caelie," she told me. "Go away."

I did. We'd all packed our suitcases the night before, and I kind of regretted that I wouldn't get to keep mine. It's the most beautiful thing I've ever owned. I ran my hands over the leather one more time, then turned away, checked for the blade in my shoe, and went down to the lake and sat quietly for an hour.

I'd given my hats away to the girls in my room last night, and hoped Charlotte wouldn't mind. In return, Jean gave me a silver and blue bracelet she'd made herself, Gurpreet, Julissa and Neveah gave me different coloured rocks they'd bored holes into over the course of the summer, and Lora gave me a braided rope in our team colours to string them on. I'd tucked them into my suitcase with all the books Charlotte had sent.

I still don't like cheerleading, but the summer was so much better than I'd feared. I was nervous about the routine today, but everybody was. In the early morning stillness, I pulled the blade out of my shoe and touched it gently, thinking about a lot of things until the gong rang for breakfast. As the last peals echoed across the lake, I slid it back into my shoe carefully and laced it up tightly before running off. My team would worry if I showed up late.

Practically nobody could finish breakfast, and for once Ms. Medley didn't make us. All summer, she worried about us trying to starve ourselves to look better for cheering, and her countermeasures were very effective. That girl and the egg on the first morning had only been one of a long series of girls she'd caught trying not to eat. Like anybody could actually get fat doing 8 hours of hard exercise a day and eating nothing but the healthy stuff Ms. Medley set out. Today, though, she relaxed the rules.

Once we were all seated and picking away at our food, Ms. Medley wandered cheerfully through the dining hall, giving bracing advice and encouragement to every team while passing out a glossy, leather-bound book to each girl.

"Go hard, Emerald," she told us, and I leafed through my book, finding formal pictures of all the teams, plus lots of candid shots of kids working on stunts, brushing their teeth, practicing tosses into the lake, giggling with friends and just hanging out. Everyone relaxed while looking through them.

There was a 'before' this, so there would be an 'after' this, too. We even managed to get a little in our stomachs before heading to the main gym at 7:45.

There were already parents arriving, lots of them. They waved to their daughters if they could see them, then claimed the seats they wanted for the show before settling in to watch the warm-up. It was a good thing the main gym was really huge because most of the stands were full before we even finished warming up.

In between warm-up times, our whole team exchanged yearbooks to sign, plus the coaches wrote stuff in them. Jean found me and took my yearbook, handing me hers in return. *Say hi to Jane Allyson for me!* She wrote. *And don't come back next year! You make me look bad.*

Jean was the only person at camp who believed I didn't like cheering, and she added her email and phone number with a heart at the bottom of her message. I grinned at her and wrote back, *Thanks for helping the new kid! I'll be counting on you to make sure they don't separate Lora and Shyan next year.* I wasn't sure how long I'd have my phone for, but I gave her the number. I couldn't believe the nice stuff people wrote about me, and I actually knew what to write back. Jean and I hugged, wishing each other good luck as the coaches began to assemble us into our teams again.

Emerald was up third, and I hated the waiting time, but once they called us, I ran out with the rest of them, clapping, yelling, bouncing and grinning like an idiot, then took my place for the routine. The lights were not just bright, but hot, and the sounds of two thousand people trying to be quiet were very intimidating. For a second I was afraid I would forget everything, but once the music started, I forgot to worry.

It really was like flipping a switch because we'd done it so many times, and provided we kept smiling, we could still talk to each other. The music in cheerleading is deafening, and nobody could hear us even when we were yelling, but smiling is a very big thing in cheering, and my cheeks hurt more than anything else at the end of a routine.

When my bases hoisted me up for our final pose and the other flyers caught me just right (I was the top of a pyramid, on top of flyers who were on top of other flyers who were on top of bases . . . pretty much my worst cheering nightmare ever), I smiled for real. It was over, and I hadn't totally screwed up!

The crowd went wild for us and we ran off to the side, where we were allowed to watch the rest of the teams. I would never have to do this sport again! I cheered on the other teams as hard as I could, and only two of them made mistakes. Both of the mistakes were flyers not getting up right and falling back down before the stunt, but at least their bases caught them safely, and they managed to get back on track quickly.

When the last team finished, there was a lot of milling around and squealing and chattering for about twenty minutes before they had the long-awaited awards ceremony. I was sobering up, because timing was going to be very important to me soon. My best chance to get away was in the first rush of campers, but everyone was still crowding around me and we were all sitting on the floor for the awards. I couldn't get out if I wanted, and I'd be too conspicuous if I tried.

Our team came in second, and there was a lot of squealing and hugging as we accepted our medals. It was even crazier after first place was announced for the red team, the oldest and most experienced team on campus, and the entire camp rushed up and hugged them, wanting to touch the trophy and congratulate the team members.

Finally, Ms. Medley got us all seated again and gave a speech to the parents about how hard we'd worked and how proud she was of us. After that, camp was over. There was a mad dash for the bleachers—I thought they might collapse under the weight of all the campers and their parents—and I got a hollow feeling in the bottom of my stomach.

It was nice to sort of blend in and not have to worry about . . . anything really, except my bases dropping me on my head and killing me. But at least it wouldn't be on *purpose*.

It was time for me to move on, intelligently and quickly. I was not going back to my dad, and I for sure wasn't going to face him in a courtroom, and there was only one way to make sure.

I melted easily into the crowd and was almost at the empty corridors that led to the changerooms when Ms. Medley stepped forward and smoothly pulled me off to the side. I'd successfully avoided her all summer, so she wasn't on my radar as I dodged hugging families and excited siblings.

It was very stupid of me, and my mind raced as I tried to reconfigure my plans. In one second, she'd changed everything. I could almost see my father's victorious leer hanging in the air before me.

"Caelie." Ms. Medley got a very firm grip on my elbow and pulled me quickly and effortlessly through the throng of excited parents and cheerleaders, "you have some visitors in my office."

I was hoping for a hint about them so I could decide what to do, but she just smiled noncommittally at me. With luck, it wasn't an armed escort or the entire media population of the city, either of which would make everything messier and a lot more complicated. We were mobbed in the hallways, but Ms. Medley smiled at everyone we passed and politely indicated that she would be available shortly.

Every parent wanted to find out if his or her daughter was the best one there, had improved a lot, or was at least good enough to come back next year, but I was politely and determinedly towed along until we got to her office. We stopped outside her closed office door, and she turned to face me.

"You've done a great job here, Caelie. You're stronger than you think you are. I know you were afraid the bases would drop you, but you didn't let that get in the way of learning more skills than any other girl has ever learned in one summer. You'll be welcome here any summer you want to come back." With that, she shook my hand firmly then raised her eyebrows and tilted her head towards her office.

She waited there, blocking any possible attempt I could have made to escape and ignoring the crowds of admirers or supplicants or whatever word you'd use to describe the parents and athletes thronging around her. There was no way out. I took a deep breath, wished I'd had time to wash my "competition" makeup off, and opened the door.

I shouldn't have been as surprised as I was to see Charlotte waiting for me behind Ms. Medley's door.

CHAPTER TWENTY SEVEN

"Let's go, Caelie," Charlotte nodded briskly at me, before I'd even had time to process her presence. It was like no time had passed since she'd dropped me off here, and camp didn't even exist.

"Where are we going?" I asked warily. The blade was still in my shoe, but I could never get it out in front of Charlotte. Why did I think I'd have more time to get to it?

"You're due in court ninety minutes from now," came Amy's voice from behind me, and I lost my breath. "There's a helicopter waiting outside, and we should just be able to make it. Your stuff is already packed and on board."

"I had stuff in the changeroom," I ventured. My mouth was operating on automatic, but my brain had completely shut down. I wasn't going to the trial. I wasn't. The trial was *today?*

"It's been packed," she said. I turned around slowly to face her. It wasn't her image on a shimmering, pearly wall. It was Amy, in person. "Think of it like ripping off a band-aid." She offered me her hand and I took it. Speaking to her on the phone had never become normal, however much I loved it, but Amy in front of me was something completely different. I was stunned, and obeyed her instinctively.

"It'll hurt either way," she told me, "but once it's off, it's off for good."

I followed her blindly out a back exit, away from all the campers and their parents, and a golf cart drove us quickly away from the buildings.

She always does everything she's afraid to do. Even knowing beforehand how much it will cost her, she does it. The one person in the world I can't let down is Amy, and a tiny part of me was betting Charlotte knew that.

"I did tell you I'd be here when you needed me," she reminded me, as we stepped out of the golf cart and crossed the grass to a waiting helicopter.

"Did you—see my routine?" I asked stupidly.

"Absolutely, Caelie," she confirmed, holding up a wig and sunglasses for my inspection, "I was incognito. You were fabulous. Still hate it, huh?" she squeezed my hand gently.

I nodded my head dumbly as she lifted me into the helicopter and then sat down beside me, helping me put in the weird earplugs Charlotte passed her.

When the blades started up and the helicopter lifted off, I thought I was going to puke, even though I'd hardly eaten anything at breakfast, and nothing at all after that. By now, Charlotte could recognize the signs and passed me a plastic bag but I waved her off, and managed to stop gagging.

Amy tucked her arm around me and held me close, which yesterday would have made me delirious with joy, but now I barely noticed. I closed my eyes and concentrated on keeping the meager contents of my stomach in place.

At least half an hour passed before I opened my eyes, and we flew for another twenty minutes in silence.

"What kind of trial?" I finally asked, my voice loud and strange through the protective earbuds. We could hear the tremendous buzzing of the helicopter only faintly.

"Everyone will be in the courtroom." Charlotte's voice arrived clearly in my ear via the joy of technology, but I didn't turn to look at her. "It is a highly publicized trial, Caelie, in its second day. Your evidence will be heard this afternoon and you'll probably be finished after that. Nobody likes to keep kids in your situation coming back day after day. Because of your age, you'll be allowed a screen so that you can't see anyone but the judge, and nobody but the judge can see you."

Of all the times she could have chosen to be forthcoming, this was the one she picked?

"Why didn't you tell me before?" I wasn't angry, just numb. My mouth seemed to be asking questions that my mind hadn't even thought up.

Charlotte paused almost imperceptibly. "We decided it wouldn't help you, and since you weren't slated until this afternoon, it would be best if you finished up camp first. It's not like there was anything you could have prepared ahead of time."

We. "Morgan," I said aloud, anger rushing through me at last. It felt better than the sick fear that sat greasily in my stomach. "Morgan decided. Where is she?" She promised she wouldn't leave me, right before she ignored me for two months. Charlotte probably lies to me all the time, but so what? She doesn't know me. Morgan does.

"You can kill her later," Amy offered cheerfully. "Caelie," she added gently, once I met her eyes, "I don't think she's had more than three hours of sleep in the last week. It's one thing to play a character who hardly ever sleeps because she's pushing herself to always be there and always be the best, but it's totally different to watch someone in real life drive herself to the point of collapse."

"Here," Charlotte interrupted, looking irritated with Jane. She held some clothes out to me. I was still in my cheering outfit. "You need to get changed."

Panic engulfed the anger, and the stupid voice in my head reminded me that it had warned me about Morgan. The nausea returned in full force. I'd been in a huge gym with thousands of other people less than an hour ago, and now I was in a helicopter on the way to the trial I'd planned so carefully to avoid.

If it weren't for Charlotte's presence, I'd have begun to question my sanity. Instead, I threw up, something Charlotte was ready for. I didn't feel any better when I was finished, but Charlotte passed me mouthwash and some ice, and waited until I'd used them.

"Do you have a cloth?" I asked Amy, struggling to wriggle out of my cheering skirt and firmly ignoring the resulting spasmic pain in my stomach. The uniforms were flexible, but really tight. "I never wear makeup and I don't want to go in there feeling . . ." I trailed off, and stood still.

"Conspicuous?" Amy suggested, a hint of dark amusement tingeing the compassion in her eyes. I nodded, and her head moved so close to mine so that I could feel her soft, silky hair brush against my face. I love her hair, as black and deep and soft as the night, and I shut my eyes to hold the moment.

"Yeah," she said quietly, her voice coming through to both Charlotte and me through the fitted earpieces we wore, "standing at the front of a courtroom in front of spectators, a judge, the media and your father won't make you feel conspicuous at all."

Charlotte looked horrified and furious, and whirled to confront Amy until she saw I was grinning.

Oh God, I love Amy. Why don't other people realize how valuable it is to just acknowledge the truth?

Swallowing hard and sitting back down very slowly, Charlotte contented herself with muttering, "It's a good thing she's already thrown up," and shifting slightly away from us, but it took several minutes for her colour to subside and her breathing to return to normal.

It was the pilot who handed me an entire tub of wipes. Apparently he has two babies at home, and keeps wipes everywhere 'just in case'. I scrubbed at my face, but it wasn't until Amy pulled some cream out of her bag and smeared it all over my skin that any of the makeup actually came off. The cream stung my eyes, but I could still see clearly enough to notice that Charlotte was carefully and thoroughly examining my uniform.

I sighed and slid my shoe off. The minute I saw Charlotte in that office, I knew it was over. "You'll have better luck with this," I told her, pulling the blade out and laying it on her armrest. Charlotte held her hand out for the other shoe, and I passed it over as well. Once she was satisfied, she put them in her own bag without comment.

"Showers?" Amy asked me, glancing briefly at the blade.

I half nodded and half shrugged.

"Nice," she congratulated me, causing Charlotte to flush with rage. Can you be shocked and delighted at the same time you're overwhelmingly terrified? I love Amy more with every passing second.

"Get changed," Charlotte said tersely, anger still riding through her voice.

It was hard to get my top off, especially in the limited space, and I almost fell back when Amy finally yanked it over my head. She pulled my undersuit off too, like I really am seven instead of just looking that way, but maybe that's normal with actors. It should have felt weird to be standing there in my underpants with a helicopter pilot I've never met, Charlotte, and the most famous actress in the world, but I didn't.

I felt separate from everything that was happening around me or to me, and Amy acted like it was totally normal to strip my clothes off me. By the time I got into the brown pants and cream coloured blouse, as well as the soft brown shoes Charlotte supplied in place of my runners, and let Amy wipe my face off one final time, we'd landed.

Charlotte's car, the deceptively dull beige one, was sitting there, only this time Morgan wasn't there and I knew where we were going: the underground parking of the courthouse. I'd waited for my dad more than once there, in what now seemed like another lifetime, because he schedules media appearances at the courthouse on a regular basis. A heavy, imposing building and a 'tough on crime' mayor go well together.

Oh, God, what had happened in the last nine weeks?

Charlotte settled into the front to drive, and Amy, back in her wig and bright red sunglasses, sat in the back with me and held my hand. She didn't look like Amy in her disguise but she did feel the way I always imagined she would, and the same way Morgan feels. I clutched her hand, and she drew me in closer.

"I want to tell you something," she whispered.

I waited.

"Char said you like Terry Pratchett, so I've been reading his books this summer."

Because of me? I looked up at her.

She nodded, her lips curving slightly in a smile before she spoke, quoting from what I immediately recognized as *A Hat Full of Sky*. I don't like the main character of that book very much, but Amy was quoting the best part in the book, where she talks about having to do things you don't want to do, and the only reason is because it's the right thing, and you know it's the right thing. Amy was word perfect for the entire quote.

"It's all right to be afraid," she added, in her regular voice. "Horrible," she added, "but all right. What's not all right is to fail because of it. The only way out of fear is through." She shrugged apologetically and then tilted my chin up and pushed her sunglasses out of the way so I could look into her eyes. "I'll be with you in there. Don't screw up."

I almost smiled at that, but was pretty sure that I was going to puke again any second, so I concentrated on taking short, quick breaths of air, panting to suppress the gag reflex. If I ever want to be like Granny Weatherwax, I have to start here.

The courthouse was only a few minutes' drive from where the helicopter landed, and we arrived at our destination way too quickly. As Charlotte escorted me to our courtroom, I started hyperventilating, and she sat me down and pushed my head between my knees. Amy hadn't left my side, nor let go of my hand.

"It's almost over, Caelie," Charlotte encouraged me, pushing a piece of paper into my hands. I looked down at it and tried to read it. "It's from Morgan. She said to give it to you before you went in there."

Amy helped me smooth it out and hold it steady. It took three tries for the words to become meaningful, but when I finally managed to get the black marks to form into words and then sentences, they were my favourite lines from the best Cynthia Voigt book ever, *Homecoming*. How had Morgan found my favourite quote in my favourite Voigt book? I'd taken so many books at the beginning of the summer.

I felt so alone, but both Morgan and Amy wanted me to know I wasn't. Did that help? I looked up at Amy, who gazed steadily back. A bit. She'd been through this herself, and she was going to make sure that I made it, too. *This isn't my fault*, I reminded myself. But it was my responsibility.

I took a deep breath, clutched the paper tightly in my hand, and turned to Charlotte. "I don't want the screen," I said, my voice breaking.

"Caelie—"

"No, it's worse to imagine things than to just see them. I don't want the screen," I repeated, not recognizing the sound of my own voice, loud and wild, rising up into the high, domed ceiling.

Charlotte looked at Amy, who nodded, and then motioned to one of the uniformed security men outside the courtroom. He spoke to someone inside the room, and we waited for a couple of minutes before I was escorted in by two of them, one on either side of me. My legs were shaking and I swallowed hard, twice, to keep from throwing up. I would have to walk past my father. *I would have to walk past my father.* The thought was so huge and so sickening that the security guys had firmly marched me past him before I could realize it was actually happening, and I didn't even look at him. Not then.

I stood up, trembling, my eyes on the floor as I weakly echoed the promise to speak the truth. None of the words I said were actually getting through to me, and my strangled voice sounded like it was coming from far away. When the woman reciting the oath paused, I repeated words I didn't know I'd consciously heard. When she spoke, a strange buzzing noise filled my ears and I was only able to hold myself upright at the thought of how humiliating it would be to pass out in front of all these people. In front of him.

Once I was allowed to sit, I breathed out shakily. My legs could not have supported me for one more instant, and I fell clumsily into my seat as they adjusted the microphone to my height. I cautiously raised my eyes a tiny bit. Amy was already seated, with Charlotte beside her, both of them as close to me as they could get. I focused on Amy. She looked a question at me and I took a deep breath and nodded slightly. I would tell the truth. I would be stronger than the fear. I would not let her down.

And then it began.

CHAPTER TWENTY EIGHT

The first thing I had to do was point my father out in the courtroom. I had to look at him then, and I was surprised to see that he wasn't looking at me; he was looking at the desk in front of him. A black tide of memories washed over me and for a moment I wished for something I'd been praying would not happen, that he would look at me.

He never had a problem looking at me when he was hitting me, but now he was avoiding me. I wanted to scream at him, "*You* did this! Not me!" but I realized that someone was asking me a question. Repeating one, really. My letters were now laid out in front of me, and I wondered how long I'd been oblivious to the speaker.

"Did you write all these letters, Caelie?"

The voice asking me questions was still patient, so it couldn't have been that long. I was unable to look at them for more than a second, but they were mine, all right. I sought Amy's eyes again, and they reflected nothing but confidence. The pity, speculation, sympathy and cruel curiosity that were present on the faces of everyone else, fanning my own fear and humiliation, were absent from Amy's expression. I didn't look away from her as I answered.

"Yes."

Amy held my gaze expressionlessly. Sympathy, support or encouragement would not help me, and all she could give me was the reminder that I really do exist, not just in the letters and not just in other people's minds. I'm not here to do what my dad or any of the official people in the courtroom want me to do. I'm here to do what has to be done, and nothing else.

"Why did you write them?"

"I didn't want to be alone with it anymore," I replied, still looking at Amy. It's okay to tell her the truth, because she already knows it.

"Why didn't you ask someone for help?"

"I did," I said, in that strange voice that didn't belong to me really. Writing to Amy was the first real thing I ever did in my life. As she listened to me, she didn't so much smile as relax a little bit more.

"Who?"

"In my letters," I clarified.

"You are aware that the person you wrote the letters to doesn't really exist?"

"The person who read them got me help," I answered, and this time Amy did smile, a very little bit.

"Why didn't you ask someone you knew?" the questioning continued, searing, flaying, personal questions asked in a measured, level voice that didn't understand or even care.

"No one believed me," I replied.

There was a pause before the voice resumed. "I see the Ministry investigated your family as a result of an anonymous call."

I'd only hinted at the truth to one person that year, so how anonymous could it be? It wasn't a question, though, so I said nothing.

"Why didn't you tell any of this to the investigating officials?"

Because I was seven and my dad was in the room with us? Because they're idiots? Because the Ministry is a system, and systems exist to protect themselves, not others? Take your pick.

"Please answer the question."

"No." What was I going to tell them? That even when I was seven, I could see there was no point? Telling the truth would only lead to more stupid questions that don't have governmentally-approved answers.

After an appeal to the judge and a heated discussion between the judge and the lawyers, the judge ruled that I didn't have to answer since it wasn't germane to this case. He did, however, warn me that there would very likely be a separate inquiry into how the Ministry had dealt with my case, should the charges against my father be proven true.

I might be going through all of this for nothing? Hysterical laughter nearly burst through the protective bubble I'd constructed around myself, but I knew that if it did, it would be just like the first night with Charlotte. Screaming or laughing, it would carry me away to someplace safe.

Would I really have to go through all of this again, for someone else? Amy caught my eye and shook her head slightly. Don't worry, she was telling me. Focus. You're still here. We both are.

I took a small breath before the next question, and she nodded slightly.

"Is everything in those letters true?"

I panicked for a second, unable to remember everything I'd written. I was pretty sure it was, but what if I'd written something unkind about someone at school? Was that still true? Was it ever? I saw Charlotte shake her head slightly, exasperated at the question instead of me, and probably still angry at the previous one.

I had to answer, "I don't know." We were all forced to wait while the judge quieted the courtroom.

"I'm sorry, Caelie," the questioner went on. "Let me ask you a different question. In your letters, you write about your father hitting you, kicking you, and choking you. Did those things happen?"

"Yes."

The courtroom was silent now.

"Did he break some of your bones?"

"Yes," I replied in a tight voice. I didn't want to cry or throw up here, but I was having a really hard time holding it in. Surface questions were bad enough, leaving only glancing blows, but now they were piercing through me, leaving open wounds from which the blood flowed freely, and the pain screamed mercilessly. The next question hurt so badly that I didn't hear it as words, but felt it as a weapon, and one that split me open.

"You describe your father attacking your pet dog. Was that true?"

Amy's face swam out of focus and all I could see in her place was Missy, hacked and beaten and pulpy. I could hear it all again, too. I threw up into a plastic bucket that someone, probably Charlotte, had put into the witness stand. When my stomach was shrieking in pain and I could gag no more, I realized I was bawling, and I *hated* him for making me cry here.

Someone handed me a box of Kleenex and some water, and I got myself back under control, more or less. I couldn't breathe except in involuntary jerks and spasms, and the tears streamed out silently without my consent, but I'd clamped down on the desperate sobbing. The bucket was taken away, and an argument that I hadn't really been hearing died down. I didn't care what it was about, and tried to force myself to answer the question. I *wanted* to answer the question.

"Yes. He killed her," I choked out.

The other voices were now silent. "Did you tell anyone about that?" came the next calm question. I hated that the person asking me these questions could ask them as if they didn't really matter. As if I didn't really matter, and nothing that had happened to me mattered.

"No."

"Did you lie to doctors to hide how you got your injuries?"

"Yes." *Shut up.*

"Did your father take you to different clinics and hospitals so that they wouldn't notice how often you had to see a doctor?"

"Yes." *Like they wouldn't have found the records by now. Stupid question.*

"Did anyone else ever ask you about your injuries?"

"Yes."

"Who was that?"

I answered the question only reluctantly. I knew where it was going and wasn't looking forward to it. "My gym teacher and a boy in my class."

"What did you tell them?"

You already know what I told them. Stop making me look like an idiot. "I lied to them."

"Are you lying to us now?"

"NO!" I screamed it as loudly as I could, trying to get that horrible calm voice to shut up, and I started crying again so hard I could barely breathe. I scrunched up behind the witness stand, pulling my knees up to my chin and tucking my head under so I didn't have to see any of them anymore.

"Thank you, Caelie. That's all for now."

Finally. I choked back the sobs, and my security escort led me out into a corridor filled with the press. Even with my head down, I could see flashes as cameras took photos of me, and I heard people shouting questions at me, exactly like they had a whole lifetime ago when we'd raced to the car just ahead of the reporters.

CHAPTER TWENTY NINE

There were other people in the room they led me to, all of them were cops, and nobody's conversations or activities even faltered. I folded my arms on the table, rested my forehead on them and felt a hot wetness as tears silently welled up and fell for the very few minutes before Charlotte and Amy came in through a door at the back of the room.

Amy put her arms around me, kissed my hair and let me cry quietly for a long, long time. I choked on the tears that wouldn't stop coming, but her arms held me solidly, safely, against her.

Finally, I slowed down into that hiccupping sobbing stage, and Amy rubbed my back softly with one hand and gently settled the other one on my hair, keeping me close as my breathing began to calm down and I slowly became aware of what was going on around me. Everyone was still there, voices quiet and calm as if people broke down in here all the time.

I heard Morgan's voice among the others and realized that she was in the room. At a different table, talking to someone else. In that instant, I hated her more than I've ever hated anyone else, even my dad. She's no different from everyone else after all, but worse because she pretended to be like me and made me think she knew me. Not just me, everything. At least my dad never lied to me. It made me furious, mostly at myself for thinking that Morgan might be different, that she might understand and like me even though nobody else ever has, and I couldn't sit there any longer. It felt better to be angry anyway.

I started to push Amy away so I could go over to her, but Amy and Charlotte both grabbed me and said at the same time, "She can't!"

I stewed silently between them for a few minutes and then loudly demanded, "So what happens next? In the trial?"

It was Charlotte who answered, in a hushed, harsh voice that was designed to make me be quieter. "It's finished for today. The next few days or so will be taken up with hearing other evidence for your case, and then the defense will have their say."

Her eyes flicked over Morgan when she talked about the other evidence for my case and I realized that Morgan would be presenting it.

"I want to hear it," I said out loud. "I'm going." I wanted to make Morgan see what she had done to me. She knew I was here and she wouldn't even *look* at me.

Charlotte and Amy were both shaking their heads at me.

"I don't care. It's about *me*. I'm going." I wasn't arguing, I was stating a fact. Charlotte and Amy both looked flustered.

Morgan was still facing her colleague and looking down at her work, but Amy and Charlotte glanced over at her. "That is not an option. Period."

For someone speaking so quietly, and apparently to someone in the opposite direction, her voice sure carried well. So did her fury, which was much more powerful than mine. The entire room, even those who hadn't heard her actual words, went silent. Charlotte and Amy stood up quickly and pulled me out of the room. I felt bad, afraid, that I'd made Morgan so angry.

Of course I was trying to, but once I succeeded, I really regretted it. I turned as we got to the doorway and was about to call out that I was sorry when Charlotte slapped her hand across my mouth and Amy hissed at me to shut up. I was mad at Charlotte, but shocked by Amy, so I did shut up. We were driven to a hotel (was I going to live in hotels and camps until I got to college?) and taken up to a room through the employees' entrance and elevators. The longer they said nothing, the more my anger built up until we finally got into our room and I turned on Charlotte, who started yelling before I could.

"What on earth is *wrong* with you?" Her face was flushed and she was actually shaking. Amy took her arm gently and looked at her warningly. Charlotte glared at me for a few more seconds and then stormed into the bathroom and locked the door.

Amy turned to me. She wasn't angry, but she was very serious.

"There's nothing wrong with you," was the first thing she said. "Not even Charlotte thinks that. And what happened in the break room was our fault, Caelie. Not yours, and definitely not Morgan's. Morgan loves you, exactly as much as you imagine anyone can love another person."

What?

"If she didn't think my being here would comfort you, I don't think she could get through this," Amy continued. "And we all need her to get through this. What do you think the defense—" she stopped and corrected herself. "What do you think your father would do if he knew that Morgan loves you?"

She looked at me steadily.

"She doesn't, so who cares?"

"Caelie." Amy took my hand and waited.

"Okay, fine, if she did, which she doesn't, he'd say that she was lying for me or that I was lying to her and she believed me because I suckered her." I was maybe willing to entertain the idea that Morgan liked me, because Amy wouldn't lie to me that much, but I had to push the whole idea of her loving me far, far away because the truth is that I love her so, so much. If she just likes me back a little bit, that'll be enough.

Amy looked sideways at me for a minute. "We all love you, Caelie, and if it takes ten or twenty years to convince you, well, we're pretty young. We've got time. You're an easy kid to love."

Yeah, right, I thought, but I managed to keep from rolling my eyes at her. She laughed anyway, and hugged me. "I love you, kiddo," she repeated, smiling but sincere.

I've been hugged more today than in the last thirteen and a half years. It's kind of weird, in a good way.

"Amy doesn't say that," I told her. Amy never talks about how she feels.

"She does when she's with someone safe," Amy told me, stopping my heart for a moment and then making me look up at her in wonder. Does she really care if I love her back?

"Trialwise," she continued, still smiling, but now giving me serious instructions. Her arm was still around me. "Morgan stays away from you and you stay away from her and we can avoid the whole mess of having you testify that you love her, which you do, and then having a bunch of shrinks come in to talk about why you feel that way and the fact that Morgan loves you too, and how it does or doesn't affect her work, and a bunch of other crap. Okay? She has to win this. For you. Acknowledging a personal relationship with you is more than just a complication. It's a threat to the case. So there can't be one. Right?"

"Right," I nodded back, responding automatically to Amy stating how things were going to be, even while the words 'personal relationship' filled my head with a pink and gold cloud of hope and wonder. She was good at that. "I'm *really* sorry," I added.

"Yeah, well, that won't make her any happier. Trust me." Amy grinned at me and hugged me tightly. "I love you, Caelie. And you got through it! She told you it didn't have to be pretty, it just had to be done, remember? It's done. You did it. It's over," she whispered soothingly as I began to tremble.

When Charlotte's cell interrupted us, I realized she'd come back in the room. Amy's only response was to shift me to her side, keeping one arm around me as she let out a very slow breath.

Charlotte pulled her phone out, and her body stilled as suddenly as Amy's had. Neither of them wanted to face this phone call, so it must be Morgan.

Charlotte looked at the display on her cell for a moment longer, glanced over at me, and then answered tersely, "Yeah." She listened for a few seconds and said, "It's too late, I already have. She was ready to yell at me too, if that's any consolation."

Charlotte only talks to one person in that tone of voice. My guess was right.

"Look, I'm sorry," Charlotte apologized. "The situation was defused, and calmer, more objective heads prevailed. Everyone is okay." Charlotte looked worried for a second, but whatever Morgan said reassured her. She looked over at me, said good-bye, and hung up.

I held her gaze for a few moments, and then we each took a deep breath and she nodded briefly. She was still a bit mad at me and I was still a bit mad at her, but we could live with that. Then she turned to Amy.

"Aren't you filming tonight?"

Amy nodded confirmation. "Yep. Helipad on the hotel roof." She broke off to look at her watch. "Right about now."

"You've been up all day to be with me and you have to work all night?" I asked anxiously.

"Really?" she asked me critically. "After a day like this, you're worried about me losing a little sleep? Get a grip, kid. Geez."

When I just stared at her, she broke into a wide grin. "I want to spend time with you. Work on at least beginning to believe that, okay? Besides, I can sleep tomorrow. I was here yesterday to testify about your letters, so I slept last night. A bit," she grinned ruefully, and I almost smiled back.

She reached down and picked me up, squeezing tightly, like she never wanted to let go. I held her back, breathing in the fresh melon-mint scent of her hair. "Keep in mind," she whispered, "some things are work and some things are life. I choose what's in my life, and you're one of my choices. You're not my damn job, and you never will be."

"Thanks, Amy," I said, profoundly happy for that one moment. She put me down and smiled at me proudly.

"Want to come see me off?" she offered. I nodded eagerly, and glanced over at Charlotte, who shrugged and picked up her jacket from the couch. So, Charlotte was my guard again. She led us back into the employees' areas and up to the roof, where the helicopter was already waiting.

"Gotta go!" Amy shouted over the noise of the blades. She hugged me one last time and I buried my head in her shoulder for a minute. "See you soon, Cael. I love you," she said into my ear, kissing me on the head and releasing me with a final squeeze on my shoulders.

I smiled at her and waved. *I love you, too.* We kept watching as she got in and got settled, and when the helicopter took off, I waved her out of sight. Amy Anderson knows me, and she came when I needed her. She was nice to me. Amy Anderson knows me. In spite of the day, in spite of the absolute horror and pain of the trial, and the rollercoaster-like nature of the whole day taken at once, I smiled, deep inside.

Charlotte let me stay there and look out at the sky for a few minutes after the helicopter was out of sight before she turned to me. "Hungry?"

"No." I shook my head at her. Charlotte again.

"Okay, then let's get back and you can get ready for bed."

"It's not even five o'clock, Charlotte," I pointed out. She gazed steadily at me and I sighed and trudged along beside her. The truth is, I wanted nothing more than to fall asleep for the rest of my life. I didn't want her to know that, though, so when we got back, I had a shower and then went to 'my' room wrapped in a towel, seriously relieved that I didn't have to do my hair in a French braid. What with the braids and the constant sweating, my hair hadn't been properly dry all summer.

I was also looking forward to letting the dye wash out.

I carried my dirty clothes with me, hoping that some of my clean clothes had made it here, but when I walked into the room that had been designated as mine, I dropped my clothes in amazement and some of my tiredness fell away. The recess in the window held about twenty of my books. There were clothes for me folded in all the drawers in the bureau. New ones, since apparently everything I owned before had been taken into evidence and processed, and my gorgeous suitcase sat at the foot of the bed, no doubt thoroughly inspected by Charlotte for safety reasons.

Sara, whom I hadn't seen since I left for camp, was sitting limply on the bed, her button eyes shining and her hands folded softly in her lap. A slow smile spread across my face and I stood there taking it all in for several minutes before putting on some nice new pyjamas, ones from Amy's show, and going out to confront Charlotte.

I found her in the kitchen area. "Thank you for the stuff in my room," I said, sitting down across the table from her and propping Sara up beside me. Charlotte was holding a mug of tea with both hands, and looked up at me as I sat down.

"It's all right?" she asked without expression.

"It's perfect," I answered, smiling.

"Then you know I didn't do it," she said dully. Man, whatever Morgan said to her on the phone must have been worse than I thought.

"I'm sure you helped." No response.

"And . . . thanks for writing to me at camp. And sending me books. I liked them. And for being at the trial," I finished. "I'm sorry for today with Morgan," I added, when no response seemed forthcoming.

"No," she said firmly. "I should have taken you out of there a lot earlier. Morgan had no choice, but I did. All I did was hurt both of you and make you both mad at me."

"What, you're not used to that?" I asked, teasing her because she looked terrible and I never like people being too nice to me when I feel awful. It's no good to have someone feel sorry for you.

"Caelie . . ." she trailed off, not sure how to react.

"Charlotte . . ." I imitated her tone of voice exactly.

Finally, she smiled. A little. "Sorry, Caelie, it just gets frustrating. I try really hard, and I always get it wrong."

"Yeah, well, be happy about that. You can understand normal people. That has to be an advantage, since there are more of them than there are of us."

"Well, I don't work with too many normal people," she admitted.

Was I really considering telling the truth to Charlotte? I bit my lip, then took the plunge. "It's frustrating for me, too, because you've read everything I ever thought or felt or did, which is totally humiliating for me, and I spend all this time with you, so I just assume that you know me better than you do."

It felt like camp was a dream and we'd never been apart. The trial was a black nightmare that would come back to me later, but if I thought about it now, I'd lose it. Completely.

The feeling of being in Amy's arms was still with me, and I never wanted it to fade.

Charlotte shrugged and looked down into her tea. Not answering wasn't helping, so I tried to explain more. She felt awful, I could tell, and I opened up more than I ever had with her before.

"I mean, Morgan can spend two minutes with me and know how I'm feeling, but I can live with you for a week and you never have any idea. Sometimes I look down on you for that," I admitted, "as if you're stupid or something, but I shouldn't. Ignorant, maybe, of things you're lucky to be ignorant of. But you try a lot harder than I do. So . . . thanks for that, too."

"Wow, is this Caelie, getting along with a normal person?" she asked brightly.

"I'm having an off day," I shrugged. Then I started laughing. It suddenly seemed ridiculous to me that this morning I was worrying about forgetting a cheerleading routine I never really cared about in the first place, and then I got to meet Amy, but in really horrible circumstances. I had my first helicopter ride, faced my father in court, narrowly escaped a million reporters, angered everyone I cared about, spent half the day in Amy's arms, and was now reassuring Charlotte, of all people.

I laughed and laughed, until Charlotte couldn't help joining in. When my stomach hurt so much I couldn't breathe any more, I finally stopped, gasping and holding on to my middle.

"One a scale of one to ten, where one is being a Soviet helicopter pilot on the day Chernobyl blew and ten is being one of Charlie's Angels for real, I'd say your day was about a two, Caelie," Charlotte acknowledged, after a few minutes of contemplation. "Maybe a one and a half," she considered.

I giggled a bit and then moaned as my stomach screamed at me. "Can we not do this again?" I suggested.

"Ever," Charlotte agreed emphatically.

"'Okay, I'm going to bed," I stood up and nodded to Charlotte.

"About time, too," she called after me. I rolled my eyes at her, but smiled before I shut my door. Bossing me around, which she knows that I hate, is her way of trying to get me to trust her. I grabbed about five of my books to take into bed with me, turned on my bedside light, crawled under the covers, and placed Sara in the crook of my arm.

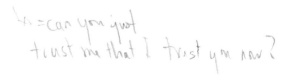

= can you just trust me that I trust you now?

CHAPTER THIRTY

We both slept in late, and the scent of French toast and syrup hung in the air long after our plates were taken out of the room.

"I know I ask you this a lot, but what happens to me next?"

She kind of answered, in the style I've come to expect from Charlotte.

"Well, you get to hide out here for a while until we know if you have to go back in and testify again. You try to avoid having the media locate you, which means avoiding having anyone recognize you. Which means, basically, avoiding anyone."

Her responses about school and where I would live were equally unhelpful, and several days passed where I sat and read, or watched the LLD episodes from Amy while Charlotte worked practically nonstop on her laptop.

Meals were brought in to us, so we didn't cook together, and Charlotte hardly spoke to me because she was working so steadily. After six days, I'd watched all my episodes, sometimes with Charlotte, who'd never watched Amy's show before and was interested enough in the characters to refrain from critiquing the police procedures, and I'd re-read all my books. I was feeling very cooped up and irritated, and I just wanted to *do* something. Anything.

I sat up and argued with Charlotte about practically anything I could think of until about midnight, when she finally ordered me off to my room. I was too wound up to sleep, so I spent some time trying to make the perfect French braid in my hair. It didn't work, just like it hadn't worked all summer, and I went to bed restless and crabby.

I woke up in a seriously bad mood the next morning and stormed out of my room to pick another fight with Charlotte, but stopped in my tracks when I saw Morgan sitting on the couch. She looked a bit like a skeleton, and her eyes had massive shadows under them, but she was smiling. I smiled back tentatively and waited.

"It's over," she confirmed.

"Is it . . . his turn now?" I asked.

"He changed his plea to guilty. Unfortunately, you're not given that much time for child abuse, unless you actually kill the kid. Still, it'll be enough time. And he's given up custody of you permanently, so with any luck at all, your new parents will be able to deal with him if he comes around after he gets out. We can't get him for murdering your mother, Cael. I'm sorry," she apologized, and her smile was gone. "It seems obvious, but the law works on what is provable beyond any doubt, and the evidence is too degraded."

"Jeez, Morgan, why do you always have to tell me the truth about everything?" I half-seriously complained. I was still a bit mad at her for not contacting me all summer, not being at the trial, ignoring me in the breakroom, and not talking to me since then. Even if it *was* all to help me in the end, it was still crummy. "At least Charlotte evades all my questions if she possibly can and practically never tells me anything bad."

Morgan started to laugh hysterically. Like, really hysterically, the way I'd screamed. I didn't know what to do, but Charlotte strode into the room, knelt down in front of Morgan and grabbed her by the arms. She looked into Morgan's eyes for a long minute, then Morgan leaned forward and rested there for a bit, quietly. When Morgan looked up, she seemed genuinely composed and Charlotte moved away without a word to either of us. I turned nervously to Morgan.

"Haven't had much rest lately, Cael," Morgan offered, by way of apology and explanation.

"Yeah, I can see that," I answered quietly, instantly forgiving her. I walked over and sat down beside her. She put her arm around me and I knew I would be perfectly happy to sit there for the rest of my life. It was worth it, even if she did hurt me again. We sat there for a long time, then I turned to her.

"Are you going away again?"

"Would you believe me if I said I wasn't?" Morgan asked.

"Would you tell me the truth?"

"The truth is always more complicated than yes or no."

I accepted the pain, and pressed her. "I still want it."

"Caelie." The quiet reprimand had come from the doorway, where Charlotte was now standing. A lot of things she wanted to say passed across her face, but what finally came out was, "Breakfast. You need to pack."

"Okay," I agreed, and went to pack up my stuff, which didn't take that long, and then I was ready to eat. Charlotte and Morgan were waiting for me in the kitchen, and neither one of them was particularly forthcoming. Morgan looked slightly less corpse-like, and was eating voraciously.

"Ready to meet your new parents?" she asked me.

I shrugged, and she smiled faintly. "I'm sorry I didn't answer your question. I can't think very well right now."

"I'm sorry, too, Caelie," Charlotte said. "We should have told you at the beginning that you'd have to be distanced from Morgan during pre-trial, but she was the best chance we had to get your co-operation at the beginning, and the most important thing was getting you free. It was wrong, but it was still the best option we had."

I nodded, not looking at her. I've never trusted Charlotte, and she'd done her job, so it was fine. Morgan had done her job, too, I guess. I just wish it didn't hurt so much when I wasn't near her.

"Hey," Morgan said softly. "I'm going to answer the question. I just can't do it yet."

It sounded like she could think okay after all.

"Are you ready?" Charlotte asked me.

"I guess."

None of us spoke again until we were in the elevator.

"Relax, Cael," Morgan told me. "You'll be okay."

It wasn't really what she said, but more the fact that she was there and thinking about me that made me smile as we stepped out of the elevator, where I was greeted by a million flashes. I heard Charlotte mutter something under her breath and grab her cell phone. The thought that ran through my head was, *I'm glad I'm not the one she's going to yell at.* Charlotte is so different at work than she is with me. I kind of like knowing that.

Morgan and Charlotte flanked me and pushed me through the sea of reporters, and now no trace of exhaustion, fatigue or starvation existed in Morgan's appearance. Instantly, she drew herself up and looked strong, formidable, and powerful. Even the shadows that haunted her face had disappeared, and I enjoyed discovering that she was different at work than around me, too.

It was a comforting thought that couldn't quite overtake the more immediate situation, with the TV cameras and microphones everywhere, and each and every person shouting something at me. Charlotte and Morgan squeezed my arms, and I knew they were telling me not to worry and not to pay attention to anyone. It wasn't like they've never drilled me about the media before, and Amy gave me detailed directions during more than one of our phone conversations at camp.

I looked down so there would be fewer pictures of my face, but when we were almost out of the crowd and I could hear sirens approaching, I heard someone yell out over the horrible cacophony, "How do you feel, Caelie?" and a white-hot rage surged through me.

I shrugged off Charlotte and Morgan and turned back. Morgan swore briefly, but inventively, and neither of them tried to pull me away. The damage had been done in that one second when I'd turned around, and I ignored the cameras that continued to whir and click and flash around me. I sought out the person who'd asked the question, and a little space cleared around one man.

I looked directly at him and replied, "How would you feel? If it were you?"

I held his gaze for a few minutes, then swept a look over all of them before I turned on my heel and strode away. What did he want me to say? I feel bad that my dad is in jail? I'm worried he'll get out and kill me? I'm desperately glad I have a break from him? I'm embarrassed that the whole world knows all my secrets? I'm terrified of having to be me, day after day for the rest of my life?

I feel a lot of things, and can't do a single thing about any one of them.

You don't have choices. You have us, Morgan had said to me once. What I felt didn't matter. Get in the car. Get through Cheer Camp. Testify at the trial. Avoid the press. Go to a foster home. Push through.

My answer did nothing to discourage the press and there was a brief rush as they tried to follow me, but by that time uniformed police officers were there, holding them back. Charlotte and Morgan bundled me into the car, groaned, and drove off.

"I'm *sorry*," I started to say, "but-"

"Caelie, reporters are like starving piranhas and words are like blood to them. You can never get rid of them once you open your mouth," Charlotte chastised me.

"She's a minor, they'll have to leave her alone," Morgan assured her. Under her breath she added, "Eventually."

"You got rid of them before," I protested to Charlotte.

"Because their actions could have influenced a legal proceeding," she said, impatient with my stupidity. "Trial's over now."

Oh. A few minutes later, my cell rang and I got to listen to Amy castigate me for a while. "Didn't I *tell* you not to say anything? What did I *tell* you? Still . . . you looked good, and your hair was back and the brown hasn't all washed out yet, and it was a pretty good thing to say. I guess. But reporters can make *anything* look good. Or bad. Don't you ever *see* the news?"

I let her go on for a while, because I figured it would keep the lectures from Charlotte and Morgan shorter. When she was finally finished, I meekly apologized and promised to never, ever speak to another reporter ever again, no matter what they said to provoke me. Ever.

She sighed, then told me to come out and visit her soon. When I hung up, Morgan and Charlotte did seem to be in a better mood.

Morgan shrugged and Charlotte sighed, and then they both said at the same time, "What's done is done." I thought it would be in my best interests to curtail the discussion before I got into any more trouble, so I bit my lip and looked down at my lap.

We drove a short way out of downtown into some nice suburbs before pulling up in front of a white house with navy blue trim. It had stone fences and thick, cedar hedges around it and some big trees in the back that looked good for climbing. It also had a pretty big yard. It was the kind of old house that I really like—all wood and stucco and lead glass windows. For some reason, that kind of house feels very safe and comfortable to me.

A tiny piece of the rigid, panicky me inside relaxed a little bit. Surely nice people would live in a house like that?

I swallowed hard, smiled determinedly at Morgan and Charlotte, and started to collect my stuff. I could feel my heart starting to beat faster as I stood on the porch and rang the bell, with Morgan and Charlotte behind me. The tones echoed in the house for a minute, and then the door was opened by a middle-aged woman who looked very kind, quite officious, and a little plump.

She smiled at me, and I tried to smile back.

"Hi, Caelie. My name is Anna. Would you like to see your room?" she asked, still smiling nicely, and standing back so I had lots of space to walk in without getting too close to her. That was thoughtful.

I nodded and we followed her up the stairs to a room at the back of the house. We passed a big, modern kitchen that looked a bit out of place in this old-fashioned house, and then walked through the living room. It was really cozy, done in navy accents and smooth, gleaming wood with a long wall of bookshelves and a huge fireplace. Blankets in colourful but muted tones draped over the backs of couches and chairs, and the staircase had a long, curving, open banister with the same soft, shining wood as the bookshelves and mantelpiece.

Upstairs, I passed a mint green and bright white bathroom that looked like it had been newly painted, and then we got to my room. It also looked newly painted and was a bright, sunny yellow with a big white bed, billowy white curtains and a white carpet. The white curtains had tiny flower-shaped holes all over them that were stitched all around with yellow thread. There were white bookshelves lining the walls on either side of the bed, which was draped in a white bedspread with blue and yellow accents.

A desk sat under the deep, recessed window that sported a carpeted ledge and two cushions—one bright yellow and the other blue. I could sit on the ledge and look out at the yard and read, or think, or study. Being in the room was like being inside a sunny, happy day with no shadows. I really, really loved the room. It was a room that cared about the person who lived in it.

"Do you think you'll like it?" Anna asked me.

I nodded fervently and said politely, "Yes. Thank you."

"Well, I guess I'll leave you here, then, if you're happy with everything." She smiled and picked up a purse and clipboard that had been sitting on the floor just inside the door.

I felt like I was in an elevator that had started plummeting towards the ground; my stomach just flew up as I turned slowly to look at Morgan and Charlotte.

"No," Morgan said, smiling as she finally answered the question I'd asked her before breakfast. "I'm not going away. We live here."

My eyes shifted to Charlotte, who shrugged. "I got used to having someone help me make dinner."

I started crying and laughing all at once, and Anna left us alone. Morgan held me for a long moment, long enough for us to hear the front door open and shut, and a car engine start up in the street, then they watched me as I wandered around my room a bit, sat in the window seat, and looked over my bookshelves. All the books I'd left behind were in there, with room to spare for new ones. I ran my finger over them, all in their rows, the only part of my life before that I wanted with me in my new one. Then they took me on a tour. The kitchen, obviously, was Charlotte's doing, but the den was all Morgan's.

"No smartglass?" I asked.

"Can you see any?" Charlotte returned.

Well, at least looking for it would give me something to do in my spare time.

Their bedroom was also upstairs but it was across the hall from mine, and looked out over the front yard. It didn't have a window seat but it did have a gorgeous, round, stained glass window over the bed. Charlotte was watching me closely when they made it clear they shared a room, but did she really think I hadn't figured it out? Watching other people closely has kept me alive this long and it's become a habit I'm not sure I can get rid of, even if I want to.

Knowing what other people are thinking and feeling at all times is not a skill you develop lightly or can just discard when you don't need it, and why else would Morgan have told Charlotte the truth about herself? Besides, all their silent cues and communication were a lot more personal than professional. It wasn't hard to figure out.

Charlotte would still be bossy, she still wouldn't understand me, and she'd still be my guard. I was okay with that.

Morgan would be everything else, but while she was sleeping—and she'd crashed in their room as soon as she knew that I was fine with her and Charlotte—I decided to explore the rest of the house under Charlotte's ever-watchful eye. More the yard than the house, really, because after being stuck in a hotel room with Charlotte for over a week, I wanted some time to myself.

There was a vegetable garden at the back, and wild blackberry bushes on one side. The rest was grass and compost and huge, old trees that looked both easy and fun to climb. Charlotte didn't stop me from going outside, and didn't come out with me, so after wandering around to find all the nooks and crannies, I did climb them, going as high as I could before the branches started bending alarmingly under my feet. When I was almost at the very top of my second one, I caught Charlotte frowning at me out of one of the windows, but she didn't say anything, and I was not going to stop climbing trees for Charlotte.

It was gorgeous and freeing outside, possibly because nature is too old and enormous to hold any memory of things as small and fleeting as my father or my letters or my life. The distant sounds of other people's lives floated gently on the air, their anonymity and complete ignorance of my presence making me safe, and reminding me of how often I wanted to be invisible.

I'm far from invisible now, but I don't need to be. Amy and Morgan want to see me. They aren't alone or wrong or different anymore, and neither am I. I'm not alone. For a moment, it felt like that first night with Charlotte, when I'd begun to think it was a dream. The sky was a pale, dreamy blue, the sun was hot for September, and the grass had just the right mixture of moss in it to make it very soft and a new, bright green. It wasn't a dream, though.

A cloud passed over the sun, chilling the air as my thoughts moved to my father. Was I supposed to do anything about him? Was I supposed to think about him now? Was this what Amy had in mind when she said I would have time to think about it? I didn't want to think about him.

The cloud blew away and I let the thoughts blow away with it, for now. I stayed in the trees for a long time, letting the sun, wind, and occasionally bird or squirrel sounds fill my mind. Hardly thinking at all had never seemed so attractive, or so easy.

When Morgan woke up, the house smelled welcoming from the dinner that had been cooking all day in the crock pot. I'd just come in from a walk around the neighbourhood with Charlotte, who had not asked me to help with dinner at all, probably because I'd been in a tree when she was working on it. I doubted that she would let me get away with that very often, but that was okay.

I had a strong feeling that Charlotte was always going to be organized and healthy as we sat down around a really good vegan stew with fresh bread and cheese. We talked about a lot of things as we ate, but there were only two things I really wanted to know, one unresolved thought besides my father that had kept popping up amid the fluffy white floating clouds, miles of blue, blue sky, and golden sunshine that'd filtered warmly through the reddening leaves to heat me that afternoon.

I decided to get my father over with first, and looked at Morgan, who was more likely to give me useful instead of practical advice.

"What am I supposed to do about my dad?" My throat almost closed over when I said those last two words, but I had to know.

"Nothing," she said, shaking her head slightly, and meeting my eyes. "He can't see you anymore. It's over, Cael, and all choices, contact and options are gone. You're supposed to walk away."

"What do you want to do?" Charlotte asked me, concerned.

Morgan answered for me, her spoon halfway to her mouth. "Oh, she wants to walk away, but she feels guilty about it." The words were anything but casual, but her voice was light and matter-of-fact.

I glanced at her gratefully.

"Some people need to confront their abuser," Charlotte put in.

Morgan rolled her eyes, entirely for my benefit. What a gross thing to say. Charlotte being so bloody normal was going to annoy me sometimes.

"The trial was enough," Morgan told her. "Along with facing him every single day of her life up until then. What more could she possibly have to prove to herself or anyone else? She doesn't owe him anything, and he has nothing that she needs or wants. There's nothing. It's over." *On the outside.*

I looked at her intently. She hadn't said those last words out loud, but I'd heard them anyway. Could she read my thoughts just as easily?

Of course. She smiled back at me, the unspoken words echoing in my mind. In both of our minds. I grinned. I don't ever want to see him again, but I didn't know if they thought I should, or if I had some societal or human obligation, or if we were tied together forever just because we share some DNA.

"Caelie, honey, there are no debts," Morgan told me. "To him, or to yourself. The bad, scary, guilty, awful stuff will never be taken away, and it's a huge part of who you are. That's okay," she assured me, "because that's what is. There's more out there, though, and it's time now for you to explore new things. It's not about erasing the bad, or changing who you are. We both know that doesn't happen. And that's okay, too."

Morgan's words were a huge relief to me, and some of the knots inside me began to loosen, just a bit. Getting to live with her was a miracle.

It actually was a miracle, literally, one I'd never dreamed about, but that they'd obviously been preparing for during the summer, at least. The new paint, the non-pinkness of my room, the bookshelves that lined the wall . . .

"Why didn't you tell me?" I asked them, looking down at my bowl as I forced myself to speak the words aloud. "You knew I could live here, and you didn't say anything."

I didn't want them to get mad, but they could have told me this morning and saved me from worrying about living with strangers. They could have told me in June, or any time this whole summer. I'm good at hiding things—nobody would have had to know I had a 'personal relationship' with Morgan, and I would have felt so much better the whole time. "When did you know?"

After a long silence, it was Morgan who answered. "Before I left Amy," she said. "The day we picked you up from school."

Before I even met her for the first time? "Then why—?"

She cut me off. "You had to know that you could stand for yourself."

"The trial wasn't enough?" I twisted her earlier words. I could see them not telling me at the beginning, but what about after I'd testified, or even this morning?

"You were forced into the trial," she explained, and the thought of it seemed to make her pretty angry, but she didn't elaborate. She didn't have to. Nothing in my life would ever be worse than the trial. Ever.

"If you'd failed there," she went on, "it wouldn't have been your fault. This was different. You had to decide you were going to live, and not for someone else, and then you had to deal with the practical consequences of that decision."

I tried to block out the thought of what would have happened if I'd failed, and how close I'd come that last day of camp.

"How did you know about the razor blade?" I asked Charlotte.

"If you're going to know everything," she said, darting a quick glance at Morgan, "and I had to, in order to keep you safe, you need to have a lot of other people telling you what they know, too. You told her in your last letter."

I hadn't really told her, not directly, but yeah, I'd been saying goodbye, and had counted on Morgan being able to figure it out.

"But how did you get it so quickly?" I wondered. Mail takes days, if not weeks to get anywhere.

Charlotte winced slightly, and took a deep breath before meeting my eyes again. "Your letters never went through the mail, Cael. The contents were scanned to our phones immediately and the originals were couriered in. It was part of my job. I'm sorry."

"And my phone?" In the back of my mind, I'd kind of wondered if Amy would keep my letters to herself, and doubted it, but I'd talked to her a lot. She belongs in my head. Charlotte doesn't.

"Recorded," Morgan acknowledged. "It was her job," she reminded me quietly.

I looked away, and she reached out to touch my chin lightly, bringing my eyes up level with hers.

"I don't want to always be a job," I whispered involuntarily.

"It's okay," Morgan told me softly, and a glimmer of smile grew deep within her eyes. "She's very good at her job."

I frowned, and Morgan moved her hand down to my arm. "Hey," she said, "you were never a job to me. The judicial system was a huge pain-in-the-neck job to me, but you were not, for one second, my job. I promise."

She waited for a moment, then grinned. "You'll always be a job for Charlotte, though, just like I am, and there's not a single thing either of us can do about it, so there's no point worrying."

"Why did it matter if I chose to live with you or with strangers?" I wanted to know. Either way was living, right?

Morgan smiled slowly and sweetly. Even sitting down at dinner after sleeping all day, the coiled power was visible beneath the ethereal beauty. "Because now we can love you and protect you all we want, and you'll know it isn't because you're weak. You belong here, Caelie," she said simply, "but we're very strong. You had to know you were, too, or you could have lost yourself."

"No, I'm not," I said, with certainty, not bothering to address the fact that losing myself was something I actually want most of the time.

"If you had a choice between having Granny Weatherwax's respect or having her help, which would you choose?" Morgan asked me, looking unconcernedly at the table, its polished wood gleaming softly beneath our plates. She, too, had read all of Terry Pratchett's books that summer.

"Her respect," I replied, without having to think about it for even a second. I would know I was a good person if I had her respect, but I'd feel guilty for taking up her time and energy if she had to help me.

"That's what makes you a strong person." She leaned back so that she could see me properly. "Cael, the hard choice is to keep living, and you've made it many times over. Having a place where you're known and loved?" she asked, shadows of emotion flickering in her eyes. "That's a gift, and your strength made it possible for you to accept it. If you didn't know the measure of your own strength, you would never have really been able to trust us, because you wouldn't have been able to trust yourself."

The light glinted off her spoon as she twirled it thoughtfully in front of her. "You couldn't take everything we have to offer you if you didn't know you could live without it."

I wasn't totally sure I understood that, but it did give me a lot to think about. Why would I want something I could live without? How could not trusting myself affect how I felt about her? She seemed pretty sure of herself, though, and she's a lot smarter than I am, so I just stored the questions away in my mind to consider later. There was one final thing we had to sort out.

I took my phone out of my pocket and laid it on the table. "Charlotte?" I ventured.

"I disabled the record and report on it once you left camp, but we'll get you a new phone if you'd rather," Charlotte said quickly.

I decided that she probably wasn't lying, mostly because Morgan's expression made that perfectly clear, but this wasn't just about the phone. "No," I said slowly. "I just . . ." *have no idea how to say this*, I thought.

They waited for me. "Well, I don't want you in my head," I blurted out, looking down at the table. It sounded ungrateful, but I *hate* it so much! Even if she's trying to help, it's painfully wrong, her presence jagged and sharp and unwelcome, and I can't live with it forever. I really can't. "It's not fair."

"I'm sorry," she said, surprising me. "It's not fair, you're right. It was my job, though."

"Yeah, but Morgan says I'm always going to be your job," I reminded her.

"Yes," Charlotte agreed, "but not like that. Look, it will always be my job to keep you safe, because that's what I do. When you were writing those letters, your life was in jeopardy from someone else, and this summer, you could have killed yourself, right?"

I nodded slowly. That was the plan.

"Well, it's my job to make sure that doesn't happen," she explained. "Caelie, I read the letters before I even met you, and I had to read them to do my job. If it weren't my job, it would have been someone else's. I can't take that back, but I'm very sorry that it hurts you."

I really, really did not want to think about my letters, and the eight kajillion people who've now read them.

"As for this summer and camp," she continued, "you were under a fantastic amount of pressure which limited my choices to a private hospital ward or extremely vigilant and invasive monitoring of you. Do you disagree with my choice?"

Yes, I thought, but the other one would have been worse. Still. "Yes."

"Yeah," she sighed, as if she were genuinely thinking about what it would be like to have a stranger walking around in her head. "Well, I can't go back and unlearn anything, but your phone, room, mail, email, journal, diaries, homework, and anything you can think of are safe from me. Forever. I promise."

She lifted her hands up in the air, but when I still wasn't convinced, she leaned across the table to get closer to me. "Caelie, we have invasion of privacy laws in this country. Of course, as your guardian, with you a minor child, many of them do not apply to me."

Did she think that was going to help?

"You can trust me, though, and I hope you will. Your thoughts, goals, hopes, dreams, ambitions, fears, worries, regrets, experiences and conversations are all your own, Caelie, unless you deliberately choose to share them with me. Nobody can live any other way, and I've gone to a lot of trouble to make sure that you can live. I'm not going to waste all that effort now."

With Morgan, that would have been a kind of joke, but Charlotte was dead serious.

I remembered the books and letters every week at camp. I remembered how relaxed she was on the Ferris Wheel, looking out at the city after a wild afternoon of rides and junk food. She'd never left me alone at that hospital, or made me feel weird or embarrassed. She'd even taken me out to the beach every day at the apartment. Charlotte would never be like Morgan or Amy, but she was okay.

I turned my phone over and over in my hands. Maybe I *could* trust Charlotte, but I don't. And that's a pretty big maybe for me.

"I think it's a bit early for trust," Morgan commented mildly, just before the silence became uncomfortable. "After all, we did some crappy things to save you. It worked, but maybe something else would have worked, too, and we can't go back."

I kept my eyes on the phone. I do trust Morgan, because I can see what her choices did to her. Even after sleeping the entire day, she looks like she needs IV fluids and a sedative more than a family dinner in the kitchen.

"Hey," she said, and waited for me to look up. When I did, I saw that she was sliding something across the table to me. It was my picture of Amy, laminated so nothing could wreck it. When I flipped it over, the message was there.

Trust me. Love, Amy.

"Thanks," I said, quietly.

"She's not ever going to leave you," Morgan told me, and I believed her. We could never go back, that was true, but I could go forward with them. It wasn't a dream, and it wouldn't be easy, but it was a million times better than any choice I'd ever had before.

When I slid my phone off the table and back into my pocket, Charlotte got up to pour us all some piping hot, steaming tea, filling the kitchen with the scent of mint. We sat around the table spooning up warm, sweet bites of blueberry crumble as the tea cooled and the conversation switched to school, books, movies and hiking.

It was like a normal dinner with a normal family, even though technically only Charlotte is normal. The three of us together are just right, and maybe that's how normal people feel all the time.

I don't know. And now I don't need to.

Read on for a preview of the second Caelie novel,
Escaping the Shadow.

CHAPTER ONE

"So, Caelie, you're an intelligent young woman. What made you think it would be okay to hurt yourself?"

This was my third session with Dr. Mettkl, a lean, well-dressed, slightly bronzed thirty year-old counselor, and I'd honestly been trying to work with him. He was my second therapist in four weeks, because the first one was this really sickly sweet woman that I wanted to hit after less than half an hour, and he was supposed to specialize in helping people work through emotional blocks.

Everyone was worried that my lack of support (ha-ha!) until this year would stunt my emotional growth, making me screwed up forever.

I'd been honest with him, even when it was embarrassing. I tried to think about my answers so I could work co-operatively with him, and I worked really hard at having an open mind going in to every session. I was even keeping a ridiculously personal and lame journal because he said it was important and would help me, but that question was the last straw. Nobody thinks it's 'okay' to hurt themselves!

What an idiot.

As he carefully calculated how much concern to project with his dark brown eyes, I tried to calm down, but failed. Something in me rebelled at the absurd injustice of being forced to open myself up to someone so stupid and alien, and I stood up.

"I have to go," I announced, ignoring the flash of curiousity he couldn't conceal. No matter what I told him or how honest I was, he never got it. He never got *me*. How can you help someone you can't even understand?

I walked out of his office and back towards the waiting room, resisting the desire to throw something at his professional 'concerned' face, which does not adequately conceal the bone-deep complacency that normal people think is their right. His banal, self-interested protests at my abrupt departure rang in my ears and burrowed into my thoughts because I stupidly can't stop myself from believing, somewhere bone-deep, that other people might be right about me.

His eyes and his shallow curiousity followed me down the hall even as his voice mercifully subsided.

Why would Morgan send me to a normal shrink?

She wouldn't.

A very brief surge of resentment flashed through me as I finally pieced together the conversations that had stopped abruptly whenever I walked into a room over the last few weeks, and the complicated glances that had passed between my guardians since I started therapy.

This whole shrink gig had to be Charlotte's idea, and she was the one waiting for me at the end of the hall.

I began to worry about her reaction to me walking out. What would I do if she made me go back in? I slowed down a bit, but the hallway suddenly wasn't long enough, and I reached the end of it reluctantly.

Charlotte, who takes her new parenting duties far more seriously than my other guardian, Morgan, was there as always in the impersonally peach waiting room, totally immersed in whatever work she had on her iPad. Her elegant fingers flew efficiently over the pad as her wide, hazel eyes scanned the display intently.

When she's angry or upset, green and gold flecks blaze in her eyes, but most of the time they are light and clear. So far, they were still clear.

Loose curls spilled down her back, but were pulled back efficiently from her face. Charlotte looks beautiful, the way I imagine porcelain dolls did in Victorian times, but no doll possesses the underlying power and efficiency that define my new guardian.

Approximately one nanosecond after I saw her, she looked up at me quizzically, but I shook my head hopelessly. I couldn't go back in there, and desperately hoped she wouldn't make me.

To her credit, or possibly as a result of all those arguments with Morgan, she seemed to accept the situation at face value.

I relaxed a teeny, tiny bit inside and stepped gingerly towards her. She just sighed and slid the iPad, whose screen goes blank automatically if I get within five feet of it, or at least that's how it seems, into its sleeve and stood up. And then further up. She's model tall and I'm way too small for my age, so she tends to loom over me when we're standing together.

As conscious of that as I am, she stepped back, simultaneously shifting the iPad to her far side.

"C'mon, Cael."

Thank goodness. I followed her gratefully as we walked out of the professionally dull office, down a communal corridor with hideously impersonal prints of flowers interspersed with bulletin boards displaying mass-produced pleas for the universal understanding of mental illness, and impatient, patronizing reminders about washing your hands regularly, especially during the current flu season.

I was glad to step out into the fresh air, which at least did not smell of people paid to pretend they care about you, and into the cool, cloudy afternoon.

My running shoes made no sound, but Charlotte's steps were accompanied by faint, efficient clicking sounds. Her smooth, chestnut hair fell neatly down her back and bounced slightly with every step. As usual, she was immaculately and beautifully dressed.

My clothes look fine too, since she picks them out, but I'll never project the grace and sheer competence that she does, and the bright red corkscrews I call hair swirled madly around my face, getting trapped in the straps of my bag as I scrambled along in her wake.

I like getting to the car first, because the mere touch of my hand on any part of the panel unlocks my door, although it's unfortunately the only part of the car that responds to me in any way. My guardians can get it to do absolutely anything, but Charlotte has stopped using it in front of me.

I think she's worried I'll figure it out, and gain access to information or programs I don't have clearance to access.

She should be.

From the outside, the car's boring, plain and beige, disguising itself as a normal, even mediocre four-door sedan, but the steering wheel is the only normal thing in a front that has no dash, no gearshift, and no visible air vents, just one smooth, curved sheet of glass. Or possibly plastic.

Whatever it is, it works exactly like her iPad, and Charlotte can do anything on it, including access sealed files, which I know because she had no choice but to work on mine in the car once. In Russian, a language she chose specifically because I didn't know it, which meant I devoted a lot of my free hours at summer camp to learning Russian on the internet.

Once we got inside and shut the doors, she turned to me.

"What's up?" Her warm hazel eyes were filled with concern, but the green and gold flecks were absent. That was a good sign.

I shrugged, but she never lets me get away with that, so I sighed and fixed my eyes on the non-dashboard. It was just empty glass until she chose to activate it, and my distorted reflection looked back at me. I quickly turned to her instead, and decided to get it over with. There's no escape from Charlotte's questioning, even at the best of times.

"I can't do it, Charlotte. I really tried. He doesn't understand me *at all.*"

She has no idea how awful it feels when professionals whose entire job it is to understand me can't even come close, and trying to make her understand is impossible because she *is* one of those professionals. A million times better than Dr. Mettkl, of course, but Charlotte wants the world to work the way she thinks it does, and her world has nothing in common with mine.

"I don't understand you at all," she commented cautiously.

"Yeah, well, I'm not that crazy about you all the time either," I told her. "You're just like him—on the other side of this nice, thick wall and you look over at me and read all these textbooks about people like me but you don't *know* me."

"Caelie." She wasn't quite reprimanding me, but it was almost the same thing.

Well, you don't. "It's just . . . frustrating. I hate therapy—it's not something I want to do at all. Ever. I definitely can't do it with someone like that and," I turned stubbornly away, "I don't want to talk about it with you. I can't *explain* it to you."

"Parent," she reminded me, saying it the same way Captain Jack Sparrow says 'Pirate.'

I like him a lot, and she has his voice down pretty pat, but the only parent I have left is in jail.

"I can't," I repeated helplessly, forcing back tears and silently cursing myself for being drawn into an exercise in futility.

Was I really going to cry in front of Charlotte?

I bit my tongue, hard, and breathed in slowly to calm down. She doesn't understand me, and she never will, so telling her the truth is useless to both of us. That's not something to get upset about, but it is something I should stop forgetting every time we have a serious conversation.

I adjusted my priorities from getting out of therapy, which I'd just done on my own, to avoiding having Charlotte become my replacement therapist.

"Caelie."

"You know, you say that a lot," I pointed out, in control enough now to face her again. Then, before she lost it, I added, "Char, you're a good guardian. I like cooking with you, I like hiking with you, and I'm learning stuff from you. You don't have to do everything, you know."

She rolled her eyes at me, and I frowned.

"Come on," I said, pleading with her to *try* to understand. "What would it be like if Morgan insisted on teaching me to cook?"

Morgan's all but banned from the kitchen entirely, and Charlotte winced.

"See?" How can she not see that her efforts with me are as consistently disastrous as Morgan's efforts in the kitchen?

"I'm responsible for you, too," was what she said.

I was getting annoyed. "Charlotte, what is up with you? You can't 'fix' me. I'm not a file you can close and put in some drawer somewhere."

Although I am, actually, and not just one file, either; she probably has an entire shelf devoted to me in the stacks at work, because despite my most recent shrink's very stupid question, I didn't come up with the idea that it was okay to hurt myself all on my own.

It took years and years of living with my dad to learn that it was not only okay but necessary to hurt me.

ABOUT THE AUTHOR

Kaija currently lives in Vancouver with her two boys, her father, two birds, and their sweet but very loud beagle. She works as a Teacher-Librarian and French teacher, and has done everything that can possibly be done in a school from Assistant Head to Duke of Edinburgh Co-ordinator, Ultimate coach, Department Head, and Humanities and English teacher. She loves history, reading, writing, working with young adults, going anywhere warm, and playing on the trampoline. In 2013, she realized a lifelong goal by competing in the National Gymnastics Championships (Trampoline), where she was definitely the oldest athlete there.

CPSIA information can be obtained at www.ICGtesting.com
Printed in the USA
LVOW13s0353261013

358649LV00001B/15/P